Desire never takes time off . . .

Six foot two. Lips to die for. And boy, can the man fill out a suit. The gorgeous stranger sending Aysia Banks steamy looks from across the bar is the perfect way for her to take her mind off her high-stress job, and maybe even forget about her ex.. An invitation to dance leads to a smoldering night, which turns into a weekend of uninhibited, toe-curling, blow-your-mind passion. Things are starting to look up for Aysia—until Monday morning . . .

Another city, another company to save. It's nothing new to executive Marcelo Diaz, who's used to calling the shots and getting what he wants. But what is different, is Aysia: the vixen he spent the weekend rewriting the entire playbook with. But before Marc can take things any further he's shocked by what he discovers . . .

Marc was hired to keep his employer's reputation squeaky clean.

Part of Aysia's job is to enforce her department's strict no-dating rule.

And they work for the same company.

Now, with their red-hot connection doused by office policies and politics, Aysia and Marc try to put their fling behind them. It should be easy. But when a behind-the-scenes power play threatens their careers, they'll have to bring their hearts to the table . . .

After Hours
Business or Pleasure

Melinda Di Lorenzo

LYRICAL PRESS
Kensington Publishing Corp.
www.kensingtonbooks.com

To Joanna:

For wanting to be an even better friend than Liv, and for selling really great fictional bath products. Thank you.

Chapter 1

Marcelo

"All right, sir. S'all done."

I flicked my eyes open, surprised to find the tech guru's face in front of me instead of his ass crack. It wasn't that he was fat. If anything, just the opposite. He was a skinny kid. His belt barely held up his cargo shorts, and I swear I'd been watching his superhero underwear slide up and down his sweaty backside for a full eight hours. In fact, a quick glance at my watch—a throwback to the classier days of zero cell phone addiction—told me it was damned close. Even knowing I'd have the most secure computer in the entire building, complete with access to every bit of browser history on every *other* computer...eight hours of sticky ass crack wasn't really worth it.

"Sir?"

"Right here," I said, schooling my voice to mask my irritation.

It was the worst Monday in the entire history of Mondays, and it wasn't even Monday. It was Friday. Things sure as hell weren't boding well for the kick start to my new career at Eco-Go Developments. Putting aside the rain that had been slamming down since the second I arrived—just one of the climate differences between Vancouver, British Columbia, Canada and Los Angeles, California—not a single damned thing had gone right. From being given the wrong key to my office to being assigned an e-mail that didn't exist to having an assistant quit without notice to losing a dollar in the vending machine at lunchtime. I was getting a serious headache. Sure, I'd come in a few days before I technically started, but that only excused about half the shit on my plate.

The tech didn't appear to be in a hurry to go, either, making my temple throb even more as he shifted from foot to foot instead.

"So…" He trailed off, cleared his throat, and tried again. "Um…"

Was he expecting something? A tip? Did people tip their computer repairmen? Hell. Maybe they did. The man in front of me was clearly waiting. My hand slipped to my back pocket, searching for my wallet. I didn't get as far as actually yanking it out.

"You know we do early Fridays, right?" the kid asked.

"Yeah, I know."

"Everyone goes home at noon."

"I'm aware."

"Some of us go to this pub down the road called The Well. If you're looking for something to do."

"I'm not."

"Okay. Just…it's almost five."

"All right."

"Can I go?"

"I'm not your mother."

"Right." He blinked, then, and moved to go, but paused in the doorframe. "Is it true?"

I mustered as much patience as I could manage. "Is what true?"

"Did they really hire you to fire everyone so Eco-Go could save money?"

"Wouldn't that be counterproductive?"

"What?"

"I draw a hell of a salary. Be pretty damned stupid to hire *me* to try and save money, wouldn't it?"

He scratched his beardless face. "Guess so."

"Are you worried about your job?"

"Me? No. I'm an intern. Unpaid. But I heard it around, so…"

I strummed my fingers on my desk, the only visible manifestation of my annoyance. "Let me give you a small piece of advice. One you can use through the rest of your internship, and through every job you have after."

His mouth twitched uncertainly. "Okay."

"Whatever the hell else you do, never, ever listen to rumors. Never buy into them, never *feed* into them, and never believe them. Got it?"

The kid stepped back, and it took me a second to realize I'd pushed to my feet and was leaning over the desk, my voice raised. Quickly, I raked a hand over my hair and collapsed back into my chair. I opened my mouth, but nothing came out. Admittedly, apologies weren't my strong suit. At all. I blinked once, and the tech was gone anyway.

Another man in my position might've called after him. Someone new to the company, like me. Someone whose primary position involved maintaining his cool and making sure everyone else did, too. Like me. But I wasn't another man. So instead of swallowing my pride, I turned my attention to my computer to get a head start on what would be *real* Monday's workload.

Working backwards—last names, starting with the Zs—I began combing through the emails in search of anything that might overtly damage the company. It was boring stuff, mostly, but it gave me some insight into what I was coming into. It also gave me a chance to get to know the employees without speaking to them directly. People didn't tend to give up their weaknesses freely. A few quick clicks, and I already had a mental list going.

Gerry Zellweger from payroll was big into cats.

Felicity Underhill from reception totally dug skateboard videos.

Antony Santori from supplies talked to his mother a *lot*.

Carl Reeves from accounting…

Well, shit, Carl.

I paused to take a closer look at what had just hopped up beside his name. A photo labeled with the words *From Carl's Phone*. A girl in a red negligee sat in a curved chair, her eyes fixed out the window to her side. She held her hair in her hands, taming a wild mane of brown hair. Though the shot wasn't particularly pornographic, it was definitely seductive, and something about it—her, really—caught and held me. I stared at the picture for a long moment, caressing her curves with my eyes.

"At least you've got taste, Carl," I murmured, grabbing my notebook from the pocket inside my suit jacket.

I jotted down the accountant's initials with a note beside it, then grabbed the mouse and prepared to move on. Instead, my hand slipped. It clicked the image and brought it to life, and the girl in the photo became a girl in a video instead. She stroked her hair gently. Up and down, up and down, in a mesmerizingly rhythmic motion. Behind my zipper, my cock twitched with interest. The more she teased her curls, the more I stared. The more I stared, the harder I got, and the sudden throb reminded me it had been quite a while since I'd put aside work in favor of play. Too long, apparently.

Fuck if I could look away now, though.

On screen, the brunette released her hair. The curls sprung free. They framed her face, and as she dragged her fingers to her ample cleavage, she turned in the direction of the cameraman.

Money shot, I thought.

I shifted in my chair as my pants grew uncomfortably tight. I leaned forward, waiting. Her eyes came up, their vibrant blue focused somewhere over the cameraman's shoulder, and her stare was clear. Not even a hint of put-on sexiness.

She doesn't know she's being filmed.

The thought popped into my mind and stuck, even as the camera blurred, then went blank. I couldn't be sure, of course, but just the idea that it was a possibility made me shift again, uncomfortable for a different reason.

"Carl, you might have good taste," I said, "but you're also a pervert. And you're quite possibly breaking a few laws."

I added a second note beside the first, thinking about how the poor computer tech would react when I *did* fire someone immediately. With a frustrated exhale, I closed the window on the computer and stood up to slide into my discarded suit jacket. It sure as hell wasn't the way I wanted to make my debut.

In with a blaze of not-so-glorious glory.

I locked the door behind me and moved down the hall, pulling up my sleeve for another look at my watch. It was nearly seven now. I'd spent almost twelve hours in the office. Not an unusual amount of time for me to dedicate to work, but I was definitely glad to have Saturday and Sunday to settle in and prepare for the upcoming week.

I moved out of the building, and the scent of frying food hit me, reminding me that I hadn't eaten since this morning. In fact, I was starving, but I hadn't taken the time yet to stock up my kitchen. I hadn't even unpacked a plate, let alone filled the fridge, and the thought of going home to my bare apartment made me grunt.

Following the scent of fried onions and sizzling spices and remembering what the tech kid had said about a place called The Well, I walked up the block.

Walked. I gritted my teeth. That was another thing that hadn't gone right today. No car. Delayed at the dealership. I hated the idea that I couldn't up and leave the city anytime I wanted. That I'd have to call a driver or a cab or take a goddamned bus.

"Nothing an overcooked steak and watered-down beer won't fix," I muttered as I found the source of the mouth-watering smell.

The Well, read the sign.

It was a pub, done up in classic, stereotypical London-style. Which meant it didn't look like a *real* London pub at all. I pushed my way through the heavy wooden doors anyway and scanned the busy floor for an empty seat. After a second, I found one.

Only one problem.

It was directly across from a stunning, wild-haired brunette with downcast eyes and a dress that doubled as a guaranteed hard-on. The very same woman from Carl's home video.

* * * *

Aysia

"I hate him." I didn't look up from the swirling concoction in my glass as I said it.

"I know."

My best friend's reply was tinged with both sympathy and boredom. I appreciated the first bit and I couldn't really fault her for the last bit. I'd been complaining for twenty minutes solid. If the drinks weren't on me, and her current boyfriend hadn't been out of town, she probably would've got up and walked away in disgust. Even the nearest and dearest of friends can only take so much bitching.

"Did I tell you that he thought I was a *temp*?" I added, just to spice up my complaint a bit.

"I know."

"A temp! I practically *run* the human resources department. I've been working here for *two* years, and I make ten thousand *more* a year than he does."

"I know."

I lifted my eyes from the drink and narrowed them at Liv. She had a decorative umbrella wedged between her teeth and her gaze trained on a group of decently dressed, decently hot guys across the room. There was no way she was paying attention to a word I was saying.

"The sex part wasn't even worth it," I said, testing out the waters.

She exhaled, making the little umbrella quiver. "I know."

"His penis was practically a cocktail wienie."

"I know."

"His testicles might as well have been shriveled raisins."

She reached over and squeezed my hand without looking. "I know."

"So. I'm going to quit."

"I kn—wait, what?" Her attention finally turned my way, her blue eyes wide and alarmed.

"I'm going to quit," I repeated.

"Aysia, you've been dreaming of working at Eco-Go since you were three years old. I think it's what you named the first sand castle we built together."

I decided to use her own words back at her. "I know."

"You can't quit over some bad dating decisions."

"Yes. I can."

"No. You can't."

"Look," I said with a sigh. "There are other opportunities out there."

"Opportunities *like* Eco-Go?"

"Yes."

"No."

"Yes."

"No."

"Y—"

"Stop it. You've said a hundred times that Eco-Go is one-of-a-kind. There are other builders out there who are focused on being sustainable. There are some that work on not-for-profit projects for low income housing. But you know as well as I do that Eco-Go is the only one effectively doing *both*."

"I can do something else. Compromise," I said.

She blinked at me disbelievingly. "Since when?"

"Since the man whose paycheck I sign told me he could help me get a permanent position with the company?"

"Is that a question?"

"No. I don't know. Am I seriously *that* unnoticeable?"

"Is *that* a question?" Liv said again. "Because right now, you don't sound anything like the Aysia Banks I know. Maybe you shouldn't have taken today off. All that extra sleep rattled your brain."

I swished my drink around and forced myself to take a little sip. She was right. About the not sounding like myself bit, anyway. A self-pitying moment like this one was rare. I didn't even *really* hate Carl. He meant nothing to me. But I just couldn't seem to shake it.

"I thought..." I trailed off, then tried again. "I don't know what I thought. Something."

"That Carl might fit your life plan?"

"Exactly."

"But he didn't."

"Literally," I muttered.

Liv laughed. "You're awful."

"No, *he* was awful. I was merely mediocre."

"So maybe *he* should quit."

I let out another sigh. "I keep getting this weird feeling that it's going to blow up in my face."

"The bad sex?"

"The bad sex with *Carl*. I mean, I'm the one who created Eco-Go's dating policy. So one complaint..."

"And it'll blow up," she echoed.

"Yes."

"Like *now*?"

"What?"

She leaned on the table and spoke in a whisper. "Don't make it obvious when you look, but he's over there beside that leggy redhead who works beside me in reception. He keeps glancing over here. Like, enough times that the redhead just glared at you, then stuck her tongue in his ear. I guess *she* didn't get the dating memo, either."

I suppressed a groan. I mean, not that I was surprised Carl was there. Like Liv and I, everyone from Eco-Go frequented the bar. *I* wasn't going to stop coming just because we'd gone our separate ways so I didn't expect him to. And it wasn't exactly shocking that he'd moved on. Hell. The morning after we ended things, I'd seen him outside a coffee shop with his hands up another girl's skirt. Clearly, a graceful waiting period wasn't in his repertoire of severely limited tricks. What worried me was the idea that he was looking at me right that second. Where anyone else could see. And notice.

"He's got balls," I grumbled.

"Shriveled raisin balls?"

"Oh, so you *were* listening?"

"I'm always listening. I'm your best friend."

"Good. So you know that I want to live my life free from the awkward, cumbersome things that go along with a romance. Especially an *office* romance."

"Aysia—"

"And now I've ruined my chances of doing that, so I've got to move on."

"Everyone has to get laid," she said. "Even you."

I wrinkled my nose. "You're so crass."

"Oh, please. You told me two weeks ago that if you did it with your vibrator one more time, you were going to name it and marry it."

"Shut up." So maybe I *had* said that. Maybe I'd even gone so far as to tentatively try out the name Francois. But I hadn't actually gone through with it. Yet.

"You're not going to quit," my friend said. "And you're not going to marry something that runs on double A batteries. You're going to drink that drink. You're going to drink another. Then you're going to—"

"Stumble around then pass out in a taxi?" I interjected.

"Stop that!"

"Fiiiine. Then I'm going to what?"

"You're going to march right past Carl, and you're going to walk up to that tall blond guy with the polka dot tie, and you're going to whisper in his ear to meet you in the bathroom in ten minutes. Then you're going to thank me for making you wear the black lace panties instead of the grannies."

"C'mon, Liv."

"Just once, I'd like to see you throw aside your plans and live a little."

"I *do* live. A lot."

"Then why is that glass of yours so full?"

"Because I've got a modicum of self-restraint."

"Drink!" she commanded.

Obediently, I lifted the lukewarm beverage and sucked it back. As Liv signaled the waitress, I craned my neck, trying to get a look at whatever poor, unsuspecting soul my friend had picked out for me. I spotted him right away.

"Curly hair, wide shoulders, and a little scar beside his nose?" I said.

"What? We're not close enough to see that."

"Yeah, I know. But that's the guy, right?"

"Polka dot tie," she repeated.

"Uh-huh. That's Gillian's husband."

"No way! Gillian from supplies? She's twice his age."

"She is," I agreed. "And I know it's him, because I've eaten dinner at their house. Twice."

"Ugh," Liv replied. "Okay. Fine. We'll pick someone else."

"You do realize that my sex life isn't yours, too, right?"

"Your *lack* of a sex life affects me directly."

"How do you figure?"

"Because when you're moping around all unsatisfied, *I* feel guilty being satisfied."

I snorted. "Right."

My friend sighed and hopped off her barstool. "I'm serious. And I'm going to the bathroom. By the time I get back, that second drink better be gone. You'd better have picked another guy out—one who's going to fuck the melancholy out of you in the most delicious way possible—or I'm going to make you ask Gillian and her husband about the possibility of a ménage."

Rolling my eyes, I took a pointed sip of the full drink that had magically appeared to take the place of the old one. Liv nodded approvingly, then sashayed across the floor, her minuscule hips swaying with the beat of the background music. It was my turn to sigh. Admittedly, my love life was pretty slow. But it was by choice, not chance.

I'd spent the last two years focused on work, climbing from an actual temp position to a director inside human resources—just a short jaunt away from my ultimate goal of running the department completely. The two years before that were dedicated to a course in personnel management, and in the three years before *that,* I'd crammed in a four-year ecology degree. So at twenty-five years old, the notches on my bedpost were a little slim. Not that I was a nun. I'd had a few short-term, strictly for-fun relationships. And few hookups. And of course, most recently, the month I'd wasted with cringe-worthy Carl from accounting. Even putting him aside, none of it was worth bragging about.

So maybe it really is *time for a change.*

Absently, I scanned the bar, searching. My eyes landed on a pair of wide shoulders immediately. He was alone. Hunched over a full beer, a scowl on his face. He looked about as unhappy as one guy with a burger could. So why my gaze stayed there, I don't know. But something about the tight line of his back made me curious. His hands—clean but strong, masculine but tidily groomed—flexed on his glass in a way that made me tingle. And when he glanced up and back at me, his gaze hit me like a Mack Truck. He stared at me just long enough to make my pulse race, and just long enough for me to note the ruddiness of his skin, the brown of his eyes, and the sexy cut of his jaw. Then he looked away again, and I wished he hadn't.

"Go for it, babe. Misery loves company."

I jerked my eyes up at the familiar voice, and I cringed. Carl had somehow managed to extricate himself from the redhead, and he stood beside my table, his smug face smiling down at me. How the hell had I ever thought he was attractive?

I opened my mouth to tell him where he could shove his clichéd observations, but a warm hand landed on my bare shoulder, stopping me. Somehow, I knew exactly who those fingers belonged to. They squeezed against my skin in the same way they'd closed on the beer glass.

"Sorry, *babe,*" said a new voice—not familiar, but deeply, distractingly buttery and touched by a hint of dark humor. "Didn't see that you'd come in."

The stool Liv had vacated slid out, and a whiff of understated cologne filled my nose as an arm dropped over my shoulder possessively.

Chapter 2

Marcelo

Talking to her was a mistake. I knew it before I opened my mouth. Before I even got as far as her table. The memory of the red negligee wrapped around her cleavage was too fresh in my mind. Her wild mess of brown curls, her seductive mouth, and her utterly curved but completely petite body were even more enticing in person.

Letting the asshole continue to torment her, though, was out of the question. A quick glance up had told me she was uncomfortable, and that he wasn't going to back down. Now his eyes were narrowed at me suspiciously. I let my mouth curve into a grin. He flinched. I grinned harder. Then I tightened my grip on the woman's shoulder again, and after a second, her hand came up to mine and squeezed back.

"I didn't see you come in either, honey," she said, her voice not wavering at all. "Carl was just leaving."

Carl from accounting, I thought, *nice to meet you. Now I'm looking* forward *to firing you.*

He opened his mouth. Closed it. Fixed an angry look at the girl, then turned and strode away.

I released her shoulder and started to pull away. Her hand shot out and landed on my knee, stopping me.

"Don't," she said. "He's still watching."

I leaned closer. "It's a shitty thing, isn't it?"

"What?"

"When a girl has to pretend to be with one guy to fend off another."

She laughed and tipped her head my way, some of the tension in her face easing. "That *is* a shitty thing. But trust me when I say that I can handle Carl. I take a particular satisfaction in knowing he's over there seething."

"So you want me to stay for selfish reasons?"

"Is that a problem?"

"Nope. Use me all you want."

"You say that *now*..." she teased, reaching for her drink.

She got the glass as far as her chin before my hand shot out to close on hers. Her skin was deliciously soft and smooth. Cool from the drink she clasped, but it still sent heat up through my palm. An image of her fingers filled my mind. Sliding over my forearm to my shoulders and my chest. Slipping down to find the buckle my belt and caress my already eager cock. It was an image that I wanted to make into a reality.

Instead, I forced the cup back down to the table, then dragged my hand away. "Don't," I said.

"Um. Why?"

I swallowed. Why the hell *had* stopped her? Maybe because the liquid sliding down her throat would be more than I could handle. Maybe because alcohol could explain away Carl and the red negligee.

Back to that, I thought, irritated by the fact that the other man had intruded upon my interaction with her.

I shoved down a reminder that he and his douchebag video were the whole reason I was talking to her in the first place and shrugged as casually as I could manage. "I don't want you to do anything you might regret."

"Like pretending to be here with you?"

"Is that something you think you'll regret?"

Her too-blue eyes met mine levelly. "No."

For a long, fiery minute, we didn't move. Our gazes stayed locked, and her succulent lips parted, her breaths shortening into near-gasps. And hell if her pink tongue didn't come out to dart across her lips.

Goddamn.

It was the hottest staring contest I'd ever had.

Forget the fucking dress as a guaranteed hard-on. Those eyes...

If a perky voice full of surprise hadn't cut in just then, I might've been tempted to toss aside the fruity drinks so I could take her on the table then and there.

"Um, hello?"

The brunette drew back, a lacy blush creeping up her throat. "Oh. Hi. This is..."

I stuck out my hand for a quick shake. "Marc."

The blond grinned. She was a pretty girl, too, I noted absently. Voluptuous and clearly not shy. Far more my type than the crazy-haired brunette whose syncopated breath I could still hear over the clatter of voices and music. But parts of me didn't twitch when I looked at the blond.

"Lovely to meet you," she said. "I'm Liv. This is my friend Aysia. And *you're* in my seat."

"He was saving me from Carl," the brunette—Aysia—replied.

"Saving Carl from himself," I corrected.

Liv blinked at me. "Oh, you're slick, aren't you?"

I couldn't help but laugh. "I'm guessing you're no less slick."

"I'm honey-tongued," she replied, then lifted an eyebrow at her friend. "Do we need to pretend to be lesbians?"

Aysia eyed me, that spark jumping between us once again. "I don't know. Do we?"

I met her gaze evenly. "Under normal circumstances, I'd encourage it. But right now…I think it'd just make me jealous."

Liv let out a low whistle. "Wow."

"*Very* slick," Aysia murmured, not taking her eyes off me.

"All right then," said her friend. "Just let me get out of your way *before* you hop up there on the table and start making a baby."

Aysia inhaled sharply, and I could tell it took real effort for her draw her attention back to her friend. "You don't have to—"

The blond cut her off. "I do. I think Gillian's husband wants to ask me something, actually. Something about three people and a bed? Yep. He's definitely waving."

I had no clue who Gillian was, but Aysia's face reddened, and Liv laughed before jumping up and dancing over to her side of the table. She leaned in to give her friend a kiss on the cheek and whispered something in her ear, a knowing look on her face. Then she waved and did a thorough hip-sway in the other direction. I watched her go, but only to give myself a moment to curb my libido. It was a useless endeavor. The moment I turned back to the sweet-mouthed brunette, the blood in my body refused to cooperate with my plans to regain a bit of control.

I shifted on the stool, and she drew in a breath that sent her chest up high enough to make me want to groan. Her fingers slid toward the drink again. Like a security blanket. My knuckles brushed the back of her hand, stopping her from getting a grip on it. I spread out my own fingers and dragged them to her wrist. God, her skin felt good. I stroked back and forth, losing myself in its silkiness. She didn't pull away. Instead, she lifted her eyes and met mine with a challenging look.

I slipped my palm up past the crook of her arm and moved my thumb over her shoulder. I leaned a little closer and inhaled. She smelled clean and fresh, making me think of unscented soap and steaming hot showers. A vision of Aysia, wild hair damp and calm, mouth dropped open in pleasure as the water beat down on her, filled my head.

Holy hell.

Any second, I was going to have to stand up and adjust. Sitting there with the throb between my legs was hitting the point of pain.

I pulled my hand back down to hers. She clutched her glass tightly now, more like a lifeline than a security blanket.

She looked up at me again and swallowed. "It was just one drink."

"It was at least two," I said before I could stop myself.

"Were you watching me and counting?"

"Maybe I was just admiring your dress from afar and happened to notice."

"My dress, huh?" She glanced down at the strapless top and the skin-tight, satin bottom. "This one happens to have been Liv's idea."

"You always let your friend pick out your clothes?"

"No. She thought I should wear it because—" She stopped abruptly, then started again. "I thought there might be dancing."

"Liv thought you should wear it, or you thought there would be dancing? Which is it?"

She glanced over my shoulder quickly before looking down at the liquid in her glass as she muttered, "Both."

I didn't really want to follow the flick of her eyes, but the compulsion to know what had drawn her attention was too much. I swiveled my head. Carl. King of accounting and illicit photography and—at the moment anyway—redheaded women. It annoyed the hell out of me that he'd taken her focus away from me again. It bothered me even more that she'd worn that sexy-as-sin dress in order to make *him* feel regret. A shot of irritation mixed with shot of jealousy, and together, they hit me in the gut. I tried to push them off. I failed.

"There *could* be dancing," I stated instead.

Her eyes flickered with surprise. "What?"

"*We* could be dancing."

"We could?"

"You. And I."

"Um." She shot a glance past my shoulder that told me she was looking straight at him again.

Goddamn, Carl.

Why the hell did she care what he thought? I bit back an urge to ask her about the video. Whether or not she knew about it. Something told me if I did, she'd simply get up and walk away. It was the last thing I wanted. But if she wanted to make it about him, I could, too.

"Let's make that asshole wish he'd stayed home," I growled.

Then I grabbed her hand, ignored the way she gasped as I pulled her to her feet, and dragged her to the middle of the hardwood floor, hoping damned well that the other man would get a suitable eyeful.

* * * *

Aysia

For about thirty seconds, I worried. That Liv would come back and see me and that she'd be far too gleeful. That Carl would be watching and wondering why I was openly gyrating across the floor with *this* man—a stranger—when I'd insisted that we keep *our* tryst a secret. I worried that my co-workers—and I could see at least three of them—would be whispering about me behind their hands.

But as Marc spun me out, then in again, and pulled my hands to his waist, my body talked my brain into letting it go. I gave in to the pure pleasure of being handled by a man who could move. And every little hip thrust, every little bump and consequent grind—all of it—made me sure those moves extended beyond the dance floor. Damn how I wanted to find out.

"Aysia?"

He's talking. Shit.

Conversation had been the furthest thing from my mind. I scrambled, trying to make my brain rewind to what he'd just said.

I cleared my throat. "Sorry. I missed that."

He chuckled. And it was more buttery than his voice. In fact, it was so buttery that it might as well have been warm caramel, kind of dripping down my body, then pooling between my thighs.

Oh God.

"Was I speaking too quietly?" he asked.

"No."

"Then maybe it's because I was too far away?"

His hand pressed to the small of my back to pull me flush against him. His fingers were warmer than both his voice and his laugh, and it was the kind of heat that traveled. It slid up my spine then trickled outwards. It spread along my shoulders and down my arms, then into my chest. There, it hovered for several seconds, expanding out in a way that made my heart thump against my ribcage. Then it skidded again and brought my skin to life. Goosebumps lifted across every inch of flesh, and under the thin fabric of my filmy dress, my nipples rose to life, too.

I could smell his musky scent and feel his distinctly caramel-y warmth. I sucked in a breath, trying to draw both in. And the inhale seemed to drag him even nearer. He leaned down and pressed his mouth to a spot just to the side of my ear.

"Maybe this is better?" he murmured.

"I can hear you," I managed to get out, albeit breathlessly. "What did you say before?"

"I just asked if the asshole was your boyfriend."

"What?"

"Carl."

"Oh."

"Forget about him that quickly?"

"He wasn't worth remembering."

"Good." He pulled me even tighter and swayed a little slower than the low beat thrumming from the speakers. "Is the dancing living up to the dress?"

"It's better."

He spun me out and gave me a slow onceover before pulling me in again. "I don't know about that. The dress is pretty fucking hot."

"I'll tell Liv you said so."

He leaned away just enough to look into my eyes, and his gaze caught and held me. His look was so penetrating that I half-wondered if he was trying to read my mind. Or maybe trying to make me spontaneously combust.

"I'd like to give you a few other things to tell her about," he said, his voice low and full of promise.

There was no mistaking the intention in his words. And my thighs shook with anticipation. But worry hit me again, harder than it had that first time.

"We can't leave here together," I said quickly.

"Why not?"

I took a breath and decided to go for the truth. "Because there are people in this bar who'd make my life harder because of it. It could affect my career."

"That really matters to you?" he asked.

"Doesn't it matter to everyone?"

"No. Some people care surprisingly little about their jobs."

"Well. Not me."

He smiled, and I was relieved to see that he looked impressed rather than concerned. "Where do you want to go?"

"Anywhere but here."

He slid his knee between my thighs and rocked forward—the dancing a clear pretense. "A bar down the street? Your place?"

My breath caught. "My place is good."

"All right."

He freed his leg, then took both my hands. His face gleamed with a wicked half-smile—a look that *just* rode the line between dizzyingly seductive and dangerously predatory.

"Let's make a scene," he said.

"What?"

"Just enough so that no one thinks we're leaving together."

He tugged on my hand, drawing me close, winked, then dropped my fingers in favor of clasping my chin. By the time I realized what he was about to do, it was too late to stop him. His mouth had landed on mine already. The kiss was warm and rough, and it drove my pulse higher. Blood rushed through my veins at a thunderous pace. I forgot about the people in the room. Nothing could possibly be more important than the feel of Marc's tongue darting across my mouth, parting my lips. When he tore himself away, the loss almost blinded me. I blinked, trying to clear my vision. He stood in front of me, his face split in a wide, self-satisfied grin.

"Now get mad," he urged in a low voice.

"What?" I said again.

"Quick."

Uncertainly, I furrowed my brow.

"Now," he commanded. "Or I'll kiss you again. And people are looking."

I didn't have to check. I could feel their eyes on me. I put my hands on my hips and turned my frown into a glare. "I asked you to *dance*. I guess that means something different to you than it does to me."

He took a small step forward, his eyes on my lips. For a second, I thought he was going to grab me for a second round anyway. My knees shook. If he thought I was going to be able to push him away to continue the charade, he was dead wrong. I inhaled, but I couldn't steady my breathing. But he just glared for a long second, then lifted his hand to flick back a chunk of his thick, brown hair.

"Back alley," he growled under his breath. "I'll get us a cab."

"Hurry," I whispered through my teeth.

"Two minutes."

Then he spun on his heel and lurched away in pretended drunkenness, stumbling into a table as he made his way up to the bar.

I didn't stick around to see if there was any aftermath. I pushed through the curious, gossip-hungry crowd and made my way to the door. From the corner of my eye, I caught sight of Liv. She stood near the bathrooms, her mouth hanging open.

Don't follow me, I willed.

But I knew she'd need me stop her. I gave her an awkward wave, then an even more awkward thumbs up. Her mouth closed.

Good enough.

I flew past the coat check area, deciding I could sacrifice my favorite jacket. It would be a small loss in comparison to satisfying my increasing need. And my fast movements were only making the want worse. My thighs brushed together as I slammed the door open, and I just about moaned.

Even the rush of cool night air couldn't calm me down. Goosebumps filled my skin where the breeze hit. I forced myself to keep going without looking back to see if Liv had followed me anyway, or if Marc had caught up yet. I found the opening between the exterior of the bar and the next building, and I slipped between and made my way to the alley.

There, I sank against the chilly brick wall and drew in a big gulp of air.

Two minutes.

It was going to seem like forever. I tried to distract myself by taking inventory of my surroundings. The bar was in an upper-class commercial area in Vancouver. It wasn't devoid of crime completely, but more prone to digital theft than muggings. I felt safe enough ensconced in between the buildings. They were tall—though not high-rise material—and modern and clean. At least a few of them had been designed by Eco-Go, so it was almost like coming home. But when a warm hand landed on my arm, I still jumped.

Marc's laugh filled my ear. "Nice girls don't hang out in dark alleys."

I met his gaze. "Nice boys don't ask them to."

"Me, not nice? You're the one who not-so-nicely resisted my advances on the dance floor. My feelings and my pride are wounded." Then his sexy half-smile made an appearance. "Luckily, I can think of a few ways to take the emotional sting out."

"Me, too."

He pushed both palms to the wall behind me, blocking me from moving. "Show me."

I'd never been so pleasantly trapped in my life. I pressed myself forward, the length of my body brushing his, then lifted myself to my tiptoes to dust his cheek with a kiss.

Then I sank down and shot him a deliberately coy look. "How's that?"

"That's a start," he said. "But I'm sure you can do better."

"You do remember that you *asked* me to send you away in there, right?"

"Do you always do what you're told?"

"Rarely."

"So if I commanded you to put your arms around me, you'd say no?"

"I'd point out that I can't even *move* my arms because you've got them pinned to my side."

"That's so very true."

"Does that mean you're going to let me go?"

"Nope."

I pouted. "Definitely not a nice boy."

His eyes flashed with amusement, and he inched closer, forcing me hard against the wall. "If you want nice, look elsewhere."

I might've countered with something clever. But his lips were on mine then. His hands came along for the ride, too, slipping over my face, caressing my jawline from chin to ear. It was sensual and intimate, and my mouth couldn't help but drop open to welcome him.

Marc took full advantage of the access. His tongue tripped between my lips to explore my mouth. He tasted sweet and delicious and tangy. And his fingers were magic. They moved from my face to my hair, tangling into my uncooperative curls and tugging at them with just the right amount of force.

He pulled a little harder, dislodging his mouth and sending my head back to expose my throat. He wasted no time going after the sensitive skin there. With an urgency that made me tremble, his teeth found the spot where my pulse thrummed in my neck. My knee came up to his hip, and my dress lifted and lodged itself up near my waist. I got the full, wonderful length of his erection as it pushed to the lace of my panties in an incredibly frustrating way. He was big and hard, and I throbbed with a need to feel him from the inside.

Where was the stupid taxi? I needed it so I could get what I craved.

But as one of his hands—the one that didn't hold my knee—slid down to my arms and lifted them over my head, I realized it didn't matter how fast the cab got there—it wouldn't be quick enough.

Marc's mouth was already moving south, first dipping low into my cleavage, then landing over top of my nipple, sucking it through my dress. I moaned at the attention. If my hands hadn't been pinned back, I would've been scrambling to pull off the bodice, fighting to give him better access. But he took care of it himself anyway. Using his teeth, he tugged down the fabric. And as his mouth closed over my taut, pink skin, I'd never been so glad to be braless in my life. He nipped and sucked and licked, and I wanted even more.

And he gave it.

He released my hands and fell to his knees.

Is he going to—oh, God.

He was. He did. He hooked his thumbs through my underwear and dragged them down, bringing his mouth to my thighs as he did. His tongue made a path upwards, heating the inches between my knees and my hips. I wanted to writhe. But I was too afraid that he might stop, so I stood as still as I could, waiting for him to make his way farther up. It didn't take long.

His hands came up to spread my legs apart, and his thumbs stayed there, moving together in a circle over my clit as his tongue darted along beside them teasingly. I was so wet with need, so weak with want, that I couldn't believe I managed to stay on my feet at all. I wanted it to go on forever. But I was throbbing with a desire for satiation as well. Pure, sweet torture.

"Please," I whimpered.

"Like this?" He punctuated the question with a sudden, long lick.

I quivered.

"Or like *this*?" He dragged a finger across my warm and waiting sex, then plunged it into me, just once.

I groaned. "Yes. Both."

"Greedy, greedy." He dipped his finger in again, then gave another little tug with his mouth before pausing. "Aysia?"

"Mmph," I mumbled.

"In case I forget to tell you later...you taste fucking delicious."

I gasped as he said it. And moaned as his tongue swiped over my clit then pushed directly into me, twirling and playing. It took only moments for me to get lost in the intimate attention. My hands landed on his head, they dug into his hair, holding tightly and urging him to keep going. My hips came forward and my head went back, bumping the wall. I ignored the little stab of pain. It was secondary. Buried under a wash of pleasure.

A building, thickening heat spiraled up inside of me. My whole body shook with the fast-approaching release. I was going to come. Soon.

Too soon? I wondered.

But the worry flew away almost as fast as it arrived. His tongue played me perfectly, his strong fingers a perfect accompaniment. Every touch brought me closer. I gave in to the rhythm. I let the pulse take me.

Hot. So damned hot.

"Marc." His name was throaty whisper, and saying it felt so good and right that I did it a second time. "Marc."

He increased the tempo, no longer teasing, no longer dragging me along, but pushing me. Faster and faster. Sweeter and harder and—

"Oh!" The sharp cry ripped from my mouth as I leaped over the edge of pleasure then tumbled down the side in an uncontrollable freefall.

I throbbed, riding the wave of the orgasm as Marc clamped his lips down and held me tightly. He cupped my bare ass with both his hands and squeezed that, too. Like he needed to fill himself with as much of me as he could. Like he needed to *possess* me. I'd never been held like that before. He didn't release me until the last of it subsided. As I slumped back, spent, he slid up my body and kept me upright as he pulled my panties back in place.

I opened my mouth to say something—I had no idea what—but the flash of headlights at the end of the alley cut me off.

"C'mon, honey," he said. "That's our ride."

And even if I'd wanted to, I would've been helpless to do anything but let him drag me across the concrete to the waiting cab. Because as sated as I was, the sight of his self-satisfied grin and the feel of his hand in mine made me want even more.

Chapter 3

Marcelo

The taste of her lingered, and I couldn't complain. Running my tongue up and down the softest, sweetest parts of her had been exquisite. Better than the single malt scotch I liked to sip at night while I watch the news. The residual sweetness did nothing to help with my need to slam her down the in the backseat of the cab, push her dress up again, and fuck her senseless. Christ, how I wanted to.

The second we get to her place.

The assurance was almost enough of a buffer.

The cab driver had already maneuvered away from the line of commercial buildings, and I could see row of expensive high-rises on the near horizon. They had to be our destination.

Her knee crept over the line to brush against mine, and I stifled a groan. My eyes drifted up the long line of creamy thigh to the edge of her dress.

Hell.

I adjusted again, trying to put a tiny amount of space between us. If I didn't, VanCity Cab Company was going to send me a hell of a bill. Maybe call the police. Or shit. Maybe they had a video feed set up, and we'd just find ourselves splashed all over the internet.

For a second, the thought made my cock ache even harder. Her body under my body, recorded on a shitty camera feed, moaning and thumping and more than a little pornographic.

Of course, video evidence of a lust-fueled evening was the last thing I needed. The exact kind of shit that got a PR manager fired. Worse even than having to fire an asshole like Carl on my first official day at work.

Carl.

Thinking of his face—probably smug as he snapped the video of Aysia—made me want to punch something.

"Eep!"

The little exclamation—the first thing she'd said since giving the cabbie her address—made me look down in surprise. The space between our knees had ceased to exist. My hand was on her thigh, squeezing tightly. Too tightly, probably.

"Sorry."

"It's okay."

"How many minutes until we're there?" I asked, half-teasing, half-eager.

"Seven or eight."

There was a little hitch in her breath as she said it, and I realized my fingers were moving, all on their own. Rubbing the spot I'd squeezed in a little circle, attempting to soothe away any pain I'd caused. Except the spot in question was dangerously close to the hem of her well-fitted dress. Which was short to start out with and made even shorter by the way she sat.

Damn again.

I tried to pull my hand away, but she had other ideas. She dropped her palm over top of my forearm and slid my fingers between her thighs and up. I didn't need any more encouragement than that. I tipped my wrist so I could stroke the edge of her panties. Then I slid one finger underneath them and stroked again, and she made a small, strangled sound that drew the attention of the cabbie.

"Okay back there?" he asked.

"Fine," Aysia said, her voice all hot and breathless.

I leaned close and teased, "Just fine?"

"Maybe better than fine."

"Maybe?" I stroked a little harder.

"Yes." It was somewhere between a hiss and a gasp.

"Yes, maybe…or yes better?" I moved my finger just inside of her.

She let out another sound—this one close to a moan—and the cabbie flicked another glance our way. I narrowed my eyes at his scrutiny. He had a ghost of a smile on his face, and I didn't like it one bit.

This show's not for you, buddy.

The thought was a possessive one rather than a modest one, and for a second it gave me pause. Being jealous over a woman I'd just met, whose last name I didn't even know, made zero sense. In fact, it was un-fucking-reasonable. Still. There was no denying the green tinge in my heart. My hand—the one that wasn't otherwise occupied—twitched into a fist.

Jesus, Diaz. Have a bit of pride.

It wasn't as though he could really see what was going on. Aysia was in the seat right behind his, and my own body obscured the rest of his view. Even a look in the rearview mirror wouldn't give him more than a glimpse of her gorgeous chest. Plus, I doubted it was the first time he'd had an overly amorous couple in his backseat. But all the reassurance in the world didn't quell my need to prove she was mine for the moment, and my next words swept away the illusion that I currently had complete control of myself.

"I liked it when you said my name," I said just loud enough that my voice carried to the front seat.

Aysia's eyes widened, and her sweet little tongue came out to tap her lower lip nervously as she glanced toward the cabbie.

I slipped my finger out and stilled it—deliberate, possessive torment. "Say it again."

"Marc." It was a murmured plea.

"A little louder, honey."

"This isn't very nice."

"I tried to warn you that I wouldn't be."

She closed her eyes and breathed out. "Marc."

I brought my finger back up. "Again."

Her gaze flicked forward again. "Marc."

"Look at *me* when you say it," I ordered.

She turned her face my way. There was nothing submissive in her look. Need, yes. A willingness to comply, maybe. Out and out want, definitely.

When she didn't speak, I bent closer and whispered into her ear. "Look at me and say it, honey, and I'll make you come again, right here, quick and hard."

She pulled back, her eyes catching mine and holding them. "Marc."

I stopped holding back. I plunged one finger into her waiting wetness, then two. I curled them up and squeezed along the upper wall, searching for the spot that would make her come undone. A gasp let me know I'd found it.

"Oh, God," she groaned. "Marc."

"Maybe not *that* loud," I teased. "Don't want out driver to have an apoplexy."

"Did you just say apoplexy?"

"I did."

"Now?"

"Yep. You wanna keep talking about it?"

"No."

"Good."

As I pressed then eased then pressed again, I brought my palm down over her clit and added some external pressure. Her hands dropped to her sides, clasping the seat, and her head fell back. She hissed in a breath and pressed her lips together like it hurt, and I fought a chuckle. I honestly didn't give a shit if she called out so loudly that we crashed. Touching her like this, watching her face, it would be worth the insurance premium.

"You close, honey?" I said against her throat.

"So close," she confirmed.

Under my pants, my cock throbbed. It ached. It wanted to spring free and put itself to good use. Hell. It wanted to be exactly where my hand was at that moment. To be inside her when her orgasm rocked her, to feel against my erection what I'd felt against my tongue. At the thought, my cock didn't just throb. It leaped painfully against my zipper.

Down boy.

The silent, crotch-directed order did nothing to tame my need. I tipped my mouth to her ear again, my eyes on the cabbie, making sure his eyes stayed forward.

"You have no clue how badly I want you right now," I said to Aysia. "I want you on me. Around me. I want to sink myself into you. Slow at first. Then a little quicker. Just like this."

I increased the tempo of my attention to match my words. Up and down, all while holding the flat of my palm firmly in place. I sunk my teeth into earlobe and tugged. She moaned out something that could've been a curse, or my name, or even just a primal, wordless sound—it was impossible to tell. Her body shook under my hand, her lips open and wet.

"Don't hold back," I said. "Come for me again."

I watched her face as she did. Her lids fluttered and her mouth quivered for a second before she bit her lip hard. Her hips lifted a little—once, twice, and a third time—then shuddered and collapsed against the seat, her thighs closing tightly on my hand.

As her breaths evened out and her eyes opened, I expected her to turn her attention to the driver. Maybe to see a hint of a blush. Instead, her bright blue gaze stayed fixed on my face. If I needed an ego stroke, there it was. Her hot, appreciative stare was all mine. With my free hand, I brushed back a strand of her loose hair, then ran my thumb over her bottom lip. I wanted to do things with that mouth. *To* that mouth.

Yeah, it's not your ego that needs the stroke, is it?

I adjusted my legs—and by extension, my rock-hard erection as much as our position would allow, which wasn't much at all. Not enough, for sure.

"How many more minutes *now*?" This time, the question was all eagerness.

"About one."

"Thank fuck," I said.

She laughed. It was a good sound. Melodic. It filled the taxi for a moment, and it made me grin.

"You liked that one?" I teased.

"I like—"

The cab jerked to a halt, cutting her off. I stared at her for a moment, waiting. What did she like, I wondered? My dry jokes? The way I made her body respond to mine? Strangely, I hoped it was all of it. That what she'd been about to say was that she liked was *me*.

Instead, she just waved to the squat but modern building outside. "Guess it was less than a minute."

I shook off the odd feeling and reached across her to fling open her door. "Guess so."

As she climbed out, I let my gaze linger on her curved ass and lithe legs for a minute before reaching for my wallet. I snapped it out, then snagged a hundred from the small stack inside.

"I don't have change for that," the driver said.

"I'm not asking for any," I replied, holding it out.

The cabbie eyed the bill—an eighty-five-dollar tip—then eyed me, too. "You drunk?"

"Sober as they come."

"Yeah?"

"Uh-huh. Better take it quickly," I added. "Before I change my mind."

He grabbed the bill as if I'd pull it away. "Thanks, man. For real."

"Thank *you*. Ride of a lifetime."

"You coming, Marc?" Aysia called from outside the car.

I swung my feet to the ground and grinned up at her before standing. "Not yet. But I hope to be soon."

"Pervert."

"You have no idea."

"Not yet," she threw back with a wicked grin. "But I hope to soon."

"Oh, really?"

She nodded. Then she lifted a perfect brow, licked a delicate top lip, and turned on a pointed heel to head up the front steps of the building. And I'm not ashamed to say that I chased after her at something damned close to a run.

* * * *

Aysia

Nerves and excitement battled as I made my way up to the heavy glass doors at the front of my building. There was no doubt in my mind that I was in for a mind-blowing night. In the last half an hour, I'd had more non-self-induced orgasms than I'd had in the previous *year*. And if he was that good with his mouth and his hands, I couldn't wait to see what he could do with the rest of his body. My fingers trembled with eagerness as I reached for my purse and my key card.

My purse.

"Shit," I groaned.

Marc's palm landed on the small of my back. "Problem?"

"I left my stupid purse at the stupid pub."

"Whoops."

"Understatement."

"Are we locked out?"

I shook my head. "I can use my password."

He swept aside my hair and kissed the back of my neck. "Good."

I moved to the keypad, finger outstretched. Then paused. For the first time since Marc had sat down beside me at the bar, I considered that what I was doing was slightly insane. I'd left the security of my favorite pub, the company of my best friend, and—apparently—my purse behind. I was glad I'd opted to use an app on my phone as a payment method, or I'd be scrambling to call the credit card companies instead of scrambling to find a way into my apartment.

Still.

Every bit of safety I could count on was back there. My phone, key card, and pepper spray. And what I'd taken home instead was an enormous hunk of man. Probably almost twice my size. Dangerous at best. Suicidal at worst.

It's not like you're the first woman to ever bring home a one-night stand.

But still…

"Second thoughts?" Marc said, his mouth near my ear.

I tried to make myself shake my head and I couldn't. I angled myself away from him instead, and met his warm gaze.

"What if I said yes?" I asked.

"To having second thoughts?" He sounded surprised.

"Yes. What if I told you I no longer want to let you take me upstairs? That I want you to forget we met and forget where I live?"

"I'd leave."

"Just like that?"

"Yeah, honey. I probably wouldn't be able to forget that we'd met, but I sure as hell wouldn't force my way upstairs, and you wouldn't find me on your doorstep tomorrow morning."

"Oh."

"Not what you wanted to hear?"

I shook my head. "I don't know."

He touched the back of his hand to my face. "If it makes you feel any better, I'd also have the bluest case of blue balls ever in the history of blue balls. And probably have to choose between calling a hooker and taking eight cold showers."

I leaned into the caress, my breath already shortening. "Okay."

"Okay to which part?"

"I want you to go."

He dropped his hand and drew back, his mouth open. "Really?"

"Yes."

"All right."

He turned away wordlessly and descended the steps to the street. I watched his wide shoulders as he started to move up the road.

He's seriously leaving. Not even going to argue.

It was that simple. All I had to do was ask. Was he going to walk back to the bar? Find someone else? The thought of that made my chest squeeze uncomfortably.

"Wait!" I called.

He stopped, then turned back to me slowly. "Yeah?"

"Don't go."

"Don't go? You going to change your mind again in two minutes?" He smiled crookedly, but I could tell he really wanted to know.

I shook my head. "No. I didn't really want you to go in the first place."

His smile widened. "A test to make sure I'm not a sex-crazed lunatic?"

"Does that make *me* crazy?"

"Possibly. Or just cautious."

I shifted from foot to foot, feeling more than a bit foolish. "Are you leaving?"

"Do you want me to stay?"

"Yes."

"Then hell no, I'm not leaving."

He strode back toward me, taking the stairs in two steps. He grabbed my face in his hands, then backed me up to the wall. Immediately, my arms came up to land on his shoulders, and my hand slid to the soft, thick hair on the back of his head. For several intense moments, we clung to each other. Forehead to forehead. Chest to chest. Our breathing quickened together, and I tipped my head up. He was several inches taller than I was—maybe six-foot one to my five-foot seven—but he was bent down enough that my move put us in kissing distance. Our lips brushed, and he pushed me back even farther. I closed my eyes, prepared for an onslaught. Hoping for one.

What I got instead was the squawk of the building's intercom. "I can hear you breathing."

Marc and I froze, and I fought a laugh as I recognized the cranky voice.

"Hi, Mrs. Fisk," I greeted, pulling out of Marc's embrace regretfully.

"Aysia?" My ninety-year-old neighbor sounded equally annoyed and confused.

"Yes, Mrs. Fisk."

"What the hell's going on down there?"

"We…uh, I…slipped and bumped into the intercom."

"It's the middle of the night."

I fought another laugh; I doubted it was even ten o'clock. "Sorry, Mrs. Fisk."

"All right."

I waited until the intercom button clicked off, then turned my attention back to Marc. "Were we about to do something?"

"You were about to open the damned door. And you were about to do it quickly."

I couldn't stifle my snort of laughter anymore. "Okay, Blue Balls."

He shot me a disgusted looked. "That is *not* going to be my pet name."

"BB?"

"No."

"Please?"

"Are you trying to make me leave again?"

I laughed again, punched in the code, and the door buzzed. Marc held it open for me, then put his hand on my back again. This time, I didn't question the possessive, natural-feeling gesture. I didn't wonder if it was dangerous. I leaned into it a bit instead, letting him guide me through my own door. But as we moved into the warmth of the lobby, I decided I did want a few extra moments to collect myself. And being stuck in a six-by-six elevator with a man who turned my knees to mush would definitely derail the recovery moment.

"I'm on the second floor," I said. "You mind if we take the stairs?"

"Do I get to walk behind you and stare at your ass?"

"Is that going help you with your blue ball situation?"

"Probably not."

"Good."

I heard his muffled chuckle follow me as I pushed open the heavy door and reached the first step, I turned and shot him a look. "Seriously?"

He blinked at me, confusion evident in his frown. "What?"

"A hooker or a shower? You couldn't just...you know. Take care of that yourself?"

He laughed, his caramel chuckle echoing through the stairwell. "With you on my mind? I'm not sure I'd be *able* to satisfy myself."

"I'm going to take that as a compliment."

"Believe me. It is."

I snorted, then slipped off my heels and ran up the stairs. I could feel his eyes on my ass, as promised. And by the time I reached my floor, he'd caught up.

"You're trying to torture me, aren't you?" he asked.

"Don't pretend you don't like it," I retorted.

"I won't. I'm just trying to think of an appropriate punishment for the torture."

My mouth tipped up, and I shoved my heels into his hands. "Hold these."

I punched in the second set of codes on my door, then pushed it open. As I flicked on the light then led him from the entryway into the open living space, I felt strangely shy.

"This is it," I said.

Marc's gaze swept the room. I liked the space a lot. I was proud of the décor, picked out to match my personal tastes. There was a wall of classic novels, and a few framed prints. I had a vintage turntable and a stack of records, and a rack full of wine that I never seemed to get around to drinking.

"It's perfect," he said after a few moments of scrutiny. "Classic but modern."

"Yeah?"

"Definitely. Is this building an Eco-Go design?"

I nodded. "You know the company?"

He nodded back. "Getting to."

I bit my lip and thought about telling him I worked there. Was it too much information? Too many details for a night like this? If I started talking, would I be able to stop? I'd probably overwhelm him with enthusiasm, all based on his simple, polite observation. After a quick consideration, I decided it might kill the mood.

Better not to say anything.

"They design great things," I said instead, then gestured toward the wine rack. "Would you like a drink?"

"Just one," he said, a sideway smile tipping up his lips. "Wouldn't want to do anything I regret."

"Ha ha."

I grabbed two glasses from the display case, then retrieved the nearest bottle and carried it over to kitchen where I searched for the corkscrew. It took me three drawers and a good dig before I finally found it.

"Aha!" I said, lifting it triumphantly.

"I don't know if I should slow clap, or wait for your acceptance speech," Marc joked.

"Maybe wait until I've actually opened it to decide."

I was kidding, but after a few minutes of fighting to get the corkscrew to cooperate, he stepped in and took over. He jabbed the curly tip into the cork expertly, twisted it, then freed it easily.

I shot him a narrow-eyed glare. "Show off."

He answered my grumble with a smile. "Twice I've saved your ass, and that's the thanks I get?"

"Saved my ass, huh?"

"Yep."

He slipped off his suit jacket and hung it over one of the kitchen chairs. Then he put one hand on the counter beside me and reached around me with the other to pour the wine. As he leaned back to hand me a glass, he kept his body pushed against mine and took a small sip from his own. The effect was instant sensuality. His lips on the rim, sucking off a drop. His thigh pressed between my legs. His eyes on mine unwaveringly. I wanted to toss aside the wine, take him by the tie, and pull him to the ground.

"Marc…" I heard the raw need in my own voice.

Clearly, he did, too. "Take what you want, honey."

So I did. Slowly, though, because I wanted to enjoy it. I set down the wine glass on the far end of the counter, then grabbed his and put it beside mine. I wrapped my fingers around the tie—silk, I was sure—and tugged him closer. Without my heels on, I had to stand on my tiptoes to reach up and drag my lips over his, and I realized he was taller than I initially thought. More like six-foot three than six-foot one.

"I like tall men," I murmured against his mouth.

"Oh yeah?"

"Mm-hmm."

I closed my teeth on his bottom lip and tugged. In response, he made a throaty noise, somewhere between a groan and a growl. I sucked it hard for a second, then let go and gave him a gentle, full-mouth kiss before pulling away again.

"What else do you like?" he asked.

I unknotted his tie, then brought my fingers to his shoulders and slid them down the length of his arms. "I like strong, capable hands."

"What else?"

I pulled his palms to my hips and pushed to my tiptoes again so I could run my tongue along his throat. "I like a man who tastes as good as he smells."

He exhaled a groan. "Fuck, Aysia."

I smiled and slipped a hand to his top button and teased him. "I like that, too. But I'm not quite there yet."

"Mmph," he mumbled.

"Sometimes, I like to be in charge. But sometimes, I like a man who takes control."

I undid the first button, then the next and the next. With my eyes on the strong line of his collarbone, I pushed the shirt open and ran my fingers over his chest. His skin was soft, but the muscles under it were hard enough that I wanted to forego my slow exploration and tear the rest of the buttons off so I could have a better look. And a better feel. I made myself refrain.

"I like the look on your face right now." My voice shook with desire as I moved to open the shirt all the way to his stomach. "I like the way your eyes keep closing and the way your lips are a little wet." I reached the last button, and my hands shook, too, as I unfastened it and moved on to his belt. "I like how fast your heart is beating and how you're trying to hold still, but I can feel your cock twitching against my leg."

"That's a lot of likes," he replied, low and thick.

"I have a long list," I said. "I keep adding to it. Usually when I'm lying in bed naked."

"Do you *like* being naked?"

"I do. Speaking of which…unzip me?"

I yanked off his belt, dropped it the ground, then spun around to give him access. I leaned my elbows on the counter and looked over my shoulder expectantly.

"Sweet Jesus," he swore, his eyes raking up and down my body for a second before he reached for the zipper.

He undid it swiftly, with sure hands, and in moments, I was standing in front of him in nothing but my panties.

Chapter 4

Marcelo

The sight of her, splayed out the way she was…it was almost more than I could take. Behind my partially undone pants, my cock jumped. As she flipped to face me, then hopped up on the counter, breasts bouncing, it practically sang a fucking song. When she crooked a finger, it added a tango.

"Come here," she ordered in a pert voice.

There was no sense in pretending I wasn't going to obey. My brain wasn't calling the shots anymore, and my little head had never been so utterly smitten.

And she hasn't even really touched you yet. When she does…

I dropped a string of muttered curses that made Aysia smile, then I stepped to the counter and put my hands on her knees.

"Wait," she commanded.

I dropped my hands to my sides. Her own fingers came up to my chest, where they traced a lazy pattern before they lifted to push off my shirt entirely. The seven-hundred-dollar, custom-fitted Hugo Boss dropped to the floor. I didn't care. I even gave it a little kick.

Next, her hands found my zipper. Then lowered it. Slowly, her eyes on mine, and a that sexy little smile hanging on her lips.

I wanted to tell her to hurry, to tell her I was dying a slow, painful death from all her teasing. Instead, I made myself say, "Take your time, honey."

Like she could read straight through my lie, she laughed, then slid her fingers into my pants, under my boxer briefs, then closed around my cock. I groaned. Her grip was perfection, her skin impossibly soft and incredibly warm. She gave a light squeeze and a little tug, and I swore again.

She slid forward to speak near my ear. "You've got a filthy mouth."

I leaned back to drag my eyes over *her* lips. "And you've got a fuck-able one."

She paused in her attentions and raised an eyebrow. "Is that what you want?"

"Yes, but...don't stop."

She let out another little laugh. "You sound confused."

"I'm not confused. I'm varied. My list of likes is just as long as yours."

"Hmm. So you'd like me to keep doing this?" She stroked me hard and fast for a second, then slowed again.

"Yes."

"But you'd also like me to do *this*?" She gave me a gentle push back, jumped down, and dropped to the floor.

As her tongue darted out to trace the smooth, sensitive tip of my erection, I couldn't even muster up a single syllable affirmation. If I'd thought her hand was warm and soft...it had nothing on her mouth. When she opened it to draw me in, I thrust forward involuntarily. I would never have thought the word *fuck-able* could be an understatement. In this case, it was. Her lips were heaven. Her tongue was an angel.

I used what little strength I had left to open my eyes and look down. The sight of her, sucking on me with firm assurance, was almost enough to send me over the edge. It wasn't submission. It wasn't a feeling of power. God knew I wasn't in control at the moment. It was something else. Awe. Appreciation. This beautiful, capable woman was on her knees for me. Not because she had to be, not because I asked her to, but because it was where she wanted to be. There wasn't a hotter fucking thought on the planet.

Well. Maybe one.

"Aysia," I groaned.

She paused, her mouth still halfway up my cock, then lifted her eyes. Her ultra-blue, willing-to-please gaze landed on me expectantly.

"I have another like," I said.

She gave me a quick, torturous suck, then released me and let me pull her to her feet. Her sweet curves pressed against my body, sending jolts of lust across every inch of me. As her firm nipples rubbed my chest and my erection brushed her thigh, a sharp breath whipped through me. Christ was she sexy. If I'd ever been this turned on by a woman before, I couldn't remember it.

"Marc?"

"Yeah, honey?"

"Are you going to tell me what that like *is*?" she asked teasingly.

"Fuck, no," I said. "I'm going to show you."

I grabbed her by the hips and lifted her from the ground, groaning yet again as her legs came up to wrap around my hips. Her little black panties were nothing and everything at the same time. A scant piece of fabric that I wanted to destroy. That I *would* destroy.

"Bedroom," I commanded.

"Through the living room, up the stairs to the little balcony, then through the French doors."

Hell. Even her directions were a turn on. I didn't waste any time following them.

"Living room," I growled, loving the way her ass bounced against me as I strode through the apartment

"Stairs." I took the first four in two steps and the next three in one, making her slam against me even harder.

"Door." I pushed it open with my foot, and carried her in, then straight to the crimson sheets of her king-sized bed.

"Bed," she said, a delighted grin curling up her still-fuck-able mouth.

"Thank God for that."

Still holding her tightly, I bent down and lay her back on the object in question. I dragged my mouth down her face to her throat, then to her chest. I gave each nipple a tiny lick, then kissed her just above her belly button before standing up to shake off my already undone pants. They fell to the floor with a nearly inaudible thump. I stood in front of her for a long second, enjoying the way her eyes played over me with undisguised want. When she reached for her panties, though, I stepped forward to stop her.

She made a funny face—midway between a pout and a surprised blink—and said, "No?"

"Let me."

Her hands dropped obediently to her sides. I kneeled on the edge of the bed and gripped the delicate fabric. Then I ripped. She gasped as they tore, then gasped again as I threw them aside and pushed her thighs wide so I could drop my mouth to her again. She was wet and swollen, and tasted as good as she had in the alley. Better, maybe. I ran my tongue up once, then twice, then pushed my body up and held myself over her, appreciating the way her chest rose and fell under me.

"Please tell me you have a condom," I said, my voice thick with need.

"In the drawer beside the bathroom sink." Her reply was throaty and desperate.

"Thank fucking God."

I pushed up and moved to the door at the edge of the room. I was oblivious to what my surroundings looked like. The cabinet might've been

wood or white or made of bubble wrap. I didn't care. I had one goal, and
I couldn't be bothered with noticing whether there was rose-scented soap
on the counter or matching towels on the rack. I slid open the drawer and
tossed aside a dozen other objects before my hands finally found the box.
Unopened.

It was stupid. Egotistical. Overly protective of my momentary woman.
But I was pleased as all hell that we were using a fresh box. Glad no one
else had intruded on the moment. I tore into the package with my teeth,
dragged out a string of foil wrappers, then carried them back to the bedroom.

Aysia was sprawled across the bed, her knees parted just enough to
give me full view of her well-groomed landing strip. Of her soft stomach
and of her full, delicious breasts.

I stared at her for so long that she turned to her side to stare back. "What?"

"You're stunning," I told her.

A pretty blush lit up her cheeks, but she still raised a sassy eyebrow
and nodded at the condoms. "And *you've* got some pretty high
expectations of yourself."

"When you look like that…how can I be anything but?"

The blush spread to her chest, dotting the expanse of her cleavage with
a tempting red that nearly matched the sheets.

"Are you just going to stand there all night, then?" she chided. "Or are
you going to come over here and do something about it?"

A grin tipped up my mouth. "Demanding, aren't you?"

"Insatiable, too."

"Hmm. I'll take *that* as a challenge."

I ripped the first condom from the strip, tossed the others to the
nightstand, then held up the package. Her eyes followed my motions, and
as I tore open the foil, any hint of teasing dropped from her face. Her gaze
grew hungry. The air began heating up. It felt as though an electrical current
had come loose around us, zapping dangerously with each little move.

I unrolled the latex slowly, stroking myself lightly. I watched her body
react. Her nipples grew even tighter. Her breathing turned shallow. That
pretty little tongue of hers came out to moisten her lips. When she lifted her
eyes, her lids hung low, and there was no mistaking the desire in her gaze.

"Marc…"

"Yeah, honey?"

"Save some for me."

I let out a chuckle, then stepped toward the bed. She came to her knees
and put her hand over my shoulders. With undisguised eagerness, she
tipped her head up and pushed her sweet mouth to mine, drawing me

into a deep kiss. When she at last pulled away, I lifted a finger to trail it over her lower lip.

"How come all of you tastes so good, hmm?"

She smiled. "Genetics? Or maybe my great dentist."

"I'll accept either one."

One of her hands moved down from my shoulders then, to trace a slow, seductive circle across my chest. Her fingers hovered for a second, then plunged farther south. They gripped my cock with just the right amount of tightness, playing overtop of the condom.

"Let's not waste this one," she said into my ear.

Then she lifted a knee and slung it across my hip. Still holding me firmly, she guided my sensitive tip into her. For a minute, we stayed that way. A torturous prelude. Then her fingers parted over her own sex, widening it for me as she thrust forward.

"Aysia." Her named slipped from my mouth as I sank into her about halfway.

"Good?" she said against my throat.

"So. Fucking. Good."

She pulled back, then thrust forward again, a little deeper this time. I swore. She did it one more time, and it was all I could take. With a low growl, I brought my hands to her ass and slid her down to the edge of the bed. Then I pulled up her other leg and did my own thrust. Hard. Thorough. Then again. And again. I lost myself in the feel of her. In her heat. In her firmness. I let myself go faster, watching as the speed made her eyes close and her head fall back. She was close. So was I. Not wanting to rush, I slowed just a little, but her hands came up to dig into my thighs.

"Please," she whimpered. "Don't stop."

"I'll come, honey. It feels too good."

"I know. Please, Marc."

I stopped holding back. I pushed into her with full force. She lifted her hips and let out a cry. Her hands fell to her sides, clutching at the sheets. As she tightened around me, saying my name over and over, I closed my own eyes and gave in to my need for release. I pulsed inside of her, reveling in the sweetness of our mutual orgasm. I stayed inside of her for as long as I dared, then at last pulled away. I did a quick disposal of the well-appreciated condom, then collapsed beside her.

Aysia let out a soft sigh, then rolled over to tuck her soft body against mine. "That was...I don't actually think they've invented a word for what that was."

I ran a finger down her arm. "Still insatiable?"

"Sated," she admitted. "For now."

"For now?"

She rolled again, this time to face me. A little frown creased her otherwise smooth forehead. I reached up and smoothed it away with my thumb.

"Was that too presumptuous?" she asked.

"Was what too presumptuous?"

"Thinking we might want to do that again later." She didn't sound embarrassed, she just sounded curious.

"Are you worried about etiquette?" I joked.

"I *was*. Until you used the word. Now I'm worried about how weird that sounds coming from you. Especially knowing what else your mouth is capable of."

I laughed and leaned forward to kiss her lightly. "Well. If you're really worried about the first bit, then I think it's safe to say that the word *might* isn't quite presumptuous enough."

"Good." She settled in again, tucking her face into the crook of my arm.

For several long minutes, she stayed that way, her ass on my thigh, her hand closed comfortably on my forearm, her scent filling me. I could tell, though, that there was more she wanted to say.

I finally decided to break the silence myself. "So…"

"So?"

"Is this the part where you tell me you don't normally do this kind of thing?"

"Yes," she admitted. "I guess it is."

"Well then I guess this is the part where I tell you I *like* that you don't normally do this kind of thing."

"Oh. So you're not totally into girls who go home with random guys?"

"I totally *don't* care what girls do with random guys. I care what *you* do."

"So if I was a deviant, you'd grab your shoes and leave?"

"No. I'd tell you I'm always impressed when a woman owns her sexuality."

"A lie?"

"Nope. But I'd be secretly trying to one-up every other random guy you'd gone home with. And be feeling sorry for myself because I *like* to feel special." I grinned, and she ran a finger along my collarbone.

"*Aren't* you special?" she teased.

"My mom says I am."

"Ooh. I love when a random guy I've brought home talks about his mom."

I grabbed her wrist and pushed her hand up over her head. "And I love when I random woman I've gone home with uses the word *love* in the first five minutes at her house."

"We've been here at *least* an hour."

"Picky."

"Factual," she corrected.

She tipped her face up for a kiss, and I indulged. I dragged it out a bit, exploring the contours of her mouth unhurriedly. It was easier to take my time now that the intense, single-minded goal had been met. Though as I deepened the kiss even further, my cock made an instantaneous recovery.

She broke off the kiss and lifted one of those eyebrows of hers. "*Now* who's insatiable?"

I shrugged. "Trust me. You don't want to make it a contest."

"Maybe I do."

"Do you have a competitive streak?"

"I don't need to, I always win."

"Until now."

"Don't think a girl can take you?"

"I think a girl *did* take me."

She let out another of her sweet, sexy laughs. "Marc?"

"Mm-hmm."

"I want you to spend the night."

I liked that she told me what she wanted rather than asking what I'd prefer.

"Happy to oblige," I said.

"Chivalrous."

"Factual," I teased.

Aysia smiled, then kissed me again. Her touch was soft. Gentle. It sent a nagging warmth through me—one that started in my chest and fanned down to my groin. For a second, the sensation made me pause. What the hell was that tug about? But a moment later, she slipped her hand between my legs, and the weird hint of emotion faded to the background as I reached for the remaining condoms on the night-stand.

* * * *

Aysia

I kind of lost track of the number of condoms we used over the course of the night, but I was pretty sure Marc was aiming for some kind of record. Olympic, maybe? Or sex god? Were there awards for sexual prowess? Or maybe there was just some kind of personal satisfaction involved in making my thighs ache as if I'd just won a mechanical bull riding competition. But needless to say, I wasn't overly stunned that I slept like a tranquilized monkey. I was, however, a bit surprised to wake up to an empty bed and the sound of water running in my en suite bathroom.

What were you thinking, Aysia? That he'd hightail it out of here as soon as your eyes closed?

Maybe I was. Or maybe I just didn't know *what* the expectation for a one-night stand should be. In my head, I imagined a torrid tussle in the sheets. Nameless. Meaningless. Instead, I had a gorgeous man— whose name had left my lips a hundred times rather noisily over the course of the night—in my shower on a Saturday morning. Possibly using my overpriced, totally organic coconut oil body wash. I narrowed my eyes, considering whether or not it would be prostitution if I demanded a fee for said use. Not that I couldn't afford it. Just that there was something to be said for certain indulgences. Then again, if the suit he'd been wearing was any indication, he could more than afford it, too. For a second, I wondered what he did for a living. But I shoved the curiosity aside quickly. Knowing too much about him might defeat the whole purpose of a one-night stand.

With a sigh, I freed my feet from the sheets and forced myself up into a stretch. My body really did ache. And judging by the growl in my stomach, it needed sustenance, too.

I snagged a T-shirt from my closet, slipped into that, plus a pair of underwear, then headed through the French doors and down to the kitchen. The general state of disarray was a blush-worthy testament to our eagerness to get to the bedroom the night before. The nearly full bottle of wine sat uncorked on the counter. One empty glass lay on its side, precariously close to the edge of the counter. The other had somehow found its way to the rug under the coffee table. We'd somehow managed to knock a framed print off the wall, and Marc's shirt was crumpled on the floor beside the breakfast bar. I didn't know whether to be embarrassed or impressed.

Settling on the latter, I bent down to pick up the shirt. But I froze, mid-grab, as Marc's deep chuckle carried down from the miniature balcony above the living room.

"I *was* a bit disappointed that you weren't in bed when I got out of the shower," he said. "But somehow this view makes up for it."

I straightened up and spun. But whatever smartass remark I'd planned on tossing back stuck in my throat instead. Marc stood on the edge of the stairs, one elbow resting on the loft's railing. He wore nothing but a bright blue towel and a cocky smile. His thick hair was more than damp, and a few droplets of water made their way down his neck to his wide, well-muscled chest.

He cleared his throat. "Are you *ogling* me, Aysia?"

"Definitely."

"Does that mean I can ogle you?"

I put my hands on my hips. "Am I stopping you?"

His eyes perused the length of my body, starting with the toes and working their way up. When he hit my chest, my nipples were already on high alert. And by the time he reached my face with his scorching gaze, my aches were forgotten.

"How's that ogle going?" I teased a little breathlessly.

He didn't take his eyes off mine, and his grin widened into the slightly predatory one. "Well. Let's see. I feel a bit like I got run over by a very pretty, very sweet-smelling Mack Truck. I'm starving. And desperately want a cup of coffee. But if you keep standing there like that, I'm going to have come down there and fuck you on the back of the sofa."

I lifted an eyebrow. "Oh, really?"

"Yes."

"I have an awfully expensive sofa."

"Is that supposed to be a deterrent?"

"I don't usually allow animals on my furniture."

"Aysia..." My name was a light growl on his lips.

"Marc." I tapped a finger on my lower lip, loving the way his eyes were suddenly glued to my mouth. "I'll tell you what. I'll make you a deal. If you can get down here and catch me before I get the coffee brewing, I'll let you do whatever you like to me."

"On the sofa?"

"On the sofa."

He took a slow step. A warning.

"Aren't you going to run?" he asked.

"Nope."

"You sure? 'Cause I'm pretty fast and there's about fifteen feet between you and that coffee pot over there."

"I'm sure."

He took another step. I stayed put.

"If you *want* me to catch you," he said, "it's not much of a challenge."

"I never lose, remember? And I'm not going to now."

Because I had trick up my sleeve. Each morning, I set up the pot ahead of time. And I had a magical—yes, I was sure it was otherworldly—app on my phone that connected to the machine. All I had to do was press a button. So I waited until his feet landed on the final step before I turned to snag my phone from its spot in my purse, which always hung over the back of one of my high-backed stools.

And then I remembered.

Oh, shit.

I'd left my purse behind at the pub. And now Marc was on the floor in front of me.

"Shit!"

I leaped backwards just as his hands snapped forward. I backed up and out of reach, stumbling over the edge of my area rug and just about landing on my ass in the process. I recovered quickly, though, and eyed the coffee pot over his shoulder.

"Wanna admit defeat?" Marc asked.

"Nope."

I feinted to the left, then ducked to the right as he tried to catch me. Laughing, I darted past him, then past the kitchen island. My arm got as far as extending toward the manual brew button. I even brushed the plastic with my index finger. Then Marc's hands were on me. With no sign of effort, he grabbed me by the knees, spun me around, and tossed me over his shoulder. I tried to wriggle free. His grip just tightened.

"Caveman," I grumbled into his back as I gave up fighting.

"Cavemen drag women around by their hair," he corrected. "They don't escort them nicely to the couch like this."

"Nicely?" I tried to sound stern, but I couldn't hold in a laugh.

"Yep. Special and nice. Just like my mom says."

"Mama's boy."

"You've got a lot of hostility this morning."

"I'm cranky when I don't get my coffee."

"It's got another five minutes before it finishes brewing," he said. "I'm sure I can find a way to placate you until then. On the sofa, of course. Because I *won*."

He turned toward the living room—carefully, I noted, so that he didn't bang my head on anything—then moved lightly over the floor. We only made it a couple of feet, though, before a startled gasp cut the journey short.

I stifled a groan. I knew without looking who was standing inside my door. The one person who wouldn't think twice about paying me an unannounced visit. And who would've grabbed my purse, and therefore currently had all of the key cards for my apartment.

Marc's greeting confirmed it. "Morning, Liv."

"Um. Hi. Um. Aysia?"

Chuckling under his breath, Marc turned so that I was facing her and I peeked out—still upside down—from beside his hip. Liv had my purse in one hand and a tray with two coffees in the other.

"Yeah. It's me." I gave her a little wave, then tapped Marc's lower back. "You can put me down."

He flipped me up, holding me tightly until I was stable on my feet, then leaned down to kiss a spot right under my ear.

"I'll give you a second," he said.

"Thanks."

I forced myself *not* to stare as he slipped back up the stairs. Just a prolonged glance. And maybe a lusty sigh. God, he was stupidly hot. But when I turned back to Liv, her eyes were narrowed.

"Well," she said. "At least I know you used the gift card I bought you for that waxing place."

"What?"

She tossed a nod at the hem of my T-shirt. "Ahem."

"Ew. Shut up. You could *not* see that well."

"Maybe I could."

"I used that gift card for a pedicure, thank you very much."

"Sure."

I tugged my shirt down, then wiggled my toes at her. "I did."

"Uh-huh."

I stuck my tongue out. "I would've put pants on if you'd called."

"I would've called if you hadn't risked your life by taking off with some guy and leaving your cell phone behind. You're lucky I didn't show up last night. But I'm glad you're not dead."

"Thanks."

"So…"

"So…" I repeated. "I brought Marc home."

"Uh-huh."

"And he's still here."

"Uh-huh."

"Stop that. Is one of those coffees for me?"

She lifted one out of the tray and handed both it and my purse to me. "I'm guessing he doesn't have a cocktail wienie under that towel?"

I snorted a laugh and slung the bag over my shoulder. "Shh. He can probably hear you. And no. Definitely not a cocktail wienie."

"Bratwurst?"

"Seriously. Shut. Up."

"I'll take that as a yes." She grabbed her own coffee and sipped it, a thoughtful look on her face.

"What?" I asked.

"I dunno. You have a weird glow. Did his super sperm get you pregnant?"

This time my laugh was a sputter. "Liv!"

"It's a valid question. I've never seen you so shiny."

I opened my mouth to tell her we'd used enough condoms to stop anything short of an alien probe from impregnating me, but the sound of Marc's feet on the stairs stopped me. I settled for shooting her a silent death-glare instead. But it was hard for me to maintain my exaggerated irritation when Marc slung an arm across my waist and pulled me in for a sideways squeeze. He made my coconut oil body wash smell even better than usual. And even though he'd put on his pants and socks—which were probably a bitch to find in the tangled mess upstairs—I was still hyperaware of his body.

"I should probably get going. You wanna sacrifice that coffee to help me along?" he asked as he pulled away.

"Not really."

"Hmm. How about if I offer to leave your sofa alone in exchange?"

"Maybe I really wanted to buy new furniture."

"Please?"

Liv rolled her eyes. "Give him the damned coffee."

"Give him *yours*," I countered.

"I've sipped mine."

"Fine." I held out the cup.

Marc took it with a grin. "Thanks, honey. If I don't start unpacking my stuff, I'll have to steal coffee every morning."

"Unpacking?" I repeated.

"Mm-hmm." He sipped the coffee, then set it down to grab his shirt from the floor. "Just moved to the city last week."

"Oh, good," said Liv. "Glad Aysia got to act as your own personal welcoming committee."

Marc laughed. "Me, too."

He finished buttoning his shirt, then moved on to retrieving his suit jacket, tie, and shoes. I couldn't quell a stab of disappointment at seeing him get ready to leave.

But I felt a little better when he sent a crooked smile Liv's way and said, "You might want to turn away."

Then he tipped up my chin with his fingers, dropped his lips to mine, and delivered a toe-curling kiss to my needy mouth. It ended far too quickly.

"Thank you," he murmured. "That was the best damned welcome I've ever received."

"You're welcome." It sounded lamely redundant, but I didn't care.

"I need to go."

"All right."

He kissed me once more, then dropped his hands down to snag his coffee. "See ya, honey."

"Bye, Marc."

True regret flooded through me as he slipped out the door. But I just kind of stood there, watching as the handle clicked into its automatic locked position.

Liv cleared her throat. "You gonna run after him?"

I shot her a dirty look. "Do I look desperate to you?"

"No. You look well-fucked and lust-struck. And you let him take your coffee."

"It was just sex. *Good* sex."

"Good?"

"Great sex. Which is why I let him have the coffee."

"Uh-huh."

I rolled my eyes. "Back to that again?"

She sat down on one of the tall stools. "No. But I do want to hear every detail of every Bratwurst inch. And then we can go shopping to help you drown your sorrows about being dumb enough to not demand his number."

"It was just—"

"Sex. Yeah. I heard you. But I'll let you in on little secret, oh BFF of mine." She looked around as though someone might be listening, then dropped her voice to an exaggerated whisper. "Some of us like to do it more than once."

"Shut up," I said for what felt like the twentieth time. "Wasn't it you who insisted I walk on the wild side?"

"Yeah. But who knew you'd take it so seriously?" Then her face softened. "You know that I'm just worried about you, right?"

I sighed. "Yes. But you don't need to be. I'm totally fine. The shit with Carl didn't scar me for life. It was just a little glitch."

"You're sure?"

"Yep."

Her eyes glittered gleefully. "Good. Then spill it."

"Fine," I said. "Do you want a play-by-play? Or just the highlights?"

"Every rock-hard detail," she replied.

"Give me a second then."

And as I poured myself a coffee from the finally ready pot, I couldn't quite stop myself from sneaking at glance at my own front door. *Was* it stupid of me to just let him walk out? I shook off the question and focused on adding enough hazelnut creamer to my cup. It was just sex.

Mind-blowing, heart-stopping, multiple-orgasm sex that's left you with a post-coital hangover, pointed out a little voice in my head.

But nothing a new pair of Louboutin heels wouldn't cure.

Just sex. Seriously.

Chapter 5

Marcelo

I smiled to myself as I walked out of the compact building and into the street, tapping my pocket as I strode to the corner, then crossed. I was pretty damned pleased with the quick switch I'd done. In fact, I was convinced it was downright genius. Neither of the girls had noticed as I dropped my own phone into Aysia's purse while grabbing hers in exchange. Yes, it was thievery. Yes, it was probably an unnecessary little ruse.

"But fuck if I feel guilty," I said aloud to myself, making some guy selling Rastafarian hats jump.

I grinned even wider. The dark rain clouds of the night before had tapered off, and nothing but sunshine and white clouds filled the sky. The weather suited my rainbows-and-unicorns mood perfectly, so I took my time exploring the city as I worked my way to my new-to-me condo. As much as I liked L.A.—and I'd spent the last ten years there, so at the very least it had felt like home—the change of scenery was good. Vancouver was green everywhere. Tall trees stuck in between every second building. Patches of grass where I'd usually expect to find rock. I paused on a corner to admire some overgrown shrubs, inhaling the piney scent. Hell. Even the air was fresher.

I continued in my slow perusal of everything Vancouver had to offer for a few solitary hours on a sunny Saturday. I grabbed some brunch at a café, then took another coffee to go. I even stopped and picked up a few things for my place. Veggies from a market. A weird piece of abstract wooden art that just felt good in my hands. Though admittedly, everything felt good at the moment.

Could be because you're just riding a high from spending the whole night locked up and sweaty with a clever-tongued, sassy-mouthed, fine-assed woman.

Which was far from shameful. Nothing better to take my mind off a shitty introduction to my new job than the company of a girl like Aysia. What *was* shameful, though, was that I'd blocked out the fact that the shitty introduction in question was the thing that had drawn my attention to her in the first place.

"Shit," I muttered, this time startling a dreadlocked girl—who was busking with a pan flute—so badly that she just about dropped her instrument. "Sorry."

She nodded her acceptance, but I was already turning away. It wasn't her I really owed an apology to. It was Aysia. I ran my hand over my chin, scratching at the day-old stubble. It wasn't fair that I hadn't told her about the video. It was a lie of omission to leave out the fact that I knew what a douchebag Carl was before I ever saw him talking to her in the bar.

Pretty fucking terrible way to start a relationship. At the thought, I just about tripped over my own shoes.

A relationship?

Okay, I wasn't anywhere near that yet. But if we *did* keep going, even to something reasonably casual, it would sure as shit eat at my conscience. The longer I kept it from her, the worse it'd be. Especially once I walked into the office and fired our mutual friend.

"Dammit," I swore, then clamped my lips shut and looked around for the victim of my latest accidental outburst.

This time, though, the street was empty. Really empty.

I stopped walking, looked up again and realized I'd gotten myself stuck on some residential cul-de-sac. My only choice was to turn around and go back out the same way I'd come in. I sighed, thinking that it had to be some kind of metaphor. I just didn't have my head on straight enough to figure out what it was.

I swung around and headed back in the direction I'd just come, my mood a little sourer. For all I knew, the phone exchange would fail. Aysia might even be pissed off. Maybe she had important calls to make to important people, and I was wrecking it like a true asshole. For a second, I questioned my sanity. Yeah, my ploy would force another meeting, but there was also a very real possibility that it wouldn't lead anywhere at all. We'd make the exchange and that would be it. She hadn't even asked for my number, after all.

Why the hell hadn't *she asked for it?*

Struck by an unusual sensation that felt suspiciously like insecurity, I pulled the phone from my pocket and glared down at it, irritated at myself. The red plastic case glittered back at me. Like a matador egging on a bull.

As I moved to shove it back into my pocket, it abruptly came to life in my hands. The screen flashed an incoming text message from my own number. No words. Just four digits. *9512.* I tapped the notification, but instead of expanding, the phone demanded a password.

I frowned for a second before clueing in. "Ah."

I tapped in the numbers, and the device's screen unlocked completely. *Hello, Aysia,* I typed back.

The reply was almost instantaneous. *Sneaky bastard, aren't u?*

I thought we agreed on slick, I replied.

Phone theft is a step above slick, I'm pretty sure.

Maybe it was an accident.

I could picture her disbelieving expression as she typed her extra-long answer, *Yeah. U just accidentally mixed up ur army-grade case with my pretty little red one. Which was in my PURSE. U should really set a password on here, btw.*

New phone.

Right.

Why r u so worried about it? Did you find my porn collection? ;)

If I had...I'd be watching it instead of talking to u.

A lick of desire made me shift in place. *Is that what ur into?*

I'm more of a live action girl.

Ah. Strippers, then? 'Cause I can take you if you like.

Ha. Ha. Funny.

I grinned. *Oh. Did u mean something else?*

Guess u'll never find out.

Damn.

There was a short pause before she said back, *Do u always give up so easily?*

I stole ur phone, I pointed out. *Is that giving up?*

Aha! Now I have it in writing.

:)

U shouldn't be smiling about ur petty theft habits.

I'm smiling because I'm imagining u all mad and riled up.

:P

Don't put it out there unless ur gonna use it.

Pervert.

Yep.

Are you home now? she asked.

Why? I replied. *You miss me already?*

Or maybe I thought I'd swing by before I headed out.

Where u headed?

U jealous?

I narrowed my eyes at the phone. I wasn't jealous. Until she made the comment. I swiped my fingers across the screen quickly.

Nope. Not jealous. I've got ur phone. I can find out pretty much anything I want, remember?

Oh, good. My exes are listed under a sub-folder called DOUCHEBAGS. U wanna put ur number in there?

Ouch, I typed.

That's what u get for wanting to go thru my phone.

I won't, I promised. *And no, I'm not home. I'm lost.*

What?

I'm on a weird, dead-end street that's stuck somewhere between an outlet mall and a bunch of stores owned by hippies.

Denton Avenue.

What?

Ur on Denton Avenue. They were going to tear it down a few years ago but the residents protested and had it declared a heritage site. Something about a tree.

Oh-kay.

Not my idea. There's a shortcut out, tho. Walk between the blue house with the fountain and the gray one with the yellow door. U won't feel like ur on a path, but u r. It'll take u out to an alley beside a soap shop.

Thx.

NP. I'll text u when I'm home so we can trade phones?

Yep. I hit send, then quickly added another message. *U still not telling me where ur going?*

Mom's house for dinner.

Send me a pic.

Why? U think I'm lying? :P

Nope. I just wanna see how hot ur gonna be when ur older.

U. R. Disturbed.

:D

BTW...don't u DARE answer my phone today. Or read my messages.

I'll do my best to refrain.

Do better than ur best.

Without bothering to point out that BEST is a superlative. Okay, I pinky swear.

Weird. TTYL Marc.

Bye honey.

I tucked the phone away again, grinning like an idiot and not caring who noticed as I followed her instructions for the shortcut. She was right. For about five steps, I felt like a trespasser. Then the space widened into a paved path that led exactly where she said it would. The scent of fragrant soap filled the air, and on whim, I stepped inside the shop.

Immediately, a tall, blond woman with smiling eyes stepped out to greet me. "Welcome to *Joyful Jo's.* I'm Joanna. Owner. Proprietress. All that jazz. Shopping for something specific today?"

"A gift," I said, not realizing it was true until the words were out of my mouth.

"Mother or girlfriend?"

I smiled. "Don't men come in for themselves?"

"Nope." She had a matter-of-fact way of speaking that put me at ease.

"How do you know I'm not shopping for my wife? Or *boy*friend?"

"No ring. And *ha.* The gay population should be so lucky."

My smile widened. "Well. In that case…it's *not* for my mother."

"Aha. Then you must know what kind of fragrance she likes already?"

"Uh…"

Joanna made a little *tsk-tsk,* then shook her finger at me. "Fragrance is very personal. Most men think they can just pick something *they* like and hand it over. But scents change when they're on a person. And if you don't believe that, then just remember…you never know if you're buying something her ex's mother wore."

I laughed. "Okay. Point taken. What do you suggest then?"

"Well. Normally I'd say go home and get her so she can pick, but I get the feeling this is a spontaneous thing?"

"Afraid so."

"I've got the perfect thing."

She stepped back behind the counter and dragged a cream-colored card and envelope from a drawer, then set them on the counter and wrote something in light strokes. When she was done, she sealed it up, tucked it into a black gift bag, which she stuffed with some silver paper before handing it to me.

"It's not a gift card, per se," she said. "It's more of an invitation. Your girl can come back anytime and redeem this for a fully personalized set. Soap, lotion, body wash, and massage oil. But you should come with her. That way you know what to buy next time."

I tugged out my credit card and handed it over. I didn't care what the cost was—the gift was perfect.

With a sincere thank you and a promise that I'd bring "my" girl back, I slipped out of the store and back to the street. The sky had darkened again, but my mood was once again light enough that I didn't care. Thoughts of Carl and his video were far from my mind. I was going to see Aysia again. Soon. And for some reason, not much else mattered.

* * * *

Aysia

"Aysia?"

"Mmph."

"You could try *chewing* your food."

"Sorry, Mom."

I slowed down my chomping and looked down at my plate guiltily. She'd made my favorite dinner—lasagna with Caesar salad—but I really hadn't been taking the time to enjoy it. After a few hours of shopping with Liv, I was tired. And if I was being honest…I was anxious about seeing Marc, too. Not in a worried way. In an excited way that made me squirm a bit in my chair.

"Aysia," my mom said again. "You haven't had this many ants in your pants since you were in second grade."

"Sorry."

"And your phone's rung about four times."

"They're just texts," I mumbled, shoving another forkful into my mouth.

My mother raised an eyebrow—the same gesture I always made when I wanted to call out the ridiculousness of someone's comment or action. I sighed. I chewed. Then I met her curious gaze. And I lied.

"It's nothing."

Her eyebrow went higher. "So it's a boy."

"I'm twenty-five years old. It wouldn't be a boy. It would be a man."

"Aha!"

"What?"

"It *is* a boy."

"Mom."

"I know you, daughter dearest, and the only time in your life that you ever lie to me is when it involves a boy."

I winced and took another bite. It was kind of true. My mom and I were close, and I thought we probably had an above average parent-child relationship. I'd even say it extended to friendship now that I was an adult. But my dad left when I was thirteen, and she'd never remarried. Or brought home anyone else. And though she never said it bothered her, I always felt awkward talking about my own love life with her. I hadn't ever mentioned Carl to her. Nor any of the few guys I'd seen casually before that. Maybe I brought up the occasional date, but definitely nothing else. And I guess I never thought about whether or not she noticed the deliberate avoidance.

But I sure as hell wasn't going to start by trying to explain that I'd taken home a guy from the bar and spent the night with my mouth on varying parts of his body.

"It's nothing," I said.

From my purse, Marc's phone buzzed again.

"It's something," my mom said. "At least look at it. The noise is driving me crazy."

With a warm face, I dragged out the oversized case and peered down at the screen. The first message was from over an hour earlier.

So I'm curious, it read. *Why didn't u ask for my number?*

There was a fifteen-minute break before the next text.

Okay, wrong question, apparently, it said. *How about...what're u wearing?*

Five minutes had gone by before the third one came in.

Fine. I guess we're in a fight.

I couldn't help but laugh. Especially when I saw the next three texts, which had all come more recently. The first was a collage created using my photo app, featuring a vaguely phallic carving in a half a dozen spots throughout an undecorated condo. On top of a gas fireplace. In the middle of a bubble wrapped coffee table. Upside down in empty plant pot, then in the same pot, but outside on a little balcony. Then balanced on the top shelf of a bookcase, and finally in the center of a bright white mattress.

Under the collage, Marc had typed, *Where do u like it best?*

Then immediately after that . . . *Shit. I just realized all of those are basically wooden dick pics. Why the hell didn't I realize I was buying dildo art?*

I looked up from the phone to find my mom watching me. She was clearly amused by my reaction. And curious, too.

"You like him," she said.

"I just met him," I admitted.

She lifted her fork and studied me thoughtfully. "You going to answer?"

"I can wait."

"Don't." Her voice was firm enough to make me blink. "He's making you smile. I appreciate seeing you happy."

"I'm always happy."

"You're always self-sufficient. And content. But you never laugh like a fool like that."

"Um. Thanks?"

"Answer him." She stood up. "I'm going to go open a bottle of wine anyway."

As she stepped out of the room, I moved my thumb over the screen and typed a reply. *I didn't ask for your number because you ran out of my apartment like your ass was on fire.*

His answer came right away. *I had to leave before ur bodyguard beat me up.*

Liv?

Yep.

She just wants to protect me from weirdos.

Hmm. Maybe I should send HER some pics?

DO NOT.

Okay. No need to yell.

I did tell u I was having dinner at my mom's, right?

Yeah. But u never sent the pic, so...

My mom doesn't selfie.

Because the camera eats her soul?

Ha ha. Because she read an article that said selfies are narcissistic.

In response, he sent his own selfie. He was lying on the same mattress from the previous picture, the phone obviously extended above him as high as he could hold it, giving a genuinely swoon-worthy view of his bare chest and sexy smile. Or at least, it *was* swoon-worthy. Until I realized he had the wooden carving tucked into the crook of his arm.

Seriously? I typed. *Now a cuddling dick pic? Definitely narcissistic.*

I was just assuming u liked it best in my bed.

Uh-huh. Let me know when u buy some sheets and I'll get back to u about that.

How about u let me sleep over again, and u can take me shopping for some in the morning?

My body heated a little at the thought of getting Marc back into *my* bed. And I couldn't exactly say that the thought of picking out his sheets was a turnoff, either.

Not sure when I'll be home, I told him.

I can wait.

My heart did a funny little jump, and as I set the phone back in my purse, I couldn't wipe the smile from my face.

"I take it the text went well?" my mom asked, setting down a fresh bottle of Merlot.

I shrugged as casually as I could. "He wants to see me again."

"Is that all I'm going to get from you?"

"Yep."

"Hmm. Let's see what you have to say after a few glasses."

"My lips are sealed."

Even though we did split the bottle over the next couple of hours, I managed to steer the conversation away from anything that came close to dating, or Marc, or wooden dick pics. Instead, we talked about work—mine and hers—and the latest political scandals. We did the dishes by hand and played a few rounds of rummy. And by the time the evening was over, I was pretty sure she'd forgotten about the whole thing. That is, until my cab pulled up and she pulled me in for a hug.

"Make sure he knows your worth as well as you do, okay?" she said into my ear.

"All right, mom."

Her words stuck with me on the short ride home. I *did* know my own worth. Smart and capable. Every report card, every performance review, every bit of self-affirmation told me on repeat that I was both those things. It was part of what made me *me*. And I didn't think there was anything wrong with owning my sexuality as an extension of that.

I thought it was funny that Liv—who was practically a goddess where all things man were concerned—and my mom—who was as prim and proper as they came—*both* seemed so concerned about my love life at the moment. I fiddled with the hem of my T-shirt, wondering if they saw something that I didn't. Liv had barely batted and eye when I went out with Carl. And my mom never asked me about men.

Until now. Why?

"Miss?"

I looked up and realized we were already in front of my building. I thanked the cabbie a little absently, handed over my fare, then made my way inside. A quick glance at Marc's phone told me it was past midnight already.

Too late to call and invite him over, probably.

I couldn't fight a stab of disappointment as I stepped into the elevator. I'd never considered myself as the kind of girl who *needed* a man. Though more than occasionally, I wanted one. And right that second, the want was pretty damned specific. It involved strong hands and brown eyes and a cocky chuckle.

I sighed as the elevator doors slid open. My feet even dragged a little as I made my way to my door. But when I actually reached it, and I looked down and saw the gift bag, my mouth tipped up. I knew it was from Marc.

I let myself into my condo, eagerly tearing out the paper as I closed the door. I recognized the logo on the little, ivory-hued card right away.

Joyful Jo's.

He'd obviously taken the shortcut I suggested. It made me smile. And before I could stop to think better of it, I grabbed the phone and typed up a message.

Thank u!

He didn't answer right away, but after I'd tidied up a bit, slipped into my pajamas, then climbed into bed, the phone finally beeped. *U like it?*

Love it, I admitted.

The owner claims that scents are very personal.

Joanna is never wrong.

Ah. So. U know her well?

What can I say? She makes good soap. A VanCity secret.

Hmm. R there a lot of those?

VanCity secrets? Maybe. I've lived here my whole life, so I'm sure I can tell u a few more.

I smiled as he told me he'd like that, then asked me a few more questions about the city and about my life. It felt strangely natural to talk with him like this. Back and forth queries and answers, punctuated with an extra helping of sideways wink-y faces and a heavy dose of innuendo. As the minutes ticked by, the ebb and flow slowed, and I knew he was probably feeling as tired as I was. I was just about to suggest we sign off when he sent a message that woke me right up.

Ever had phone sex, Aysia?

No.

Ever wanted to?

Not until right this second.

LOL.

Don't LOL @ me. Have u ever had phone sex?

No.

His reply made me a little bit too happy. *Ever WANTED to?*

What makes u think I'm not doing it right now?

Pervert. But the thought of him touching himself while he talked to me made my breath quicken.

A little perversion is called for, I think. Tell me what ur wearing, Aysia.
I could practically hear his bossy tone.
Lie? I answered. *Or the truth?*
The truth.
I lifted my sheet and looked down before typing, *Kinda boring. Little black shorts and matching tank top.*
Not boring on u. And not as boring as what I have on.
Which is?
Nothing.
My responding groan echoed through my empty room. And I didn't get a chance to say anything back before the phone came to life again, this time with a ring. My own number was on the call display, so I pressed the answer button, then lifted it and waited for his voice to fill my ear.
"Hi, honey."
"Hi, Marc."
"Red sheets still on the bed?" he asked.
"Yes."
"Pillow smell like me?"
I inhaled, dragging in just a hint of his lightly spiced scent. "A bit."
"Makes me a little envious," he said with a chuckle.
"Why?"
"Because I don't have anything here that smells like *you.*"
"Sorry. I guess I should've offered you a souvenir."
"You'd really reduce me to one of those creepy panty snatchers?"
I smiled. "I didn't say panties. You did."
He laughed again, low and sexy. "Yeah. But now that's what I'm thinking about."
"That's a shame. Because right this second, I'm not wearing any."
He paused, his deep breath carrying through the speaker. "Christ, do I want to be there."
"You'll probably want to be here even more when I tell you where my hands are." I balanced the phone against my shoulder and ran them up my thighs as I spoke.
"Put me on speaker." Now his voice was rough. "I want to hear you."
I fumbled for a second before finding the right buttons. "You there?"
His reply came out a little fuzzy, but still audible. "I'm here. Where'd you put me?"
"On my pillow."
"Good. I've got you on mine, too."
I closed my eyes, picturing it. "Okay."

"Are you imagining me?"

"Yes."

"Good," he said again, a little thicker this time. "Think about my hands being on your knees."

The mental picture filled my mind immediately.

"Got it?" he wanted to know.

"Mm-hmm."

"Now they're moving up, hitting the bottom of your shorts."

My own fingers followed his guided tour of my body. I was already alight, already slick with desire.

"They start to slip under the shorts, then pause and go up farther instead," he said. "They slide back and forth across the soft, sweet spot at the bend of your leg."

His words were so soft. So seductive.

"My fingers move up now." His voice was a near whisper. "They reach your waistband and then slip inside."

In my head, his thick, sure figures caressed the sensitive skin just below my currently non-existent panty line.

"They keep going," he added. "Touching and teasing. Just one finger, slipping to roll over your clit."

I couldn't hold in a gasp as my hand found the spot he suggested. And on the other end of the phone, Marc groaned. My mind moved involuntarily from him touching *me* to him touching *himself.*

"Oh, God," I gasped.

My hand moved faster, and I couldn't stop it.

If someone had told me just a half hour earlier than the thought of a man stroking his own erection would be the thing to drive me over the edge, I would've laughed. But this was a whole other story, and there was nothing funny about. It was just straight up hotness.

So.

Damned.

Hot.

"Marc," I said, startled to find the first sweet spirals of an orgasm already licking across my abdomen. "I can't hold on."

"Don't," he replied. "Please don't."

So I gave in to my need, letting his voice and my hand take me to the precipice, then toss me over full force. My hips lifted, and I shuddered. It was quick and intense, and it took me several long moments after to recover. I could hear Marc, too, breathing heavily on the other end.

It was him who spoke first. "You there?"

"Nowhere else to go," I said back teasingly. "And I'm pretty sure my legs wouldn't work anyway."

He chuckled. "I do have that effect on women."

"Hmm. Are there a *lot* of women in your life?"

I expected a hesitation. I didn't get one.

"Nope," he said. "None."

"*None?*"

"Well. I did meet one girl just the other day, and I'm kind of hoping—" A noisy beep cut him off, and he swore.

"What was that?" I asked.

"I think your phone is about to die."

"You didn't plug it in?"

"You plugged mine in?"

"We have the same charger."

"Oh."

"Yeah."

The beep sounded again, blaring into my pillow.

"Sorry, Aysia, I really think it's going to—"

And that was it. The phone died. With a frustrated sigh, I set the device back down, then put my head on the pillow beside it.

What had he been hoping? I really wanted to know. Like, really, really. I tucked my sheet up around my chin, thinking about it. Though the night before I hadn't cared enough to ask, I was glad he had no other women in his life. Not that I thought for a second I was a piece of side action. Just that a man who had moves like Marc couldn't be hard up.

Then I smiled. My own moves weren't exactly shabby, either. As evidenced by the fact that he'd stolen my phone just to talk to me again. I hugged myself a little giddily. The bubbling excitement made me wonder if I'd be able to fall asleep at all, but after a few minutes, drowsiness crept in. I drifted, Marc's sideways smile filling my mind pleasantly.

I rolled over once, sure that sleep was just a breath or two away. But before I managed to grab a hold of it, an insistent buzz forced me to wakefulness again.

The door.

I frowned and pushed to a sitting position. The buzz came again. A glance at Marc's phone told me it was now nearly two in the morning.

Marc.

Had he made his way back to my place after the phone died? It would've been a pretty quick trip. I made myself get up, and I stepped down the stairs and moved to the long window in my living room. It faced the front of the building, but my view was obstructed by the tall hemlocks that lined the walk. I squinted and angled my gaze downward, trying to get a look at the concrete patio. What I saw instead was the shiny sign on the post emblazoned with Eco-Go's logo. And reflected in the sign was a face I knew.

Carl.

"Shit," I muttered, jumping back.

The buzzer sounded again.

Please just go away, I willed silently.

It wasn't the first time he'd shown up at my place unexpectedly. But it was the first time it'd happened in the middle of the night. Did he really think I'd answer?

If his persistence is any indication...

Asshole.

I took a breath, then checked the door. It was soundly locked. Bolted. I wiggled the handle, just to make sure, then cast another glance toward my window and hurried back up to my bedroom, praying that he hadn't seen any movement inside.

I reminded myself that Carl didn't know the key code and that I wasn't scared of him. Or of his miniscule manhood. And as I climbed into bed again, the buzzing finally ceased.

But I couldn't shake my unease.

I pulled up my sheets, this time forcefully. I knew it was going to be tougher now to get back to sleep. I'd be worrying about Carl and what he wanted.

My fingers crept to Marc's phone. I considered calling Liv. Or the police. But I knew doing the former would cause more worry than I wanted to deal with. The latter would make me seem like a victim. Which I definitely was not. I didn't want to deal with the fallout if *that* got back to anyone at work, either. I could just imagine the drama. And of course—technically—buzzing me at two in the morning wasn't illegal. It was just annoying and freak-tastic. Typical Carl.

I exhaled and pulled my fingers away from the phone and admitted that if I was being totally honest anyway, the voice I really wanted to hear wasn't my best friend's *or* that of a too-patient cop. It was the one that belonged to a man I'd just met.

Chapter 6

Marcelo

I scrubbed a hand over my freshly-shaved face and stared irritably at the list of names on the side of Aysia's building.

The morning was bright and sunny. I, on the other hand, was not.

It wasn't that there were all that many names listed. The compact condominium only had six floors, and each floor had only four units. It was just that they were *last* names, and I still hadn't asked what hers was. The only one I recognized was Fisk, and I was sure as hell that the missus attached to it wouldn't be interested in hearing any more of my breathing.

I tugged Aysia's phone from my pocket and glared at it. The moment our conversation had cut off last night, I'd tried to plug in the damned thing like she suggested. All I'd succeeded in doing was breaking off the end of my charger. It left me feeling…I don't know what.

"Un-fucking-finished," I muttered.

Not because I *hadn't* finished. I sure as hell had. In a way that would've been embarrassingly quick in person. But our *moment* had been cut short.

What more I wanted, I don't know. A cuddle? A few sweet nothings and her hand threaded through mine? Yeah, okay. Possibly. I admitted I'd been tempted to leave my apartment in favor of hers, middle of the night be damned. I'd made myself stay. Reminded myself the beauty of phone sex was rolling over and falling asleep in the comfort of my own home *without* having to talk about it.

Didn't stop you from wanting to do it, though, did it, you big suck?

"Shut up," I said aloud to my asshole of a conscience, then turned my attention back to my current problem.

I stepped down the front step and onto the patch of grass, and I craned my neck up to look at the second floor. Was it unreasonable to throw rocks at a living room window? A minute later, though, I realized I wouldn't have to. Up above, a curtain of brown curls tipped over one of the balconies. The sun framed her face and even though it was impossible, I could swear that I could see the dazzling blue of her eyes from where I stood.

My bad mood eased considerably at the sight of her. "Hey, honey. Sensed my undeniable presence, huh?"

Her mane of hair shook back and forth. "No, you ego maniac. Mrs. Fisk just knocked on my door and told me there was some lunatic on the front step."

"Ah. Get a lot of us maniacs down here?"

For a second, her face clouded, then she shook her head again and it cleared. "I try to keep it to a minimum."

"You wanna let me in?"

"I guess it's better than letting you stand out there being all maniacal."

She disappeared back into her condo, and a moment later, the door buzzed. I jogged back up the stairs and yanked it open, an uncontrollable grin already on my face. By the time I actually reached her door, my cock had joined my face in having a mind of its own. It was busy making plans that my brain hadn't even caught up with yet. And it sure as hell didn't calm down at all when she opened the door and greeted me in nothing but a tiny pair of running shorts, a sports bra, and a minuscule white crop top.

I eyed her up and down. "I don't know whether to be disappointed that you're not in your pajamas or thrilled that you're in that outfit instead."

Her already-flushed face went a little redder. "Just got back from a jog."

"You wear *that* when you run?" I did another onceover, starting with her currently bare feet and ending at her mess of curls.

"Minus the insane hair—which is the result of a broken hair tie—but otherwise…yes."

"Where?"

She raised an eyebrow. "Wherever I want. Is that a problem?"

"Nope. I just want to know where so I can come."

"You run, too?"

"I do. But in this case…I just wanna watch *you*." I held out her phone.

"Ha ha." She took the cell, then shot me a look as she saw the blank screen. "Still dead? Really?"

"Don't ask. It's a boring story that ends in swear words and a hangnail."

Her mouth tipped up. "Fine. I won't. Not because I mind swear words but because I hate hangnails."

I watched as she took a swig of the water, envious of the bottle. Then I watched some more as she swallowed, her tongue darting out to suck off any wayward drops.

Christ.

Every move she made managed to be sexy.

I fought an urge to toss aside the water bottle—and my dignity—so I could throw her over the counter right that second.

She took another sip, and when she pulled the bottle down this time, a drop of liquid hung on her upper lip. I waited for her tongue to come out to claim it, and was sorely disappointed when it didn't.

You are more than a set of overactive balls, I told myself firmly, and I cleared my throat. "You still up for shopping?"

The water droplet trickled down her lip to her chin, distracting me so badly I almost missed her reply.

"Bed sheets?" she asked.

"Uh. Yeah."

"Sure."

Now the drop slid down her chin to her throat, settling for a second in the small, kissable spot just above her first rib.

Hell. Maybe I am *nothing but a set of overactive balls.*

I continued to stare for a long moment before lifting my eyes to meet her mildly amused gaze.

"Good," I managed to say.

Three seconds went by before I sought the water droplet's path again. "Gotta charge my phone for a bit first," she added.

The drop was just above her cleavage, hovering. "Okay."

"Probably eat."

"All right."

"Stretch a bit."

"Yeah."

"And take a shower."

"Okay."

"Maybe have some sex. If the right guy shows up."

The drip disappeared under her low-cut, form-fitting shirt. Why the hell was that single bit of moisture so damned alluring?

Wait.

I looked up. "What?"

She was already on the move, one foot on the little stairs that led up to her bedroom in the loft. She tossed me a smile over her shoulder, then

reached down and yanked off the tiny shirt. For a second, she held it on
the tip of her finger. Then she dropped it.

Damn.

Why wouldn't my own feet move? She laughed like she knew how stuck
I was, then reached for her bra. In an instant, she was topless.

My eyes dragged hungrily over her bare back. I clearly hadn't spent
enough time just looking at her two nights earlier. She had light muscles
under her soft curves and smooth, beautiful skin. Tan lines emphasized
how much time she spent in the outdoors, but the contrast wasn't so strong
that it was startling. I lifted a hand—maybe just to prove I could still
control some small part of my body—and ran my fingers over my chin. I
was half-surprised to find that it wasn't covered with drool.

Aysia's hands moved to her shorts. She lowered them. One inch. Then
another. She cast another look my way, but it barely registered. I had a
perfect view of the dimples in the lowest part of her back, and I could
just see the top of her heart shaped ass. But she'd stopped moving, her
striptease paused.

"Something you want, Marc?" she asked archly.

"Take them off," I said, my voice full of need.

"Say please."

"Please," I growled.

"You don't sound like you mean it."

"I don't think I've ever meant anything more."

She let out another laugh, wriggled once, then let the shorts fall. For a
blissful second, my cock and my brain were in complete agreement. Her
ass was everything that makes an ass perfect. Then she was gone. Running
up the stairs and slipping from my line of sight.

"Shit."

I finally convinced my feet that they needed to do some work, too. I
strode across the room and hit the steps in my usual way, taking two at
a time. Even so, when I reached the top, I could already hear the shower
running in her en suite. I pushed my way through the bedroom and into
the bathroom just in time to see her slide the stall door shut. Immediately,
I pressed my hand to the glass and opened it again.

She gave my fully clothed body a critical glare. "You are *not* getting
in here like that."

I shot a pointed look around the shower stall. "I don't know how to tell
you this, honey, but I don't think you can stop me."

She crossed her arms over her chest, pushing her cleavage to epic proportions, and I fought a laugh. The gesture did nothing to make her glare any more convincing.

I took a small step closer and ran my thumb across one of her wet, on-display breasts. "It's cute that you think getting mad is gonna work."

"I swear, Marc—"

I dropped my mouth to hers cutting her off forcefully. The water rained down on me, and I didn't care. I moved forward again, encircling her naked body with my clothed one, and I deepened the kiss, parting her lips with my tongue. She tasted fantastic, salty with a hint of leftover sweat and fresh with the water pouring down our faces.

Still exploring her mouth, I lifted a foot and stepped into the stall, sliding the door shut behind me as I did. She wasn't pretending to fight me anymore. Her hands were on me. Running across my back, digging into my hair, then pulling away just long enough to drag my T-shirt up and toss the sopping thing aside before tilting her head back up and cementing her lips back to mine. She hooked her knee over my hip and pushed into my thick erection.

Growling against her mouth, I reached down to grab her ass and lift her up. I pressed her against the shower wall and thrust against her in a quick circle. One way. Then the other.

"Pants," she gasped, pushing a hand between us to snatch at the button of my jeans.

As she fought the tiny space between us, her finger hit my cock, again and again, making me groan. God, how I wanted her. Now.

"Too slow," I muttered, then pushed her aside to free myself.

Quickly, I flicked open my button and zipper. She helped me along by shoving down my pants to my hips. I groaned again. I was so close to where I wanted to be. So ready to take her, hard and quick.

"Condom," I said, loath to let her go, but knowing I had to, just for a moment. "Hurry."

I released her and stumbled from the tub, pulling of my shoes and my waterlogged pants as I did. I slid open the drawer, found the box, and tore it open. By the time I got back to Aysia and the shower, I was sheathed and ready. And she was no less eager. Before I even reached the edge of the bath, she had her hands on me once more, pulling me closer.

I tried for a futile second to slow things down. I put my palm on her hip, thinking I might restrain myself for a moment longer. I couldn't. When my fingers closed on her soft skin, she tipped her head back with a gasp.

The sight of her with the water pouring down on her face—her expression wanton and her hair plastered to her shoulders—was all I could take.

Without any pretense of holding back, I grabbed her by the ass and lifted her from the ground again. I pushed her to the wall, sliding my cock into her as I did. Just entering her almost undid me. The way she fit me so perfectly. How she was tight and slick at the same time. The fact that she cried out my name as I rocked inside her, again, and again. It was all too much.

"*So* fucking good, Aysia," I said against her mouth.

"Yes!"

I don't know if it was an agreement or just an exclamation, but as soon as the word slipped from her lips, her grip on me tightened. Her fingers dug hard into shoulder blades and her knees hugged my hips and her ass clenched under my hands. All around me she tensed up.

"Christ," I swore. "I can't—now, Aysia. Fuck. Please."

She called out another affirmation, then quivered under me.

"Now," I said again, and her reply was a wild noise that drove me over the edge—that drove *us* over.

Together, we came—her pulsing around me, me throbbing inside of her. I held her there against the wall until our breathing evened out, then released her to the ground slowly and gave her a half a dozen slow, warm kisses before I pulled away.

She looked up at me, her face shielded from the water by my body, a little smile playing over her mouth. "That was the dirtiest shower I've ever had."

I chuckled and kissed her again. "You want me to clean you up?"

She shook her head, then nodded, then shook her head again. "You can try. But I might be forever sullied."

"Well. At least let me give it a solid effort before you decide I'm incapable," I teased.

"All right. But I can't say my hopes are high."

I spent the next five minutes making sure every inch of her received a thorough, soap-laden rub down, then moved on to grab her bottle of coconut-scented shampoo. She studied my face for a second before turning so I could massage the thick liquid into her head.

"This is another first for me," she admitted softly.

"Which part? Letting a very manly man wash your hair, or letting the same manly man fuck you silly in the shower?"

She let out a breathy laugh. "Well. Both, actually."

"Is either a bad thing?"

"No. You're good with your hands."

"Just my hands?"

"I think you know the answer to that," she said, leaning back and closing her eyes so I could rinse her curls. "In my head, this should be weird."

"In your head? Do you spend a lot of time imagining this particular scenario?"

"No. I mean, I *might* have fantasized a time or two about having my stylist at my beck and call, but I draw the fantasy line at showering with a sixty-seven-year-old gay man."

I grinned. "There goes my dream."

She jabbed a playful elbow into my stomach. "Shut up."

"Resorting to violence already? That's cheap." I kissed her tilted-back forehead, then grabbed the conditioner. "What about the other part of the fantasy? You think shower sex should be weird?"

Under my hands, she nodded. "Mm-hmm. All the water and awkward positions and the slipperiness."

"That's what makes it good."

"I think *you're* what made it good."

"Flattery?"

"Fact."

Smiling, I smoothed the conditioner through the length of her hair, then started to rinse. "This is a first for me, too."

"To quote you...which part?"

"Both," I admitted.

"What? No crazy hot shower in your old hometown?"

The question sounded casual, but I could hear the serious undertone. The weird thing was, it didn't bother me. Not that my sex life was a secret, but I usually didn't have much interest in obligating myself to share my history. Especially with a woman I'd just met.

But my answer came easily.

"My ex definitely added some craziness to my life for the year we were together," I said. "Not sure it translated to *hot*. Not in a good way, anyway."

"Is she the reason you moved?"

"Nope. I came out for work. Doing a favor for a friend of my dad's. Things ended months ago between me and Janie. It wasn't pleasant, but it was just a breakup."

"Not a broken heart?"

I thought about for a second, then shook my head. "Maybe I thought I loved her at one point. But her priorities were different than mine. I work hard for what I get. She wanted things handed to her. I think I was just relieved when it was over. What about you?"

"I'm glad it's over, too. I hate having shower sex with another woman's man."
I laughed. "Not what I meant."

She turned and reached past me to twist the shower to the off position,
then stood up again to meet my gaze. There was something a little guarded
in her eyes, but she sighed and spoke anyway.

"I've never made time for a traditional relationship. Work's been my
focus for as long as I can remember. The last guy I was with…" She trailed
off and shrugged.

Carl.

I locked my jaw for a second to keep from telling her that I was well-
aware of the man's douchebag status, then made myself relax and say, "He
didn't appreciate awkward, slippery sex?"

She offered me a small smile. "I don't think he would've been *capable.*"

"Good." The word came out a little more forcefully than I intended,
and Aysia blinked up at me in surprise.

"Do you have a *jealous* streak, Marc?" she asked.

"I have a need-to-be-the-best streak."

"Me, too."

I kissed her. "Trust me. There's no fucking competition."

A blush crept up under her skin, and she slid open the glass door to
reach for a towel. The one she pulled off the rack, though, was soaked. She
paused and surveyed the disaster in the bathroom. Everything was wet. The
floor. The countertop. My clothes, of course. Even the mirror was dripping.

"Shit," Aysia said.

"Pretty damned impressive." I stepped past her and out of the tub.
"Extra towels under the sink?"

"Yes."

I opened the cupboard, grabbed one for her and one for me. "You go
do whatever you have to do. I'll clean up."

"Seriously?" She shook her head. "You know what? Never mind. I'm
not going to argue. You do your thing, slippery, sexy manservant. When
you're done, there's an extra robe in my closet and the clothes dryer is
downstairs beside the other bathroom. I'll be in the kitchen waiting for
you to cook me naked breakfast."

I pulled her in for a quick kiss before I let her escape, then turned my
attention to tidying up. Admittedly, back in L.A., I had someone come
and do most of my housework for me. Putting in a ten- to twelve-hour
day most of the time didn't allow much time for laundry and dishes. Of
course, I never made much of a mess at home since I spent such a minimal
amount of time there. I wondered if Aysia was the same. She definitely

seemed like the driven type. She'd mentioned how important her job was to her. Did that mean she had someone scrub her floors? I can't say the thought of her bent down on all fours doing it herself didn't appeal to me. Especially if she happened to have a kinky little maid's costume kicking around somewhere.

Yeah. But then the floors would never actually get *clean,* I thought. *You'd be too busy taking advantage of the position.*

I grinned to myself and finished wiping the mirror. Maybe if she *wasn't* an avid housecleaner I could talk her into a little role play. I stepped back and checked out my handiwork. Things were mostly dry and mostly tidy. I grabbed my clothes, wrapped them in a towel and stepped into the bedroom to search for the robe. I paused, though, in the doorway.

Aysia was sprawled across the bed, one arm over her head, one tucked against her stomach. Her eyes were closed, her lips parted just slightly.

Sound asleep.

Moving quietly, I slid the sheet from the bottom of the bed and tucked it up over her body. She barely shifted in response.

"Sorry, honey," I murmured. "Can't pretend I didn't enjoy wearing you out."

I let myself out of the bedroom and got to work on the rest of her snarky little instructions. I put my clothes in her dryer, then made a much-needed pot of coffee. Next, I dug through the fridge and helped myself to the ingredients I needed to put together a 'naked' breakfast. Still smiling, I set everything out on the counter. As I put down the final item—one of those *as-seen-on-TV* no-stick pans—I accidentally knocked over Aysia's purse. Which in and of itself wasn't a big deal. As I bent down to retrieve it, though, a business card slipped out, and what I saw made my heart smash against my ribs.

What the fuck?

With suddenly stiff fingers, I lifted the card.

Aysia Banks. Human Resources, Eco-Go Developments.

My eyes flew from the embossed letters to the stairs that led to her bedroom. She was a goddamned employee. Why the hell hadn't it occurred to me? It made sense. That was how she knew Carl. It was why she'd been at the pub recommended as a favorite of the staff. Even the fact that she lived in an Eco-Go building should've been a hint.

"Fuck," I muttered, at a loss for a better word to describe the panic setting in. "Fuck-fuck-fuck."

I ran a hand over my hair, unsure what to do. Part of me knew I should wait for her to wake up, then explain it all. From Carl's video to the pub to this moment right now. A bigger part of me had no interest in dealing with it.

Selfish coward.

I eyed the stairs again.

"Fuck." This time it was a snarl.

I forced in a breath and began putting away everything I'd just taken out. I needed time to regroup. To think about what I wanted to say. To convince her that I *wasn't* a selfish coward.

I didn't know where to start, but I did know I had to leave. No way could I get the head space I needed with her so close.

I tucked the eggs back into the fridge, then scrawled a hasty note telling her to enjoy her nap. I hesitated, not sure how to close it.

Call you later?

See you at work?

Apparently, I'm an asshole?

Finally, I settled for a simple—copout—letter 'M'. Then I grabbed my still-wet clothes from the dryer, forced them on, and pulled the most chicken shit move of my life. I slipped out as fast as I could without looking back.

* * * *

Aysia

I made my way down the stairs, rubbing my eyes. I'd been stunned to roll over and see that the late-afternoon sun was already dipping down over the horizon. My first thought had been of Marc, and I half-expected to find his muscular form beside me. Instead, I found an empty bed.

And now that I was downstairs and a little more awake, I discovered an equally empty main floor and a vague note.

> *Enjoy your rest.*
> *Talk soon.*
> *M.*

Not that I could blame him for taking off. Hours had passed. But I could think of a few very pleasant ways for him to have woken me up. My stomach growled, and I acknowledged that yes, food would've been one of them.

I swung open my fridge, puzzled to find everything out of order. My cheese was in the fruit drawer, and my egg carton was upside down. Overall, it looked a little like someone—Marc—had knocked the whole thing over, then shoved it back in as hastily as he could.

"Weird."

I grabbed an apple, then my phone, and moved to the living room where I dropped down onto the sofa. I scrolled through all the messages from Marc's phone to mine, noting that he'd programmed his name into my address book, complete with a copy of the picture of him and his oh-so phallic carving. Then I moved on to everything I'd missed while he'd had my phone, laughing at the texts from Liv.

Hey. What're you doing?

Hello? BFF here!

Oh. Right. Shit. Forgot you didn't have your phone. You did tell me that. And Marc, if you're reading this. Stop it.

There was a voicemail from my mom, sent before I called to let her know I couldn't be reached at my regular number. There was another from my boss, letting me know the senior team needed to come in for a meeting on Monday morning with our new PR manager. Normally, that would excite me. But not today.

I sighed and sat back to take another bite of my apple. Work—for once—was the last thing on my mind. What I really wanted was a funny, sexy message from Marc. So I typed one to him myself.

*So. Rearranging fridges...*I wrote. *Is that a fetish, or...?*

I hit send and waited. Surprisingly, an answer didn't come right away. In fact, one didn't come for hours. It gave me time to catch up on some reading, to go through my emails, to run a few errands, and even grab a coffee with Liv.

Which was where I was at the moment, staring down at my decidedly silent phone.

My friend finally snatched the device away from me, clicked through my messages over my protests, then raised both of her perfectly shaped eyebrows at me.

"You had *phone* sex with him?"

"Possibly."

"Holy shit, Aysia. I'm impressed."

"Shut up."

She looked down at the screen again. "And then he rearranged your fridge?"

I tried to grab my phone from her, but she yanked it back quickly.

"C'mon," I whined. "Why are you being such a jerk-face about this?"

"Because I care. And it's weird to see you acting like some teenaged girl. Hell, Aysia. Even when you *were* a teenager girl, you didn't act like this. You're practically moping."

"I'm *not*."

But maybe I was. Maybe I was letting my hormones—and okay, stupid, girlie *feelings*—get the better of me. I exhaled and met my friend's eyes.

"I don't know," I said. "I've had more sex in the last three days than I've had in probably three years. It's not an exaggeration to say that Marc's phenomenal in bed. But it's not just that. He's funny, too. And thoughtful. He bought me a gift card for Jo's, and when I fell asleep today, he tucked me in."

She let out a low whistle. "You've got it pretty bad."

I didn't see the point in lying; my best friend knew me too well to buy it anyway. "I *like* him, Liv. And I think I could get to like him even more. I've had this weird, bubbly feeling in my chest since I woke up Saturday morning."

"That would be what all the kids call infatuation."

"It hasn't been long enough for it to be infatuation."

"Okay then. The anticipation of infatuation."

I couldn't suppress a sigh. "Fine. I'll concede to that description. I'm excited about the idea of connecting with someone like this. We feel…compatible."

It was a lame description. But I couldn't bring myself to say that when I closed my eyes, his delicious face filled my mind and made my heart jump like a drunk frog.

Liv narrowed her eyes at me. "Stop making it sound so reasonable."

"I *am* reasonable."

"Just admit that you like his butt."

"It's a very nice butt."

"Can't say I didn't notice."

She finally handed over my phone, and I looked down at the screen again with a mix of irritation and forlornness. "He hasn't answered my last text. And maybe my brain's been turned to mush by all the sex, but I genuinely think he likes me back."

"Aw. Cute. And also…gag."

I wrinkled my nose at her. "I'm serious. I didn't ask for any strings or anything, so it's not like he had to impress me with his powers of commitment. He could've walked out Friday night and not come back."

"Aha. So you've now beguiled him. Maybe he's out buying your engagement ring." Liv laughed at the expression on my face, then added, "I know, I know. Shut up."

"You said *beguiled*."

"Are you mocking my mad vocab?"

"I'm mocking your *weird* vocab."

She stuck out her tongue, making me grin. "Back to Marc. You said he just moved here, right? He's probably just busy unpacking or whatever."

"Yeah. But why not text and tell me that?"

"Because he's a dude. And dudes can be dicks."

"That's so reassuring."

"Will you feel better if I tell you they don't even *know* they're being dicks?"

"Um. Not at all."

"Fine. I won't tell you then." She took a sip of her coffee. "But…"

"But what?"

"Don't call him."

"I'm infatuated! Not desperate."

"It's a fine line to ride."

I offered her each one of my middle fingers. "By the way…does *Peter* know you think all guys are dicks?"

"Pretty sure I told him last night when we broke up."

I groaned. "You guys broke up and you've been letting me sit here and talk about Marc's perfect ass?"

She shrugged. "Priorities. I'm a good best friend."

"You're the *best* best friend," I corrected, stuffing my phone away where it couldn't distract me. "Now. Tell me what happened."

I sat back to listen to Liv tell me all the things she'd—unapologetically—said to her now-ex boyfriend. I loved her to death, but she was a serial dater and a serial heartbreaker, so she'd had lots of practice coming up with insults. Usually I tried to reason with her, pointing out that she wasn't perfect, either. But for once, I was content to just nod and let her rant. It made it easy not to think about Marc and what he might be up to. But when Liv exhausted her very full repertoire, and we'd consumed every drop of two more lattes, and I finally found myself back in my condo, Marc jumped back to mind again.

I wasn't into games, and if he wanted to play them, I was definitely out. Nice ass or not. If the one-night stand turned sex-capade weekend turned out to be nothing more than that, I'd be disappointed. But also fine.

Not wanting to dwell on it any more than I already had, I climbed into bed and settled in to binge watch something mindless on my phone. As I scrolled through my list of favorite comfort shows, several text notifications pinged along the top of my screen in quick succession.

Marc.

His name flashed insistently, and I considered ignoring him. But it would've been a childish move. And not a very genuine at that. I *wanted* to see what he had to say.

The first one made my heart skitter a little. *Hi, honey.*

"Promising start," I murmured, then scrolled down to the next one.

Sorry for not answering u sooner.

"Even better."

Stressful thing came up at work, added the third message.

That was something I could understand.

I want to make it up to u and I need to talk to u in person, read the fourth text.

"Hmm." That one made me a little nervous for some reason.

Can u take a coffee break tomorrow at about 10? Meet me at Yellow Fin's?

I bit my lip and did a quick calculation in my head. My boss wanted me at the meeting first thing, which probably meant just after eight. How long could an introduction go on? Not more than two hours, for sure. And the coffee shop—Yellow Fin's—was literally right beside my office building.

I lifted the phone and typed. *Can we make it 1015?*

This time, his reply was quick. *Definitely. Thank u.*

The fridge...? I prodded.

Tomorrow, he sent back.

I set down the phone, genuinely puzzled. He clearly wasn't trying to just run out on me.

If Liv were here, I thought, *she'd be telling me now's the time where he reveals to me that he has three wives and wants make me to be the fourth.*

"I think you'd be wrong," I muttered to my absent best friend.

Something was up. And even though my gut told me it didn't have anything to do with another woman, I had an uneasy feeling pretty much everywhere else. I rolled over and gave my pillow a solid squeeze. Ten fifteen was less than eleven hours away. But it seemed like an awfully long time.

Chapter 7

Marcelo

I glared down at the screen on my computer, willing the words to stop swimming in front of me. Pleading silently for the world to implode. I hadn't slept for a fucking second. Not one. Guilt mixed with dread, and the combo was enough to keep me up the whole damned night. I felt like shit. A glance in the mirror before I left the house told me I looked like it, too.

Exactly the way I want to start my new job.

Though if I was being honest, then I had to admit that I was more worried about how Aysia was going to react than I was about making a good first impression with everyone else. After two shots of scotch and three hours of pacing, I'd finally come up with a plan I hoped would work.

First things first. Fire Carl. Second things second. Avoid Aysia until our coffee date. The third thing. The worst thing. Try to explain away my ability to be a total ass.

The imaginary conversation made me sweat. Every fictional scenario ended with me getting a door slammed in my face and a possible harassment suit.

I didn't ask you about the video because I was living in the moment. Slam.

I wasn't sure you knew and didn't want to embarrass you. Or myself. Slam-slam.

By the way...we work together. I found out yesterday. And ran from your house like a giant baby. Slam-slam-slam.

I ran my hand over my hair and directed my attention back to the monitor, searching for Carl's direct line. It took me several too-long seconds before I found it, and several more before I picked up the phone on my desk to dial it. I didn't make it more than the first two digits, though, before a light rap on my door made me pause.

"Come in!" I called, wishing the damned office assistant hadn't quit—hiring a new one was just one more thing I'd have to do before I could really get started.

I forced a smile onto my face—probably reminiscent of a serial killer in clown makeup—and lifted my eyes to greet the intruder.

Not intruder, I corrected quickly. *Co-worker. Get your shit together, Diaz.*

Although it turned out to be neither. The man who stuck his head through the door was Eco-Go Development's founder and CEO, Mike Roper. A man I'd known all my life. He'd rescued my dad's business from financial ruin years ago, and I respected him more than most people in the world. My smile turned genuine.

"Uncle Mike," I greeted. "I wasn't expecting to see you here. Shouldn't you be on a boat somewhere?"

He stepped into the office. "Postponed my trip by a couple days. You didn't get my e-mail?"

I shook my head. "Kid from tech said he got everything sorted out on Friday, but I didn't see anything come through over the weekend."

"Damn."

"Is there an issue?"

"I called together the senior staff for a meeting this morning. Wanted to give you a formal welcome."

"Not necessary."

"Maybe not. But it's too late. They're all in the boardroom waiting."

Shit.

I opened my mouth, then closed it. I couldn't very well argue with him about it. Years of seeing him as a second father prevented it, and even if that hadn't been the case, when I'd signed on for the job, I'd agreed that Mike Roper would be the one and only person to whom I was accountable.

So much for hiding in my office.

"All right," I said through barely-not-gritted teeth.

"Everything okay, son?"

"Yep." I pushed back my chair and stood, then gestured for him to lead the way.

The older man studied my face for a minute before turning back to the door. I was grateful he didn't pursue it, but there was no way I could relax as I followed him down the hall. I could feel every eye on me as we stepped along. It wasn't the kind of thing that normally bothered me. Hell. I usually *liked* drawing attention. Hard to work in PR if I couldn't handle a bit of public scrutiny. This, though, felt like a walk of fucking shame. And no one else even knew what I'd done.

As we hit the boardroom, I paused to take a breath and straighten my shoulders.

Composure. Grow a set of balls and maintain it.

I threw a relaxed, welcoming smile onto my face and let Mike push open the door for me. I strode confidently into the office and reminded myself I'd spoken to crowds of a hundred at a time; a table of seven or eight people was nothing.

Nothing. Except when one of those people is a woman who's had her mouth on your cock.

Because there she was. Right near the front of the room, her petite but curvy frame settled into a high-backed leather chair. Her clothes were professional now, but that made them no less seductive. Under that chic, cream-colored top and hot pink, hip-hugging skirt was a body that made me want to shove aside the stacks of paper and throw her down right there, audience be damned.

For a second, my eyes held hers, and I saw surprise register on her face. A flash of fury followed. Then she covered both so quickly that I knew I was the only one who'd seen.

Yeah. Also because you're the only asshole staring at her.

I ripped my gaze away and strode to the head of the table. Vaguely, I was aware of Mike's introduction. He went around the table, announcing the names and positions of each of the department heads.

I only heard two.

Aysia Banks, acting Manager of Human Resources.

Carl Reeves, Manager of Accounts.

In spite of the way I tried to control it, my stare flicked up the table, searching him out. He was looking right back at me, a smug little smile of his face. He turned a tiny, knowing glance Aysia's way, then looked back toward me.

Fuck.

Things were going from bad to worse. The king of douchebags wasn't just some asshole crunching numbers. He was a department head. One who'd seen me with Aysia on Friday night. He knew something was up, and whether it was big or small, it still complicated the situation. His imminent demise wasn't going to go as smoothly as I'd planned.

Fuck with a cherry on top.

Mike's hand clapped me on the shoulder then, forcing me to focus on the moment.

"Saved the best for last," he said. "This is the man of the hour, Marcelo Diaz. I'm sure you're all aware that he was coming onboard, and I've heard the rumors just as much as you have, so I wanted to take this time to clear up a few things."

He went on, explaining my personal connection to his family, and asking the team to rest assured that the relationship hadn't influenced his decision to hire me, it only gave him a leg up in convincing me to join on. The rest of his speech was a blur of accolades on my behalf, an explanation of how he wanted me to help bring Eco-Go to a new level, and a discussion of how he wanted to see his vision carried through to the next generation as he transitioned to retirement. All of it was overshadowed by Aysia.

She held her face pointed in my direction, but she didn't look *at* me. Just through me. Her blue eyes were two flecks of ice. In the three days since I'd met her, not once had I seen her look so thoroughly cold.

It cut through me. Like a goddamned iceberg.

At last, Mike finished his speech and turned the floor over to me. I cleared my throat, my mind temporarily blank. I got as far as a ten-count before managing to shift to autopilot, spewing out my PR philosophy with as much enthusiasm as I could muster.

"Image is everything, but it can't just be skin-deep," I made myself say.

It was one of my favorite lines. Not quite snappy enough to be a personal motto, but close enough that I rarely spoke about my work without bringing it up. Right now it felt like bullshit.

"*You* have a public persona." I said. "Your *company* has a public persona. They need to be in line, and they need to be genuine." *Fucking liar.* "So from here on out, for every aspect of your job, I want you ask yourself just one question. Am I doing this because I mean it, or because someone told me I have to?" I stepped back from the table and smiled a wooden smile. I fielded a dozen questions—none of which came from Carl or Aysia—then gave the reins back to Mike, who closed off the meeting and dismissed the whole group.

I didn't *run* back to my office, but I sure as hell didn't stick around for coffee and doughnuts, either. I'd barely sat down, before my door swung open without a knock. I was unsurprised to look up and find Carl Reeves staring down at me, his arms crossed over his chest and smiling his self-satisfied smile at me.

I swear to God, I thought. *One wrong fucking move, and I'm going to smash my fist through those teeth.*

"Mr. Reeves," I greeted, my anger carefully restrained.

"Let's skip the bullshit," the other man replied. "Go straight to whatever it is you want to say to me."

"All right, Carl. You're fired."

"Fuck you. I'm not fired."

I leaned back in my chair and kept my tone neutral. "Your priorities aren't in line with Eco-Go's. I'm going to have to let you go."

"You can't fire me just because you fucked Aysia Banks."

"Let me show you something." I slid forward to my computer, tapped away for a second, then tilted the monitor toward the asshole. "That right there, Carl, is why you're fired. Eco-Go doesn't condone this kind of footage being shared on our server. Especially not when a female staff member is concerned. You do know that your emails here aren't really yours? They're company property. You're just lucky *I* got to it before someone else did."

"Someone else…" He trailed off and narrowed his eyes at me. "Someone else *is* going to see it, if you fire me. In fact, *everyone* else will."

"Are trying to blackmail me?" I couldn't keep the incredulity from my response.

He didn't bat an eye. "And if *that* video isn't enough…I've also got *this*."

He yanked his phone from his pocket, flicked his finger over the screen, then held it out. I took it, and another video came to life in my hands. The tinny sound of poorly recorded bass hummed through the small speakers. The thumping music was familiar, and in a moment, I saw why.

Shit.

On the screen, Aysia and I were locked together on the dance floor at The Well Pub. There was no mistaking the intimacy of our interaction. As it cut off, I lifted my gaze to meet Carl's.

"That's just a copy, by the way, so don't bother wasting time trying to delete it." He was all smugness. "And I know what happened next, so don't bother denying it, either. After the kiss, you faked a fight. She ran, and you snuck out a few minutes later. Then you got yourself a *taste*."

Every part of me tensed. My hand clutched so tightly around the phone that I don't know how it stayed in one piece. The thought of the disgusting fucker watching us made me want to break everything in sight. It took all of my willpower to keep from diving across the desk so I could take him by the throat.

"The video is just a dance," I growled. "Nothing more."

"True. But when *it* gets out, and the other one gets out, too…" He offered me a shrug. "People will draw their own conclusions."

"You're still fired, Carl," I said again.

"You really want people thinking that Aysia slept her way to where she is? You think *she* wants people to think so? You might not know her well yet, but I can guarantee you that this job is everything to her. If you fuck it up, you'll ruin any chance you have of getting near her again. And you'll destroy her."

I met his even gaze with a seething one of my own. He was right. I didn't want him to be. I wished even a part of what he said was untrue.

But wasn't. It *would* destroy her. It *would* ruin my chances.

I slammed the other man's phone onto my desk, then flicked it toward him. "Get out."

He smirked. "Not firing me, then?"

"Trust me," I said back. "I'll find a way."

Carl snapped up the phone and tucked it into his pocket. "Let me know how that goes."

He shot me a fucking *wink,* then slipped out of my office without closing the door. I didn't get up to close it. I was too busy worrying about what the hell my options were.

I wasn't going to let the douchebag blackmail me. Not on my first day. Not ever. I just needed to come up with a way around it. Something that wouldn't hurt Aysia.

"Fuck."

Just moments later, I regretted not shutting myself in. If I had, at least I'd have given myself a second to prepare.

Because Aysia now stood in my doorway, her frigid gaze pinning me to my seat.

* * * *

Aysia

I had to force myself to meet Marc's eyes.

Marcelo's eyes, I corrected silently. *Marcelo Diaz. The man you* knew *was about to start. Whose resume you perused.*

Why, oh, why hadn't I made the connection? It hadn't even crossed my mind.

But it doesn't matter now, I told myself. *What matters is doing something about it.*

And at that moment, it meant keeping my cool and not jerking my gaze away. I wished I didn't know so well what those eyes of his looked like in middle of a passionate moment. I wished I wasn't so aware of how they got shiny and crinkled up at the corners when he laughed. But I had to be strong. And strength required eye contact.

Keep it together, Aysia. He's a dick who played you.

I took a breath. But instead of saying something that would put him in his place, a question slipped from my lips.

"Did you know? When you came up to me in the pub. Did you know already that I was an employee at Eco-Go?"

His expression darkened. "No, Aysia."

"Ms. Banks," I corrected.

"What?"

"Ms. Banks," I repeated. "You need to call me *Ms. Banks.*"

"Why?"

He was frowning like I'd grown a third boob. And like the boob in question was in the middle of my forehead. So maybe it *was* a ridiculous request to make. But I wasn't going to back down. Not now.

"Because we need to be professional here, Mr. Diaz."

He shook his head like he was trying to clear it. "I didn't know you worked here. It would've been a hell of an ethical breach for me to keep that from you, *Ms. Banks.*"

"Is that the truth?"

"Of course."

After studying him for a second and decided he was being honest. I exhaled, relieved that he hadn't crossed that line. I also wished it didn't sound so sexy when he addressed me formally.

You're pissed off. Don't turn it into something deviant, I chastised silently.

"Now that you *do* know that you're my boss—"

He cut me off. "I'm not your boss."

"But you will be, when Mr. Roper retires. Everyone knew when he made the announcement last week that he would be grooming the new PR manager as his replacement. And speaking of everyone...I did a tiny bit of poking around, and thankfully, it seems like no one else noticed us at the bar the other night. No small miracle, considering that it's usually packed full of people from Eco-Go. Anyway, when Mr. Roper does hand things over, you should be safe. We both should be."

"It could be two more years before he cuts strings, Ay—Ms. Banks."

"You'll still be my boss." I refused to back down. "So that being said..."

"Aysia." He stood up and stepped around the desk, one arm outstretched like he expected me to take it.

Do not *go to him,* I ordered myself.

But I could already smell his intoxicating scent, and it made me want to close the gap between us so I could drink it in. I settled my urge to move by crinkling my toes up inside my high heeled shoes.

"*Ms. Banks*," I replied firmly.

"For crying out fucking loud," he muttered, dropping his arm.

"How long?" I made myself say.

"How long?" he repeated.

"When did you find out I worked here? Because I don't think it was the second you walked into the boardroom. You weren't surprised to see me."

"Yesterday," he admitted.

"How?"

"Your business card fell out of your purse."

"And you didn't tell me because...?"

For a second, Marc looked torn, and I couldn't help but wonder what thoughts were battling in his head. Was he trying to come up with a lie to cover his own ass? My mind soured at the thought. But after a second, he just shook his head again.

"It was a cowardly fucking move," he said.

"No shit."

"I told you last night that I wanted to talk to you."

My anger level was creeping up again. "You *texted* me."

"Aysia."

I let his use of my name slip this time. "No. Seriously. Why wait until today?"

He stepped closer again, and I braced myself for his touch. But instead of reaching for me, he walked straight *past* me. And closed the door.

"I was upset," he replied as he faced me once more. "I needed to cool off."

For some reason, his calm, reasonable statement set me off even more.

"*You* needed to cool off?" I repeated angrily. "Do you have any idea how self-centered that sounds? Don't you think maybe *I* would've liked a heads up? That maybe *I* might be upset, too? What if I'd lost my shit out there instead of in here?"

He let my tirade of questions run their course. And when I was done, instead of telling me I was acting like a crazy person, he met my eyes and said, "I already said it was a cowardly."

It made me even angrier that he seemed genuinely contrite. "So you think that makes up for it? You lied to me."

"I know."

"Why did you do it then? Aside from the fact that you needed to cool off."

He ran a hand over his hair. Slowly. Like it pained him a little. "I didn't want this to happen."

"You had to know I'd be upset, too."

"That isn't what I meant."

"Then what *did* you mean?" I asked, genuinely confused.

"I didn't say anything because I don't want to stop seeing you, honey. And I knew you'd insist that's what had to happen."

The honesty in his voice cut my breath away for a second. He wanted to keep seeing me. That giddy little bubble in my chest threatened to overtake all sense of reason. I forced it aside and gulped in a much-needed hit of oxygen.

"You were right. I do insist. We can*not* keep seeing each other," I told him.

"Why?"

"Because this is my *job,* Marc. My career. I worked my ass off to get here. I'm next in line for manager of human resources. And as unfair and stupid and sexist as it is, people tend to look down on girls who sleep their way to the top."

"You're stronger than that."

I bristled. "I *am* stronger than that. I *could* rise above it. But I'm not willing to. I won't let a single thing mar the path I'm on. So as strong as I am, I'm not willing to take the chance that this will get misconstrued."

For the first time, his calm exterior slipped. "*This*?"

"Us."

"Which is it, Ms. Banks? This? Or us?"

"This. It was a weekend, Marc. One weekend out of fifty-two in a year. So there isn't really an 'us', is there?"

His face grew stormy. "Because all we did is fuck. For a weekend."

"Yes." It wasn't much more than a whisper, and it felt like a lie.

He inched forward. "You're sure about that, honey?"

I swallowed. I could smell him again. That musky, thick scent that made my mouth water. No one had a right to smell so damned good.

"Yes," I managed to say again.

His hand came up to my arm. Just a whisper of a touch, his fingers moving up and down in the bend of my elbow so lightly that maybe I shouldn't even have been able to feel it. Except it was *all* I could feel. Had it only been a day since he touched me last? Heat swept up under my sleeve. It fanned out everywhere at once, and I felt a sudden need to grab something to use to hold myself up.

This is a swoon, I realized. *An actual, literal swoon. Oh, God. Any second my lady-in-waiting was going to have to come in and loosen my imaginary corset.*

I had to tell him to let me go. Except I couldn't do it. My body wasn't interested in obeying my brain. My eyes closed, all on their own. It made things worse. My other senses filled with bits of Marc.

His scent, of course.

His inhales and exhales.

And his warmth. Oh, God, his warmth.

It was awful and wonderful at the same time. A shiver threatened, and I could feel myself growing wet.

Stupid, stupid, and stupider. So weak.

"Aysia." Both his voice and his hot breath filled my ear, and I knew without looking that he'd leaned down to bring his mouth close to me.

I forced my eyes open and tilted my head up to meet his scorching gaze. I hated that I was fighting with myself to stop from giving in to the desire. I hated even more that I still wanted him at all.

"I can't do this," I whispered.

But I still took a step forward. My body was flush with his, his full erection pushing into the slight curve of my stomach. His hands landed on my arms and slid up to my shoulders. One stayed there, but the other slipped down to the small of my back where it turned in a circle.

He tipped his face down and pressed his cheek to mine. "Tell me you don't want me, and I'll leave you alone."

"I'm not a liar."

"So then. Tell me you *do* want me."

I leaned into his rough stubble. "I do, Marc. As mad as I am, I definitely want you."

His palm trailed down to my ass. "So take me."

"No." I shook my head. "Even if I forgive you right this second and put everything else aside, Eco-Go has a policy."

"A policy?"

"Yes, a policy," I made myself say. "An anti-fraternizing one."

"Fuck the policy," he said roughly.

I leaned away so I could look him straight in the face. "You don't mean that. And it's not what I want, either."

"Is that what you told Carl?" he countered.

It was like a stab in the gut. It'd slipped my mind that the other man's bad behavior was the reason Marc had approached me in the first place.

"That was different. It was a mistake. And it's a damned good argument in favor of the policy anyway."

He let me go and stepped back, his face an unreadable mask. In my chest, my heart squeezed painfully. Like it was kind of breaking. Which was ridiculous. Overdramatic. The wild infatuation I felt wasn't something that warranted such a thick, terrible sensation everywhere inside of me. Even the *might've-been-more* feeling didn't deserve that kind of attention.

That didn't mean I could quite shake it. Now I was fighting a need to apologize. I steeled myself to not do it. I didn't owe him a sorry. Not at all. So why did I feel so badly like I should?

I swallowed against the giant lump in my throat. "This past weekend... It didn't happen. At all."

"Saying it doesn't make it true."

"Believing it does."

"Aysia."

"Ms. Banks."

"Ms. Banks." I could hear the way his teeth were gritted. "You just told me you weren't a liar."

"I'm not."

"This past weekend." The three-word sentence was pointed.

"Didn't happen," I replied.

"Because you believe it."

"We *both* have to believe it, Mr. Diaz."

I could see a fight raging inside him, just under the surface. His strong jaw was tight, his eyes flashing so dark they were the color of coffee. Was he railing against me, or against something internal? I wasn't sure I wanted to know. I almost closed my eyes again when he spoke, not wanting to hear what he had to say.

"And if I choose not to believe it?" His voice was still strained. "If I push you against those big windows over there and slide my hands up your skirt while I put my tongue in your mouth?"

I stifled a little moan. If he did those things, I'd be lost. Completely.

"Completely?"

I blinked, clueing in that I'd admitted that aloud. I made myself nod.

"Well." He flicked his gaze past my shoulder—staring at something, anything other than me, I thought—and paused for a painfully long moment. "Then I guess it never happened."

A heaviness hung in the air. Breathing it in made me feel like I wanted to choke.

"Okay, Ms. Banks." Marc was staring at me, waiting. "I'm sure I'll see you around the office, Ms. Banks."

Oh. He's waiting for you to leave.

"Yes. Okay. Um." I'd never felt so awkward. "See you."

I turned and fled. I didn't stop until I'd reached my own small office on the other side of the building. There, I closed the door and collapsed against it. I was relieved that he hadn't followed through on his sexy threat. But only because I'd wanted so badly for him to actually do it.

I felt wrung out. Both in my body and my head.

"Get over it, Aysia," I muttered.

But as I pushed off the wall, I realized something. Even though Marc had said he hadn't confessed to knowing about our mutual employment because he wanted to keep seeing me…he hadn't used it to his advantage. He hadn't stayed in my condo and climbed into my bed. He hadn't asked for more phone sex. And I would've been in favor of either.

Chapter 8

Marcelo

My week was terrible as all hell. Monday dragged to Tuesday. Tuesday led to a farewell dinner at Mike Roper's house, where he felt the need to tell me about how he had a fantastic management candidate in human resources. Aysia Banks. Who he wanted me to get to know. The repeated mention of her name led to a green face and a serious inquiry into my health. The only silver lining about that was that I got to cut out early and go home. Where I could wallow in some self-loathing.

Tuesday became Wednesday, and Wednesday was a blur of meetings. The meetings were also a blur. Of Aysia. Dressed in a sleeveless shirt made of something soft and airy, a skirt that touched her knees, and a pair of sheer stockings that begged to be torn off. The worst part of it wasn't that she ignored me, but because she *didn't*. She spoke to me whenever the occasion called for it. She was polite. Distant. Nowhere was there a hint that she regretted cutting me loose from the weekend that didn't fucking happen. She treated me exactly the way she treated Carl. It made me sick in a different way than hearing her praises sung over and over. I wasn't the same as that asshole. Mostly because I *cared* whether or not I made Aysia feel like shit. Christ, how I wanted to punch that fuckwad. I was very, very glad when Wednesday was over.

Thursday, though, didn't turn out much better. I spent most of the morning trying to come up with a way to get rid of Carl. Unfortunately, he'd wiped his e-mail clean. There wasn't anything nefarious on it at all anymore. Not even a cat in a bikini. His performance reviews were clean, his record exemplary. It was almost too perfect, and I was half-tempted to call in the kid from tech to verify that it was all real. And if it *was* real, I thought I might ask him to fabricate something. Which is about the point where I decided that I was going crazy and threw in the towel.

With no intention of going back to work, I packed up my stuff without a word and headed to The Well for a midday beer and a thick burger. The former was quick to come, and before the latter even arrived, I'd already started in on my third drink. I was well on my way to forgetting Aysia's sexy legs and succulent lips. Until the text came in.

I yanked my phone from my pocket and glared down at the blurry screen. *There's a girl here for you.*

I blinked, confused. The name on the display was definitely Aysia's, but the message made no sense.

Marc.

Slowly, I typed back. *Ms. Banks?*

There's a girl here for u.

A girl for me WHERE?

At the office. Where else? Her text screamed of exasperation. *She's here for the office job.*

Shit, I typed, recalling vaguely that I'd set up an interview.

Where are u?

The pub.

The Well?

I tried three times to type the word *yes,* but my fingers kept slipping, so I finally settled for a thumbs up. Several seconds went by, and I took a solid swig of my beer. Then my phone chimed again.

MARC.

What?

This isn't a joke.

I'm not laughing, I told her.

What's wrong? she wanted to know.

Nothing. U said it wasn't a joke. Look. I'm on lunch. And I'm not coming back.

U have to interview this girl.

No.

Yes.

Send her home.

U have an obligation.

I thought about it, twirling my finger over the top of my pint glass. *Fine. Send her here.*

I'm not going to—u know what. Never mind.

I tried to lift my drink defiantly. Instead, my hand slipped. So did the phone. And just like that, they were one and the same. A cell phone flavored cocktail. It shouldn't have been funny, but I laughed anyway, then signaled the server for another drink. She brought it—and my burger—just a few minutes later. As I lifted the burger to my mouth for a serious bite, my gaze happened to shift across the room. Where I happened to spot *Ms.* Aysia Banks about three seconds before she spotted me.

Shit.

She was wearing some kind of crazy, polka dotted dress that swished temptingly at her thighs, hugged her narrow waist perfectly, and scooped conservatively—just the barest hint of cleavage—at her chest. Hot enough that everything else in the room kinda disappeared. Helped along by the beer, of course.

Her blue eyes found me then, and widened in surprise as they took in my state. Suit jacket tossed across the back of my chair. Top button undone and tie loosened. Stupid grin on my face.

The she spotted the phone in the pint glass and her eyes narrowed. She took a few short, high-heeled steps, and she was at my table.

"Marc." Her tone was hard to read—annoyed, maybe...or concerned?

I took an obnoxiously large bit of food. "What?"

"The interview."

She stepped aside, and for the first time, I noticed that she wasn't alone. A tall, slim woman in a white dress stood to her left. When she saw me, she smiled and smoothed back a lock of honey blond hair. I offered her a smile, too, then turned my gaze back to Aysia. Irritation flashed through her eyes, this time unmistakeable.

"This is Kitty Ulrich," she said stiffly. "Here to interview for the office administrator position."

"Okay."

"Do you want to move this back up to the office?"

"Here is fine." I nodded at the honey blond. "Have a seat, *Ms. Ulrich.*"

She slid into the chair closest to mine, adjusted her skirt, then smiled at me again. "Thanks."

"No problem. Gotta make sure you're comfortable in that position. There's a lot of sitting involved in being an office assistant."

She laughed a tinkling little laugh. "A lot of answering the phone, too. You want me to retrieve yours from inside that glass?"

"Thanks. But I think I'll just get a new one."

"No, really," Kitty replied. "It can be salvaged."

"You drop a lot of phones in beer?"

"Wine," she corrected.

Then she slid her hand past my arm to drag the beer closer. She reached a manicured hand into the glass, dragged it out delicately, then plopped it down on a napkin and sucked a drop of beer off her index finger.

"Next, we need some rice," she said.

"Rice?"

Aysia made a weird little noise, and I lifted my eyes from the drippy phone to her face. Her expression was neutral, but her blue eyes were dark.

"You don't have to stay," I told her.

"I think I should."

"Why?"

"I'm acting manager of human resources."

"That's true. Actually…why didn't *you* just do the interview yourself in the first place?"

Her eyes flicked to the blond. "Seriously?"

I nodded. "Yeah, seriously."

"Because it's in your contract that you get to approve your assistant."

"You read my contract?"

"I'm acting—you know what? Can we speak alone for a second?"

"Sure." I excused myself politely, giving Kitty my best apologetic smile, then followed Aysia across the bar and into the hall.

"What the hell's going on, Marc?" she demanded immediately.

"I'm interviewing Kitty."

"In the most unprofessional way possible! She's going to get the wrong impression of you *and* of Eco-Go."

"You insisted that I do this now. I told you I was taking the rest of the day off. She could've come back tomorrow or on Monday."

"That would've been extremely inconsiderate."

"Kind of like leaving her out there by herself?"

She glared at me. "You can't go back until you agree to stop flirting with her."

I blinked. "I'm not flirting with her."

"Everyone knows about the rice trick!"

"So?"

"So…pretending it's a new idea…that's flirting."

"That's flirting?" I echoed.

"Oh, come *on. 'You've got to be comfortable in this position?'*" she mimicked. "How is that *not* flirting?"

"That wasn't intended to be innuendo," I said honestly.

"Licking the beer off her fingers?" Aysia countered.

"She licked the beer off her own fingers."

"Technicality."

I fought a laugh. "Are you going to drag her back here, too, then? Let her know she shouldn't be flirting with *me*?"

"No. You're the potential boss. You need to let her know that flirting isn't appropriate."

"Aysia...grownups flirt. Sometimes not even on purpose."

"It's un—"

"Professional. Yeah, I get it. That's important to you."

"Just sort it out, Marc."

"I will."

She spun on her heel, and my hand shot out automatically to stop her. God, how I wanted her to stay. For a second, she let me hold her there. Her skin felt soft and right and warm under my fingers.

So damned good.

Blood rushed through my body with no disguising its intended destination. My cock jumped to life, straining against my suit pants.

Christ on a stick.

I breathed in, relishing the touch. Savoring it. Her eyes met mine, and she shook her head slowly. Like she had to fight to do it. Then she opened her sweet, full lips, and I waited for her to say something that matched the heat in her gaze. Anything. I'd take whatever she offered. Instead, she just let out a heavy sigh, then snapped her mouth shut, shook me off, and strode away.

More frustrated than ever, I watched her go before taking a moment to compose myself. By the time I got back to my so-called interview with the girl whose name I couldn't even remember anymore, Aysia had left the bar completely. But my mind was a different story. There...she stuck. There...she kissed me and demanded that I leave *with* her. There...she lifted that polka dotted dress and let me touch her. Through all of the banal questions I directed at the potential office assistant, through all of her well-rehearsed responses, what I was doing in my head was running my tongue over the length of Aysia's body.

"Marc?"

The honey blond woman was looking at me expectantly, and it took me a second to realize she was waiting for me to close the interview.

Fuck. So much for composure.

"Marc?" she said a second time.

"Mr. Diaz," I corrected.

For a second, she looked taken aback, but her look quickly turned sultry. "I didn't realize you were so old-fashioned."

"It's just professional," I said coolly. "Thanks for making the extra effort today."

"No problem." She stood. "You'll call me if I've got the job?"

"I will."

She turned to go, but paused to look over her shoulder. "Even if I don't get the job...you can still call me."

Damn Aysia for being right.

I made myself nod politely. "Have a nice afternoon."

The moment she was gone, I paid my tab and left. I was furious at myself all over again. I couldn't shake it either. With each step closer to home, I got angrier. When I reached my own street—a full five and a half miles away—I was ready to fight a team of karate-trained bears. The internal tirade wouldn't ease up, either.

Since when are you the kind of man who gets this worked up over a woman? Especially a woman you spent exactly one *weekend with? One who clearly isn't interested in reciprocating your—*

My thoughts cut off abruptly as I reached the front step. On the edge of the top stair, with her polka dotted dress fanning out all around her, sat Aysia Banks.

* * * *

Aysia

"Don't hire her," I said, hating myself.

Marc's brow crinkled. "What?"

"Don't hire her," I said again.

"Who?"

He sounded so utterly puzzled that a nearly hysterical giggle escaped my lips. "Kitty Ulrich, who else?"

"Oh. Can we talk about this inside?"

I shook my head, then changed my mind and nodded. It would be easier to present my craziness from the comfort of a couch. To rationalize it. And being inside had the added bonus of ensuring that he couldn't just get rid of me by walking away. So I followed him into the condo—another Eco-Go design—and trailed behind him wordlessly as he led me to his door.

But once we'd stepped in, I couldn't stop myself from blurting, "Hire a ninety-year old woman who has a neck that could possibly be turned into a purse."

"A…what?"

"Purse."

"Aysia."

"Preferably a happily married lesbian grandma."

"That's pretty specific."

"Seriously, Marc. If you hire a girl who looks like that, I'll be sitting around my office the whole day just worrying about whether or not she's trying to climb into your lap."

He didn't answer right away, and I knew it was because I'd gone too far. Here I was, insisting that he *not* take an interest in a flirty, attractive woman, while also insisting that he and I not see each other. Clearly, I'd gone bat-shit crazy. Clearly, I was a now a selfish bitch. With zero self-control. Somehow, sex with Marc had flipped a switch in my brain.

I waited for him to tell me to leave, watching nervously as he slid his feet out of his shoes, deposited his keys in a basket on a shelf beside the door, then removed his jacket and his tie. Each step was painfully slow. I fought an urge to help him along. If just to get the process of having me forcibly removed over with.

But when he was done, he just said, "I'm not going to hire her."

My reply was a relieved squeak. "You're not?"

"No."

I followed him from the entryway into the sparsely furnished living room. He gestured to the only seating option in the room—a wide leather chair. I perched on the edge of it, still tense and anticipating an attacking accusation of some kind.

"Don't mind the lack of mess," Marc said. "Every time I order something, it goes wrong."

"That sucks," I replied lamely.

"The furniture store sent me a red couch."

"I like red."

"This was *not* a nice red. More like a two-dollar-hooker kinda red."

"Oh. You're right. That's not good."

Marc shook his head and leaned against the windowsill closest to me. "Nope. Not at all. I ordered some art, too. A couple of framed prints. Got a set of Disney-themed posters instead. Nothing like a grown man with a giant cartoon mermaid on his wall."

Some of my tension eased as I laughed. "You probably need to stop shopping online. Didn't you bring anything with you when you left L.A.?"

He shook his head. "Sold my place furnished. Stored my personal items at my parents' place. It was kind of last minute. Mike said he needed me pretty damned quick."

"And you dropped everything that easily?"

"I don't know if it was easy. But Mike's family. If it hadn't been for him, my parents would've lost everything."

He went on, explaining how his father had been caught in a scam, and how the resulting fraud cost him his life savings. Mike Roper, a friend since the two older men were children, swooped in with not just a bailout, but with a team of people to repair the damage that had been done. Without hesitation and without judgement.

"There were a lot of people who *said* they were sympathetic," Marc told her. "But they couldn't get past the fact that my dad was naïve enough to fall for a real estate scam. My parents lost friends as well as money, but they never lost Mike. I was only twenty-two when it happened, so I remember it all. Stuck with me."

My heart swelled with renewed admiration, and in spite of the way I told it to keep calm, it thumped a little harder. I didn't want to like him anymore than I already did. But I couldn't seem to help it.

"So is it a short-term thing? You aren't really expecting to take over Eco-Go?" I asked, not sure if I was more worried that he would say he'd be leaving, or if I was more scared of what it would mean if he was staying.

He pushed up from the windowsill and paced the room. "I'm going to tell you something, and I don't want you to think of it as me betraying Mike's trust, okay? He hasn't asked me not to tell anyone, but I'd really prefer you to think of it as *me* confiding in *you*."

"All right."

"Mike's wife—Ruby—is sick. Terminally ill."

Now my heart squeezed. "Oh, no."

Marc nodded, his face full of undisguised sadness. "They found out a few weeks ago. This four-day boat trip they're taking is the first thing on a three-month bucket list. I don't know if Mike is expecting me to take over as CEO, or if he'll want to dive back in after Ruby goes. I'm not going to ask. But they have no kids of their own, and they're like a second set of parents to me. I'll do whatever Mike needs me to for however long he needs me to do it."

Before I could even think about, I was on my feet, moving to wrap my arms around him. I tucked myself against his body and pushed my hands into his lower back squeezing him tightly. He stiffened for a moment, then gently dropped his chin to the top of my head and hugged me back. We stood that way long enough for me to notice again how well we fit together. Like sliding two pieces of a puzzle together.

I might've felt bad about enjoying the closeness so much when I'd really meant just to offer a sympathetic shoulder. But it was hard to feel guilty about taking a little pleasure in the embrace with a distinct bulge pressing against your hip.

Oh, God.

It was far too easy to remember how that particular bulge fit me. Under my dress, my thighs quivered with a breathtaking need to be reminded even more. I could hear the rapid beat of Marc's heart against my ear, and that didn't help things either. The beat was a rhythmic thrum.

"Aysia."

He pulled back a little as he said it, and I tipped my head up to look at him. His eyes were glassy with emotion. He slid one hand free and cupped my cheek in his rough palm.

"I want to kiss you," he said. "But I won't, if you ask me not to."

"I want you to."

"Thank God."

He dipped his lips to mine. It was a soft touch. At first. But it quickly deepened, his lips devouring mine as I surrendered to the attention. He kissed and nibbled. He tugged and teased. And even though there was no mistaking the passion in the way his tongue danced through my mouth, there was something more in the kiss. Something deeper. A need for comfort. An outpouring of feeling. It almost wasn't fair that he could put so much into one kiss. But it lit me up.

My arms came up from his waist to land on his shoulders, and my hands dug into the short, thick hair at the back of his neck. I kissed him as hard he kissed me. I tugged his lips with my teeth and explored the contours of his mouth with my tongue. I drank in everything he offered, not breaking contact until it became necessary to gasp in a breath. Even then, I immediately went back for more. Or I would have, if Marc hadn't eased his hold on me and pulled away.

"I want to talk about Carl," he said.

"Um. Okay." I flushed; the other man was the last thing I felt like discussing.

But Marc seemed determined. He pulled himself free and ran a hand over his hair.

"I'm not going to hire Kitty Ulrich," he told me. "But I can't seem to find a way to fire that asshole."

"You want to *fire* him?"

"Of course I do."

"Because of *me*?"

His brown eyes flashed. "Because he's a complete douche with no morals."

I shook my head, desire taking a backseat to surprise at his vehemence. "I'm aware of his finer qualities. Better than you are, I'm sure. He's done some despicable things to me that I'd rather not even acknowledge."

He dropped back into pacing mode, this time with an edge. "And I can't stand that fact. It's a ridiculous fucking feeling, I know. But every time I look at him, I think about it."

"I can't change the fact that I dated him," I said slowly.

Marc paused in his efforts to wear a hole in the floor. "I know. I acknowledged that it was a ridiculous fucking feeling, didn't I?"

"What do you want me to say?"

He started pacing again, his eyes flicking back and forth between me and the floor, then muttered something about the wrong moment before he stopped abruptly and dropped into the leather chair.

"I want you to stop treating me the way you treat him," he said roughly.

"What?"

"At the office. You're too damned polite to both of us."

I stared at him for a long second. Then a laugh burst from my lips. I covered my mouth, trying to stop it, but I couldn't.

"You think it's *funny*?" Marc sounded incredulous rather than mad.

I stifled another laugh. "No. It's not funny. But…"

"But what?"

"Liv *told* me to treat you like Carl. She said it would make things easier if I approached this thing between us the same way I approached the thing between him and me. I didn't realize I was succeeding."

"That girl really hates me."

"Maybe she hates you a little. But only because she loves *me*."

"Thanks, Liv," he muttered.

"I didn't know what else I was supposed to *do*," I admitted. "When I walked in and saw you there in that boardroom Monday it was…I don't know what it was. Like a bit of my world imploding? I kept telling myself it was just a weekend. That had I hadn't even known your last name. But I honestly couldn't deal with it. I told Liv, and she gave me the suggestion. Just to help me breathe."

"I'll buy you a respirator. But please, Aysia. I'd rather you treat me like shit or pretend that you don't know me at all than have you treat me the same way you treat him."

I met his sad gaze. "You're nothing alike. It's not even a comparison."

"Yet you *did* make an exception for him. You broke the rules."

I sighed, took his vacated spot on the windowsill, and told him something only Liv knew. "Carl caught me at a vulnerable moment. My dad—who I hadn't seen in over a decade—died a few months ago. The news hit me way harder than I expected. Harder than I thought it should, I guess. By the time I came to my senses and realized Carl was the exact opposite of what I needed, it was too late to take back my own stupidity."

"You're far from stupid."

I shook my head. "You don't have to stroke my ego. Sneaking around with Carl *was* stupid. He was such an asshole that he couldn't even be faithful for the short month we were together. And when I called him on it, he was convinced it was *my* fault. I think he still doesn't understand why I broke it off."

"Fucker."

"Yeah."

Without warning, Marc swept to his feet. He closed the distance between us, dragged me up, and pushed me to the wall, where he kissed me again. Long and hard. Like he had something to prove.

When he finally pulled back, he growled against my mouth. "I'm not Carl."

"I know."

"So sneak around with me."

"Marc…"

"Or *don't* sneak around with me. Tell everyone and let them think what they want. I'll make sure human resources doesn't fire you. I know a girl, and I think I can pull some strings."

"I can't."

"Pull strings?"

"Break the rules."

"Isn't that why they made them?"

He took my bottom lip between his teeth and pulled while at the same time slamming his hand to my knee, then sliding his palm up under my dress to my thigh. I gasped at the contact, and moaned when his fingers wasted no time making their way to my underwear, which he promptly pulled aside so he could stroke me lightly.

"*This* is breaking the rules," he said.

"Yes." That was a moan, too.

"Say you'll break the rules for me. Don't make me beg, Aysia."

One finger slid over my clit, and I thrust against it, and I was pretty sure that I was a lot closer to begging than he was. I could barely form a coherent thought. It took everything I had just to form a sentence.

"I can't break them, Marc," I said.

His finger moved faster. "Do you want me to stop?"

"No!"

"But you won't say yes."

"I just…"

He hand added a small circle and a bit more pressure.

"Marc," I gasped.

"You know I love it when you say my name," he replied.

He shifted, just a little, and his finger slipped inside and his thumb took its place. His body rocked into me, too, driving me higher. Closer.

"Please," I whimpered.

"*Please??*"

"Make me come."

"All right, honey."

He stopped talking then, and focused on touching me. Just right. Just hard enough. My head tipped back and his mouth fell to my throat. And his lips on my exposed skin was the scale tipper. My hands pressed to the wall behind me, pushing my hips forward, driving his finger into me farther. With a shuddering cry, I came undone against his hand. When the last waves of satisfaction had released, he slipped free and framed my shoulders with his arms.

"The weekend," he said.

"What?"

"Give me the weekend," he said. "Just give from now until Sunday. Break the rules for three days."

He leaned back, his expression boyishly hopefully. Sweet and sexy at the same time. I didn't stand a chance in hell of saying no.

"Okay," I whispered, my eyes dropping down guiltily at the vulnerability created by my inescapable acquiescence.

Immediately, his fingers came to my chin and lifted it up so I couldn't look away.

"Not because you have to," he said. "Because you want to."

The look in eyes had changed from hopeful to concerned. I made myself study that look, memorizing it. He cared what *I* wanted. That mattered to me.

"Let's break the rules," I said firmly. "Just for the weekend."

Relief replaced worry. Then a devious glint took over. And Marc scooped me up from the ground and carried me straight to his bedroom, where he held me pleasantly captive for a number of hours that I was too preoccupied to count.

Chapter 9

Marc

Friday morning came far too quickly. Though as I dragged myself into consciousness, I couldn't really complain. My arms were wrapped around a beautiful girl. Her soft scent filled my senses. Inch after inch of her silky skin pressed against mine. And one of her hands was moving slowly between my legs on my already hard cock.

My eyes flew open as I realized the last part wasn't just a bit of residual dream. Aysia's too-blue gaze was fixed on my face, a satisfied little smile playing on her lips.

"Took the rest of you long enough to wake up," she teased.

"You've been molesting me for a while now?"

"Hmm. From the way *this*—" She gave my erection an emphatic and oh-so-fucking sexy tug. "Was nudging my ass when *I* woke up, I figured maybe a bit of reciprocal violation was in order."

"How very deviant."

"You arguing?"

"Fuck no."

She laughed, then tipped up her mouth to mine. She tasted like peppermint, and when she pulled away, I shot her a suspicious glare.

"Did you get up and brush your teeth?" I asked.

"Maybe."

"Did you use *my* toothbrush?"

"I'm deviant, not weird. I found a spare, unopened one in the drawer."

She lifted her face again and ran her minty tongue over my lip. Her hand was still closed on my cock, stroking it a little faster now. I fought to control myself. My balls were already tightening in anticipation. If we didn't dial it back a notch—or maybe *two* notches, if I was being honest—I was going to embarrass myself.

I leaned back a little and lifted an eyebrow her way. "What made you so sure that toothbrush didn't belong to the previous owner? I've only been living here for a week."

Her eyes widened for a second and her hand went still. "Did it?"

"What if it did?"

"It was *sealed.*"

"Still be weird."

"Marc...tell me it was *your* new toothbrush."

"It was my new toothbrush," I replied obediently.

"Thank God."

Her hand started up again, and I fought a laugh. My amusement was quickly forgotten, though, when her thumb swiped across the sensitive head. Then back again before she returned to wrapping her fingers around me. She held me a little looser now, her hand rising up and down on my full length, quicker and quicker. I groaned and pushed forward with unrestrained eagerness.

She wriggled a little closer, pressing me to a spot just above her pubic bone.

"Holy hell," I swore as her other hand dropped between my legs, too.

She cupped my balls tightly with her palm, one finger pressed just underneath them.

"Aysia." Her name was a guttural noise, ripped from my chest, and I could barely make the subsequent warning come. "If you don't stop—"

She cut me off by dropping to take me in her mouth.

Fuck.

With her finger still pushed into the sweet spot underneath me, and her lips closed on my cock, I was helpless. She sucked me hard, then soft, then hard again, and that was it. I couldn't take anymore. My hands tore into her hair, and I bucked up underneath her. In a series of throbs that rocked my whole body, I exploded into her mouth.

"Aysia." Now her name dropped from my mouth as a groan.

Then as a thick, heavy sigh. "Aysia."

She gave me a final tug with her lips, then dragged her body up and tucked her head against my chest.

"That was...I don't...fuck." I mumbled incoherently.

"You're welcome," she replied cheekily.

One of my hands was still tangled in her hair, and I tried to give it a punitive yank. My fingers were far too weak.

"Having a recovery issue?" Aysia teased.

"Mm. That's putting it nicely. Give me a minute. I promise I'll be back in action."

"You don't have *time* to be back in action."

"I've always got time to be back in action."

"You start work in thirty minutes."

"Shit. Seriously?" I tried to push up, failed, then thumped back onto the bed. "What about you?"

"*I* have the day off," she said, stretching out beside me.

"How'd you make that happen?"

"I'm owed a bunch of vacation hours, so I took off four Fridays in a row. But you have fun."

"Maybe I'll take the day off, too."

"Can't."

"Why not?"

"Not approved with human resources. And since the acting human resources manager is planning on sneaking around with you all weekend, she'd like to act in a way that's above suspicion."

"That has an extremely sexy ring to it."

"Twenty-seven minutes."

"Fine."

I tried again to get to a sitting position, and this time I succeeded. I swung my legs over the bed and turned to look at her. The only thing covering her body was the corner of my sheet, and that offered just the barest hint of modesty. A triangle between her thighs, a little piece of white fabric over her taut nipples...

As I watched, she smiled then pushed her knees apart. The sheet slipped up. My cock twitched, clearly forgetting its recent, one-on-one celebration with Aysia's mouth. Or maybe remembering it all too well.

"Twenty-five minutes," she said.

I made myself back up and reached for my underwear drawer, fumbling for the nearest pair without taking my eyes off her. "What are you going to do all day?"

"I think I'll stay here."

"And do...?"

Her hand slid to her thigh. "Things."

"What kind of things?"

"It's a half day, today. Only four hours and twenty-four minutes until it's over," she said. "How much trouble can I get into?"

I shoved my feet through my boxer briefs, then moved toward my closet. I grabbed a suit and worked my way into that, too. Aysia's hand was under sheet, and I could see it caressing her stomach.

"You're going to fucking kill me," I groaned.

"That would be a real waste. There's things I want you to do to me when you get home."

I buttoned my shirt, still watching her. "How many minutes now?"

"Twenty-two and a half?"

"You sure we can't—"

"No."

"Killing me," I repeated, doing up my tie.

She pulled the hand free and used it to blow me a kiss. I couldn't decide if I was relieved she'd stopped, or disappointed.

"Behave yourself while I'm gone," I said, "and when I get home, I'll show you the one thing I ordered that they got right."

"Ooh. A surprise."

I bent down to give her a light kiss. "You like surprises?"

"Nope. Hate them."

I chuckled. "Okay. Then feel free to look in the bathroom. Just don't use it without me."

She lifted an eyebrow. "Now I'm worried."

"Don't be."

I tried to kiss her again, but she put a finger up between our lips.

"Less than twenty-one minutes," she told me. "If you don't call a taxi now, you won't make it on time."

I reached for the nightstand—my phone's usual spot—then remembered. "My cell met with an untimely demise yesterday."

"Mine's on the kitchen counter."

Moving quickly out of necessity, I exited the room. I placed the call and tossed a piece of bread in the toaster at the same time.

"Seventeen minutes!" called Aysia from the bedroom.

"Got it!" I hollered back, mouth full.

Cursing the fact that there was no time for coffee, I snagged a bottled water from the fridge, then made my way back to the bedroom.

"You've got peanut butter on your chin," Aysia informed me as I searched through a still-unpacked box for a fresh pair of socks. "Come here. I'll wipe it off."

Socks in hand, I kneeled down on the mattress beside her and tipped my chin her way. I anticipated a swipe of her thumb and maybe a succulent, post-swipe lick. Instead, she got onto her own knees and pressed her nearly naked body to mine as she sucked the peanut butter off directly.

"There," she said when she was done. "All better."

"Great," I groaned. "Now I'll be thinking about that all day, when I should be thinking about how to get Eco-Go prime magazine-advertising space without violating our sustainable resources mandate."

"Online editions." She leaned back. "You make that a condition of the ad space you buy. Ask for a discount. And approach some smaller companies, too. They'll appreciate the business more."

I flopped down beside her and closed my eyes. "Perfect."

"What are you doing?"

"You did my work for me. Now I don't have to go in."

She gave my knee a playful shove. "Fourteen minutes."

I cracked one eye. "Are you even wearing a watch?"

"I have a perfectly tuned internal clock. Unless that taxi's already outside, you're going to be late."

"Pushy, pushy."

I dropped a final kiss on her cheek, stepped to the en suite to brush my teeth and hair, then moved to leave. I made it all the way to putting my shoes on and grabbing the door handle before her voice stopped me one more time.

"Marc?"

I turned to find her standing in the hall wrapped in the bed sheet.

"Yeah, honey?"

"When you're thinking about the peanut butter…think about this, too." She dropped the sheet, stood there for just long enough that I could devour her head to toe, then grabbed the sheeting and strutted away, laughing.

Christ.

With a renewed hard-on that I knew would last the day, I forced myself to leave before I gave in to the need to take her right then and there.

Hell, I thought as I climbed into the cab. *This is day is going to be absolute hell. A better kind of hell than the rest of the week. But still hell.*

Except it wasn't. It was amazing.

Carl called in sick, and I didn't care if it was because he'd died, was faking it, or had come down with a very unpleasant case of syphilis. He wasn't in my way. Two hours in, and I felt like I'd been there for minutes.

It only got better.

As I sat down for a quick coffee break, a messenger showed up with a padded envelope, and when I opened it, I found my phone and an accompanying note from Aysia.

Some guy found this in a beer, the bubbly, girlie handwriting read. *He put in it RICE. When it dried out, he found your address in the contacts and very kindly dropped it off here. (Told you everyone knew about that trick.)*

Even better than *that*...when I powered on the phone, I saw that she'd changed my screensaver. In place of the generic blurry bubbles that had been there since I bought it the week before, was a picture. It was her. Or a piece of her, anyway. I would've recognized that delicate hand of hers in a sea of a hundred. In the photo, she held it pressed to her stomach, her thumb and forefinger curved in a half-heart around her bellybutton. It was sexy as fuck. Sweet, too. I stared for a long time, smiling so I hard I expected someone to offer me a straightjacket.

When I finally finished ogling my own phone and drank the rest of my coffee, I managed to interview and hire a perfect office assistant. Since the woman was not only old enough to be my grandmother, but also a retired drill sergeant, who'd been married to another woman for the last thirty years, I was sure Aysia would approve. I snuck in time to buy a half a dozen online magazine ads at a fraction of Eco-Go's budget, and I booked a speaking spot at a conference in Seattle.

As I packed up at noon along with everyone else, I decided to upgrade my day from amazing to fucking awesome. It stayed that way through the cab ride home, and up the elevator to my floor. To my front mat and through my door.

"Aysia?"

Into my living room.

"Honey?"

Then the bedroom.

"Aysia?"

It wasn't until I realized my apartment was empty that my high finally came crashing down.

* * * *

Aysia

I slid the door shut, waiting for the automatic lock to click before angling my suitcase in the other direction. I could feel the smile on my face. I knew Marc would be home by now, wondering where I was. Maybe he'd found the note I'd stuck to the living room table and was trying to figure out what the mystery was.

As I pulled the wheeled bag up the hall to the elevator, I had a tiny moment of self-doubt. After all, my plan kind of hinged of the fact that I'd accidentally answered Marc's phone right before sticking it in the envelope to send to the office. I hit the answer button without thinking about it. And I'd been too embarrassed to correct the guy from the car dealership when he addressed me as *Mrs. Diaz*. Or maybe I liked it a little bit. But I hadn't started out with a devious plot in mind. Really. It just kind of fell into my lap.

Marc had a car. A very sexy car. The car needed picking up from some dealership forty kilometers east. In Chilliwack. Just far enough away that our weekend together could be a little more out in the open without quite losing its clandestine appeal. And the thought of walking down a public street while holding Marc's hand made my knees almost as weak as the memory of the way his hand felt all over my body. But we'd have time for that, too. The bed and breakfast I'd booked had a giant bed. And it promised luxury in the heart of the country.

The elevator door slid open and my self-doubt slipped away. If Marc was bothered at all by my unintentional pry into his business, I'd make up for it in other ways. Starting with a wood-burning fireplace and ending with one of the many pieces of lingerie I'd packed in my bag.

I stepped through the sliding doors and pressed the button for the lobby. Just because I didn't like receiving surprises didn't mean I couldn't enjoy doling them out.

The elevator came to a halt and I started to move forward. Without a warning, a rough hand came up to my shoulder and stopped me. Startled, I stumbled sideways. I flailed, trying to catch myself before I hit the ground. But my imminent fall was aided and abetted by both my suitcase and my three inch heels. The shoes made an effort to spin me and make me wobble, while the bag worked its hardest to get in position to trip me.

My head flew backwards, smacking the handrail that lined the elevator. My ass hit the floor. And for a second, I sat there stunned. Then an unpleasantly familiar cologne filled my nostrils. It made me choke, and before I even looked up, I knew who I'd find standing over me.

"Carl!"

"Aysia. I'm *so* sorry." His voice was dripping with false regret, and one of his hands dropped down in an offer to help.

In an automatically defensive reaction, I skidded away. Out of reach. And farther into the elevator.

Shit.

The doors slid shut behind him, hissing ominously as they met. Carl's presence filled the small space, and not just because of his cloying cologne. He held his feet set apart, and his shoulders seemed wider than I remembered. Like he'd juiced himself up on steroids and asshole growth hormones with his toast this morning. The intimidation factor grew worse when he turned and slammed a finger into the button that kept the elevator from moving.

You are not *scared of him,* I said to myself. *He's just your asshole ex with something to prove. Little dick syndrome.*

But as I glared up at the jerk, my pulse thundered with the nerves I couldn't quite settle. How had he managed to get in the building?

And just as importantly...

"What are you doing here?" I demanded.

"Obvious, isn't it? I came to see you. All I want is a second to talk."

"Not that it matters...but *why*?"

"Because you're making a mistake."

A tickle of worry tugged at my heart. "I don't know what you're talking about. And I have somewhere I have to be."

"Some*where* to be because some*one* is waiting for you?"

"That's none of your business."

"I think it is. One name. Marcelo Diaz."

I fought to keep from sucking in a breath. *He knew. How?*

"What about him?" I said with careful indifference.

In reply, he reached into his pocket and dragged out a piece of yellow paper. I felt the blood drain from my face as he held it up.

"Found this little gem outside on the ground."

Shit.

I kept my face impassive. I could swear I'd left the note in the middle of Marc's coffee table. But there it was. In Carl's slime-ball hands.

"So?" I made myself say.

"Let me read it aloud. *Good news. Our weekend is about to get sexier and less secretive. Pack a bag and I'll explain when I get back to your place.*" He looked up and smiled derisively before finishing. "*Smiley face. A.* You're denying that's you?"

I pressed my lips together. After all, there was nothing in the note that gave away who it was to. Or who it was from.

"Nothing to say?" Carl pushed.

"No."

"So you're just going to stay down there?"

My face warmed. "Maybe."

He narrowed his eyes. "Well. You might want to get up. Because I'm not going anywhere until you admit that I'm right. And I know how bad you are at doing that."

"Did you just come here to insult me, Carl?"

"No. I came to let you know that *I* know. And I don't like it."

"I have no clue what you mean. But I'd like to get out of the elevator."

"I don't think so."

The tickle of worry became a rush of fear. I fought it.

"I have a line," I told him. "And you're crossing it all over the place."

"Really, Aysia? You want to tell me that *conversation* is a line for you, but letting your boss—*our* boss—put his tongue between your legs isn't?"

Now my face wasn't just warm. It burned. In fact, my whole body sizzled unpleasantly. Like it'd been dipped in acid.

Violated.

That was the word that suited my feelings at the moment.

"I'm going to tell you again, Carl, to let me out," I said, sounding a lot stronger than I thought I could manage.

"And if I don't?"

Oh, God. "I'll call the police."

"You could do that," he replied. "But then you'd have to explain your relationship with me. And your relationship with *him*. And I know you, even if *you* want to pretend like this that I don't. You'd rather sacrifice… well…almost *anything* to save a little face and keep on your career path."

I hated that he was right. I hated that he knew enough about me to know what mattered most. Which is probably why I lost my patience.

"Fuck you," I snapped.

"Nice language."

"Fuck you again."

"We've been through that, haven't we? You wanting to fuck me. Again and again."

His abruptly lascivious tone—and the matching look in his eyes—made me swallow nervously. Not that I'd liked anything about the situation to start out with. But the new expression was darker. His eyes moved over my body, touching each point with far too much interest.

Don't let him win.

I took a breath, then grabbed the railing, and pulled myself to my feet, hoping the new position would remind him that I wasn't some weak girl he could just push around. Not literally. Not figuratively. And sure as hell not sexually.

"I know you, too, Carl," I said coolly. "And if one of us is going to get blackmailed here, it isn't going to be *me*. I remember everything, not just the bits and pieces that are convenient."

His smug smile dropped, and I felt more relief than I wanted to admit. *That's right you bastard,* I thought triumphantly. *Suck on that.*

I reached around him to press the button that would force the elevator back to life. I even managed not to cringe as my arm brushed his. And as we dropped through the two floors, Carl was silent until we hit the lobby.

"This isn't the end of this, Aysia," he announced, sounding more like a surly stereotype rather than a real person.

I fixed a sweet smile on my face and shot back an equally trite comeback. "It was over before it even started, Carl."

Then I grabbed my suitcase and marched out of the elevator with my head up. I managed to get all the way out the front door without turning back. I made it to the bushes at the side of my building. And there, one of my heels gave out on me. And so did the ability to handle my emotions. I couldn't even look up to see if Carl had followed, or if he was watching. I slumped down onto my suitcase, tears spilling so hard that I didn't notice the legs in front of me until he was already crouched down and lifting my face. Warm brown eyes met mine. Puzzled. Concerned. Everything I needed right that second.

"Marc." His name came out ragged with relief.

"Honey. What the hell happened?"

Unable to answer, I threw my arms over his shoulders and tucked my head into his chest. And for a long moment, he just held me like that, one hand rubbing up and down my spine while the other held the suitcase steady. With each of his gentle strokes, the heartache eased away. The memory of Carl and his words and threats and slimy face faded.

Thank God.

At last I composed myself enough to pull away. Marc's hand immediately moved from my back to my face, his expression growing even more worried as he eyed my forehead. His thumb stroked a tender spot just above my eyebrow.

"You've got a bruise," he said.

I reach up to put my fingers over his. "I bumped it in the elevator."

He frowned. "How'd you manage that?"

"It's..." I trailed off, then tried again. "It's nothing."

"Nothing?" he repeated, sounding disbelieving.

"Nothing," I said firmly. "But could you help me with this bag?"

"Aysia..."

"Seriously. We have a reservation that I haven't even told you about yet." I made myself smile. "But before we go, I want to take advantage of that big, giant mistake in your bathroom."

He studied me without smiling back. I braced myself for another question. I didn't want to lie. But I would.

Or...you could just tell him what happened, urged a small voice in my head.

But I couldn't make myself do it. Talking about Carl was the last thing I wanted to do. So I pushed up to my tip toes and kissed him instead.

"You." *Kiss.* "Me." *Kiss.* "A lot of bubbles..." *Longer kiss.*

"All right." His acquiescence was anything but convincing.

But I decided to take it anyway and pretend I didn't notice. This weekend was supposed to be Marc and me. It was supposed to be simple. Then it was supposed to be done. I was sure that if I explained the altercation in the elevator, things would grow immediately more complicated. And I was strongly suspicious that walking away on Sunday night was already going to be hard enough.

Chapter 10

Marc

I didn't buy her *nothing's-wrong* act for a second. I could sense something underneath it. But whatever that something was…I was damned sure if I pushed, it would make her turn and run. Like whatever the hell messed up her hair and makeup had somehow made her a little more fragile. Which was definitely not a word I would've used to describe Aysia Banks up until that moment. So I kept my mouth shut. I tucked her under my arm, pretended the bruise on her forehead didn't make my gut clench, and I brought her back to my condo in a taxi. I ran a bath in the ridiculously oversized tub they'd added to the bathroom by mistake, poured her a midday glass of wine, and sat on the toilet lid while she soaked. I waited until she was ready to say something on her own. Even though it was fucking killing me.

"How did you know?" she finally asked softly without opening her eyes.

"Know what?"

"To come to my place?"

"To be honest, I thought you were trying to renege on our agreement."

"So you thought I was being a jerk-faced bitch and you were still coming after me?"

"We had a deal. A really sexy deal. I thought maybe I could talk you out of running off."

She sighed. "Sorry, Marc."

Hating the soft, sad tone of her apology, I reached across to squeeze her wrist. "Don't be sorry, honey."

"I can't help it. I'm sure you didn't expect to sign on for any baggage when you came home with me last weekend."

"My parents have been married for thirty-five years. Pretty sure they've got a full set of damned pricey baggage. Matching carry-on luggage, too."

At the statement, her eyes opened wide.

Shit.

I hadn't meant to bring up my parents' three-and-a-half-decade long marriage. Why the hell had it even crossed my mind?

I cleared my throat. "What I mean is…whatever's going on with you… I've seen worse."

As soon as the words were out of my mouth, I realized two things. First. They were a lie. It wasn't what I'd meant at all. Second. *My* parents were both alive. Her father wasn't, and she'd already told me that she hadn't spoken to him for more than ten years before that.

"I'm such a self-centered, entitled bastard," I muttered.

Aysia was still staring at me, and now her eyebrows were pressed together in a deep frown. "Um. I don't know whether to shower you with compliments, or ask you if you inhaled too many of these bubble fumes."

I didn't laugh. "I wasn't trying to compare my upbringing to yours. I have no idea what it was like for you. My parents had the usual stuff going on, but they were always there for me."

Her face cleared. "Are you asking about my daddy issues?"

"No. Yes. Fuck. I don't know. I'm not very good at offering comfort."

"Marc."

"Yeah?"

"Come here."

Obediently, I inched off the lid of the toilet, then moved to the edge of the tub.

"Closer," she said.

I dropped to my knees and put my elbows on the wide lip, just out of reach of the bubbles. Aysia leaned forward, the suds that had been covering her sliding away so that her breasts floated temptingly along the top of the water, and she lifted her hands to my face. With rivulets of liquid pouring down her arms and dripping onto my dress shirt, she pulled me in for a kiss. Long and slow. Steamy and sweet. Her fingers never left my face as she explored my mouth. When she was finally done, I was soaked. My shirt clung to my chest, my silk tie was a total write-off, and I was damned sure my pants had absorbed half the bath water. Somehow, even my hair managed to be dripping.

I was also turned on as all hell, my worries about being a good listener pushed to the side.

"Are you trying to distract me with sex?" I asked against her mouth.

"Sex? That was just a kiss." Her voice was laced with false innocence.

"Just a kiss? No such thing with you." I pulled away so I could look at her.

"I was merely trying to demonstrate that I'm not using you for comfort."

"That *sounds* like a compliment. But I'm pretty sure it's an insult."

"How so?"

"It makes me seem like a plaything."

"Oh. You don't *like* being a plaything?" she teased.

"I don't mind it. So long as I can be something more, too." The words came out with more meaning than I intended, and for a second, her playful smile dropped.

She recovered it quickly, and tapped my chest with one of her slim fingers. "So demanding."

I grabbed her hand and pressed it down to my chest. "It's give and take, honey."

"So...take."

"What if I don't want to?"

She pulled away, a surprised look on her face. "You don't *want* to?"

I chuckled at her expression. "Try not to sound so stunned at the fact that I'm capable of thinking with something other than my dick."

She colored. "I know that."

I ran my thumb over the pink blush along her cheekbone, then twisted a lock of her hair around my finger. "I can listen, if you want me to. I might suck at the comforting words, Aysia, but I can provide a pretty good ear, if you wanna unload some of your so-called baggage."

"I don't know if I can," she admitted softly.

There was too much hurt in her voice. Too much fucking wistfulness. I hated that I was right about the hint of fragility. I hated the desperate need I felt to know where it came from. What the hell had happened in between the time I left for work and the moment I found her crying on her own doorstep?

"Make some room," I ordered roughly, loosening my tie.

"What?"

"I'm evening the playing field." I tossed the tie to the floor and started to unbutton my shirt.

"I thought you didn't want to have sex."

"I don't."

My shirt joined my tie, and I moved on to my pants, which slid down, quickly revealing my undeniably swollen cock. I heard Aysia's breath catch, and it made me twitch.

"You don't?" she asked.

"Well. Obviously, I *want* to. Every time I get near you—or think of you, for that matter—I want to. But that's not why I'm getting in."

"Um. Okay."

She tucked her legs up and slid to the halfway mark in the tub. I loved how she looked right that second. Her back curved as she hugged her knees, her face turned over her shoulder to study me. Blue eyes wide, and her bottom lip sucked under her teeth.

I slid my boxer briefs off and stood still. Just long enough to see that as she got an eyeful, her gaze turned heated.

Don't want to...fuck. No. Not even a possibility.

As I climbed in behind her, though, I slid almost all the way to the back of the tub—arms reach, but far enough away that I'd be less likely to just give in to the temptation. I grabbed the wash cloth and soap from the built-in holder, lathered up, then set to scrubbing Aysia's back in a slow circle.

"This is your idea of a level playing field?" she asked, leaning into my touch.

"Both naked. Both vulnerable."

"You naked is the least vulnerable thing I've ever seen."

I laughed and dipped the cloth into the water, then squeezed it over her shoulders, rinsing away the suds. "What if I told you that this is the first time I've ever been naked in a tub with a woman?"

"Hmm. I'd say it's a real shame, then, that you're pretending you don't want to have sex." She wriggled back a bit so that her ass was between my knees instead of my calves.

"Aysia..."

"Just getting comfortable."

"You're so full of shit."

It was her turn to laugh. "Sorry. Did you want me to pretend that I'm not as affected by you as you are by me? Because I just kind of assumed we were past that."

"Clearly, I'm *more* affected."

"Why? Because your arousal is visible? Give me your hand for a second and I'll show you that I'm just as turned on as you are."

"If there was a contest..." I said, widening my legs to pull her back so she could feel the full length of my erection pressed between the top of her ass and the bottom of her back, "You'd lose. But that isn't what I meant."

She let out a breathy squeak. "What did you mean?"

"I meant that only *one* of us is willing to talk. The *other* just wants to fuck."

"Hey!"

She tried to pull away, and I held her fast. She wiggled and jiggled against me so hard that I could swear I was two seconds away from coming right then and there.

Like she could sense it, she slowed her movements and added a little grind of her hips to her movements. "Which one of is which, again?"

"I can control myself," I said through gritted teeth, fighting the animalistic need for release and waiting for her to go still again.

"Fine." With that grumpy-sounding acquiescence, she collapsed against me, her back to my chest. "What do you want to *talk* about?"

"Anything."

"Anything other than how good it would feel to turn around and—"

I cut her off. "Anything but that."

She was quiet for a second before sighing and saying, "Favorite movies?"

I grinned at the barest tolerance of her tone. "Of all time, or in general?"

"In general."

"Anything action-packed."

"Typical."

"What do *you* like?"

"Porn."

I couldn't fight a laugh. "You're a demon."

"Goddess," she corrected. "Favorite music?"

"Classic rock. And Spice Girls."

She snorted. "Shut up."

"No judging. This bathtub is a safe space."

"Uh-huh."

I brought my thumbs to her shoulders and massaged them gently along the ridges of muscles. "Favorite childhood memory?"

"Disneyland when I was six. Hands down."

"Same here," I said. "Something about those mouse ears is so damned sexy."

"Shut up. Again."

I kissed the back of her neck. "Least favorite childhood memory?"

She tensed. "The day my mom told me my dad wasn't coming back. But I'm pretty sure you knew I was going to say that."

"Might've guessed a little."

"And now you want me to disclose my deepest, darkest fears? The ones that turned me into the woman I am today?"

I didn't let the bite of her words get to me. "I just want you to know that you *can*."

She went silent again. For so long that I thought maybe she really wasn't going to say anything more about it. When I opened my mouth to change the subject, though, she spoke again.

"It was another woman," she said softly. "A client he met at the ad firm where he worked. My mom was devastated. It blindsided her. She'd put aside her own career for his—they were competitors in the business and one of them had to leave it. She once told me she didn't even blink when he asked that it be her. She loved him and would've done anything for him. And that was how he repaid her."

"Sounds rough."

"It was pretty awful," she admitted. "I was almost fourteen when it happened. I never spoke to him again. Twelve years. I didn't go to his funeral. I didn't send a card to the other woman when he died. I think Carl was probably my punishment for that."

My throat tightened with a weird combo of sympathy and irritation. "Your dad left you. Not the other way around. I don't think some cosmic karma came your way in the shape of that asshole."

"Logically, I know that. But sometimes things happen, and I question it. I even question the course of my life. Like, would I be so driven if my dad had stuck around? Or am I just trying to prove something?"

"Even if you *are* trying to prove something… Why does it matter? You're not destructive in your ambition. As far as I can tell, you just push yourself. You're not stomping on people and sacrificing goats to get where you're going."

She laughed, and her hand came up to close over top of mine. She dragged her palms down to her stomach, then tilted her head to the side and kissed my throat. "Just so you know. You don't suck at comfort."

"Don't I?"

"No."

"You feel a bit less melancholy?"

"A gazillion times less *melancholy*. Weirdo."

"Hmm. Maybe it wasn't me. Maybe it was just the talking."

"Could be. But I doubt it. I don't feel this good when I talk to Liv."

"You sure?"

In response, she guided my hand even lower. In spite of all the water around us, I could still feel her own unique wetness under the tips of my fingers. I couldn't have *not* stroked her if I wanted to. She arched up into the attention, and I forgot about my resolve to keep from making this particular moment about sex. She was just too damned hot. Too fucking eager. No way could I deny her the pleasure she wanted.

I brought my hand down even more, and her thighs parted. It wasn't quite as much access as I wanted, so I grabbed her leg with my other hand, and I lifted it over the edge of the tub.

Much better.

She gasped as my fingers plunged into her. Back and forth. In and out. She felt so fucking good. Having her ass jammed against my cock wasn't half-bad either.

Her arm came up to circle the back of my head, and I dipped my mouth the parts of her I could reach. Her forehead. Her cheek. The spot just below her ear. I couldn't get enough.

I drew in a breath and lifted my eyes. And realized that what I couldn't get at with my mouth, I could get with my gaze. The full length mirror on the wall opposite the tub gave me the perfect view.

"Open your eyes, Aysia," I growled.

Her lashes fluttered, and her answer wasn't much more than a mumble. "What?"

"I want you to watch me make you come."

At that, her lids flew open. Her stare locked on mine in the mirror. Then it slid low.

I watched her watching the slow circle I made with my forefinger.

I watched her watching as I hooked it inside her and pressed up.

Her gaze didn't move. Not an inch. But her body did.

Up came her hips, driving me in farther.

Her thighs quivered as I added a second finger.

Her nipples drew into two hard points, jutting out above the water.

I could feel how tightly wound she was; I could *see* it, too. She was on the edge. All I had to do was nudge her over.

"Now, honey," I ordered. "Let go."

Her muscles clenched around my fingers. So tight. So perfect. Then she thrust up a final time, cried out my name, and released. Just for me.

* * * *

Aysia

I collapsed against Marc, breathing heavily. His erection was still pushing into my back, but I needed a moment to recover. A *few* moments. Okay. Maybe a full minute.

Every time he touched me, I thought it couldn't get better. Then it did. Even the way the tips of his fingers were running up and down my face right at that moment felt phenomenal. And sent another stir of desire through me. It wasn't a small one, either. It was a more like a wave had receded, then come back again immediately, stronger than before.

I wondered if this was how addiction felt.

I shifted sideways, and he helped me the rest of the way along, lifting me so that I faced him. My thighs straddled his, and the tip of his cock brushed my stomach just under the water. His eyes were on my face, and they were full of a longing that made me ache.

"Honey."

Even the endearment held meaning. Or maybe it was more than meaning. A question? A need? A request for something I was sure I couldn't even give? That thought made me ache even more.

I pushed up, hovering just over his rock hard length. Then I dropped just enough that it slid between my legs without actually entering me.

"Aysia." My name was a ragged breath on his lips.

I rocked forward. It was a slow, torturous move.

"Aysia." This time it was a warning.

I pushed up again. Then down.

"This isn't safe," he growled.

Still poised over him, I bent down and touched my lips to his. Ghostlike. I turned in a soft circle, my clit rubbing over his head, still without penetration. Already, I could feel the heat building below the surface.

"You don't like this?" I teased.

"Fuck yes, I like it."

"Sooooo…" I dragged the word out to match my tiny hip movement. "Should I stop?"

"Yes."

Surprised by his vehemence, I almost fell right onto him. In fact, if his hands hadn't shot out to stop me, I might literally have accidentally driven him into me. It was almost funny. Except the look on Marc's face made it anything but.

"You're really serious," I said.

"I'm serious enough that I'm telling you—the sexiest fucking woman on the planet—to stop. Even though my dick is telling me I'm a lunatic. Even though a sane man would be begging you to keep going. Hell. A crazy one wouldn't stop you, either. But I have to."

I felt a blush climb up my cheeks, both at the compliment and at his accompanying speech, and all I could manage to say was, "Oh."

He lifted his hands from my hips and put his elbows on the edges of the tub. "Honey…if you don't stop, I'll lose control."

"Control...hmm. Do you need that?"

"No," he admitted easily. "I'm happy to let you have it."

"But?"

"Even *this*..." He inclined his head down to the non-existent space between us. "Is a gamble. And you're after a weekend, not a lifetime, remember?"

His words weren't teasing. They were as serious as his request for me to stop. And I noted—because I couldn't help it—that he'd said *you're* and not *we're*. What did that mean? I swallowed a need to ask him.

But strangely, I couldn't help but picture it. An older him and an older me. A lifetime of getting there with moments like *this* as interludes.

And suddenly I wanted him even more. I wanted every inch of him in me. So badly that it was dizzying. I swayed a little, driving him closer again.

Marc muttered something incomprehensible, then reached up to push his fingers into my damp hair, and he pulled my face to his. His tongue dove into my mouth. Thoroughly and aggressive. Claiming ownership.

And I met the claim with one of my own.

Hands on his chest. *Mine.*

Teeth on his lips. *Mine.*

Thumbs over his face and down his throat. *Mine, mine.*

Fingers down between us to clasp his erection under the water. *Mine, yes, please, God, yes. Mine.*

Once more, I pulled myself over him. I angled him toward me. In a second, there wouldn't be anything accidental about having him fill me. There would just be *us*. Skin to skin.

He groaned. "Aysia. Honey."

This third time...my name wasn't a breath. It wasn't a warning. It was plea, plain and simple.

I started to ease down, anticipating how sweet he was going to feel. But before I could get so far as actually finding out, a noisy buzz filled the bathroom.

Marc's eyes flew open. "What the hell is that?"

"The door buzzer." I groaned. "Shit. The car . . ."

"What car?"

"*Your* car."

He frowned. "My Quattroporte?"

"Yes. That, too. But also the car I arranged to get us to the private dealer in Chilliwack. And you need to pack a bag."

"A bag?"

"An overnight bag. Two nights, actually."

The noisy buzz sounded again.

"That's probably the driver," I said.

"So we should probably answer it."

"Yes. Assuming you want to pick up your Maserati."

"I do want the Maserati." His eyes ran over me slowly, and he met my gaze with a raised eyebrow. "But not half as bad as I want you."

"Suck up."

"Is that an option? Maybe while *in* the Maserati?"

"Marc!"

"What?"

The buzzer went off a third time.

He sighed. "The driver's not going away, is he?"

I shook my head. "Doubtful. I didn't prepay."

He slid back and gestured to the bathroom at large. "Ladies first."

Regretfully, I climbed out and grabbed two towels. I wrapped myself in one and handed the other to Marc.

"Do you want me to answer the buzzer while you pack?" I offered.

"Sure." He finished his quick towel-off, moved toward the door, then paused. "Aysia?"

"Yes?"

"There's a box of condoms in my nightstand. I won't be forgetting to bring it."

I sucked in a breath as he left the bathroom. Prior to the moment of reckless abandon, his statement would've been a sexy one. Now, it just sounded like a warning. And I couldn't blame him for issuing it.

What were you thinking? Unprotected sex? Seriously?

But he didn't bring it up again as we made the trip from downtown, through the suburbs, and out to the more rural neighborhood. In fact, he was remarkably relaxed considering the fact that we rushed out with some pretty specific unfinished business. He joked with the driver and teased me in the back seat. He acted suitably impressed by the expanse of farmland along the highway and the perfect view of Mount Baker as we headed east. He grinned like a maniac when we picked up his sleek new vehicle and laughed like crazy when the first thing we did was take it through a drive-thru.

But my own brain was a mess.

Having unprotected sex wasn't something I'd done before. Ever. Or even considered. And it wasn't like we hadn't had the option. We weren't stupid teenagers getting overexcited in the backseat of a car. We weren't stranded in the woods at the height of the zombie apocalypse. The condoms were in the very next room.

The whole day it bothered me. I owed Marc one hell of an apology for pushing the risky behavior. And saying I was sorry was something I was actually pretty terrible at doing. But when we were finally settled into our luxurious bed and breakfast room, with its four poster bed and its private fireplace and panoramic, I knew I wouldn't get away with avoiding it any longer. My conscience wouldn't let me.

So as we cued up a movie and balanced a bowl of popcorn on our knees, I opened my mouth to deliver the apology in a rush of awkward words.

But Marc spoke first. "She thought she was pregnant."

"I—what? Who did?"

"Janie."

I struggled for a second before placing the name. "Your ex?"

"Yeah." He tossed up a piece of popcorn and caught it in his mouth. "Was fully convinced."

I wasn't sure what to say. "But…she wasn't?"

"No." Up went another kernel. "She *thought* she was pregnant. And she didn't want to keep it."

I remembered, then, what he'd said about the breakup. Different priorities.

"And you *did* want to," I ventured softly.

A third buttery piece went flying, and he snapped his lips shut over top of it. "Of course I wanted to. But she printed a shit-ton of adoption information off the Internet before she even told me. Before she went to the doctor, for Christ's sake. And when I suggested that *maybe* we should consider keeping it, she went ballistic. Told me I was selfish bastard. *Me.* With a good job and a good family and all the resources to do *right* by a kid…I was selfish for wanting to keep my own child and provide a more than decent life. I lasted the week it took to find out it was a false alarm. I lay awake every night, thinking about a paternity suit. About keeping my kid, even if it meant losing Janie. Just because she wasn't ready to be a parent didn't mean she should make that decision for me. I told her I was leaving her right before she told me she wasn't pregnant after all."

My heart squeezed with sympathy. With understanding. And with that much more guilt about my actions in the bathtub.

"Marc…" I trailed off, fighting the thick lump in my throat.

He shook his head, reading my intentions perfectly. "I don't need you to be sorry. Not for me, or about the situation, or for wanting to be a bit wild. You didn't know. No one does, honey. Not even my parents. But I thought I should tell you, so you get where I'm coming from. Okay?"

The lump was so thick now that all I could do was nod.

He leaned back and tossed an arm over my shoulder. "Good. Let's get the movie started before I change my mind about watching the cheesy romance one and insist on the one full of guns instead."

I let him pull me in, but I stole a quick glance at his profile before I turned my attention to the screen. And for that second, I let my imagination run far wilder than it had in the tub. I let it envision the same thing it had earlier—an older me and an older him—with one small added detail. A crazy one. A kid. With his strong jaw and my blue eyes and a funny smile that was all his own.

And I wondered how his ex could possibly have wanted to give that up.

Chapter 11

Marcelo

So.

Apparently the best way to cleanse one's system of a girl like Aysia Banks is *not* to spend the entire weekend with her. Not to wake up wrapped around her. Not to go to sleep that way. Sure as hell wasn't to eat picnic lunches together while fighting over whether apples and peanut butter were better than apples with caramel.

By the time Sunday evening rolled around, all I could think about was how shitty Monday was going to be. Then Tuesday. And every other fucking day after that.

My mood mustn't have been as obvious as I thought, though, because as we made our way over the last stretch of highway, she turned to me and said, "You're awfully pensive."

"Pensive?"

"Quiet. Thoughtful. Reflective."

"Thanks, Little Ms. Thesaurus. But my concern wasn't what the word meant. It was whether or not it's an accurate descriptor."

"You're staring out the windshield so hard I'm kind of worried you're trying to break it with your mind. I think that warrants an observation on your pensiveness."

My hands tightened on the steering wheel. "I'm not pensive. I'm royally fucking disappointed that the weekend is done, and I'm trying to find a way to either make it last, or to convince you that we should keep seeing each other."

She was quiet for a second before answering, and when she did speak, it was in a very soft voice. "We had a deal, Marc."

"Deals get amended all the time."

"Is this how we're going to end it, then?"

End it. I hated the way that sounded.

"Is *what* how we're going to end it?" I snapped back irritably.

"In a fight."

"I don't want to fight."

"Could've fooled me."

"This weekend was basically a romantic montage," I said. "I don't understand why you think that's a *bad* thing."

I could see that she was fighting a smile, but her reply didn't give me any hope. "The only reason it was a romantic montage is because we both knew it was going to be over today. No strings means no expectations. No expectations means no awkwardness."

"Fuck the expectations, Aysia. I want the goddamned strings."

She drew in a breath so hard that it echoed through the car. "Are you going to quit your job, Marc? Walk out on Mike Roper?"

"I—Christ." I ran a hand over my hair in frustration. "Why does that have to be my only option?"

"Because *I'm* not going to leave Eco-Go. And the only way for us to keep seeing each other is if one of us does."

I opened my mouth, then snapped it shut again quickly. I wouldn't—couldn't—leave Mike's company, even if I wanted to. No way in hell would I ask Aysia to do it. Even if she wanted to. Even if she hadn't disclosed the details of how things played out with her parents. Not after a lust-filled year let alone a lust-filled week.

"I hate the goddamned rules," I muttered.

"But they exist for a reason. And it's not just as a cock block."

I couldn't muster up a smile. We'd turned off the highway, in just a few minutes, we'd be at her place. Where I somehow doubted she was going to invite me up for a nightcap.

She let out a sigh. "Eco-Go matters to me."

"I know."

"And the dating policy is there to protect it, as a company."

"I get it, honey. I really do. I just don't like it. And I'd be a pretty shitty PR person if I didn't push to get what I want. But I'm not a shitty person in general, and I'm capable of taking *no* for an answer. The problem is that it feels so fucking wrong to just let you go." My voice had an embarrassing hint of raw emotion at the end of the last sentence, and I had to clear my throat before continuing. "I'd be lying if I didn't admit that. I'd also be lying if I didn't admit that working beside you is going to be tough."

"But imagine how much harder it would be if it went on for months, then ended badly."

We reached her street then, and I pulled over in front of her building and turned to face her. "Do you always assume the worst is going to happen?"

She shook her head. "No. But I have to assume that the worst *could* happen. And *I'd* be lying if I didn't say it."

"Fair enough," I conceded. "But does that mean you also assume that the best could happen?"

"Of course."

Her tone was as soft as her expression and, automatically, I brought my hand up to caress her face. She flinched. Just enough to tell me that no matter what I said, she'd come back to this same thing. The rejection stung. I pulled back without completing the touch.

"I guess this is it, then?"

She nodded. "Yes."

She stayed there, unmoving. Staring at me like she was trying to hold onto the moment, trying to memorize what I looked like right that second. In spite of my wounded pride and disappointed heart, I did the same. I studied the sweet curve of her lips and the untamed curls that framed her face. I committed to memory the tiny, paint-dab mole high on her left cheekbone. I drank in the flush that crept down the slope of her throat then dipped to her cleavage. Even though I knew I'd be seeing her the very next morning at the office, I made sure I had every detail of right now filed somewhere safe in my mind.

When she finally opened the door without kissing me good-bye and without telling it was the best weekend of her life, I managed to hold my shit together in the manliest way possible. I even pulled my car out without looking back. Yeah, I cranked up the generic rock radio station. Maybe I cursed out a loud a few times. Altogether, though, I took the weird breakup of our non-relationship like a fucking champ.

At least I *thought* I was taking it like a champ. Until Wednesday morning when my phone buzzed from its spot on my desk, and her name flashed across the screen. The decorum of Sunday through Tuesday slipped away, and I became a kid on Christmas. One who didn't even know it *was* Christmas until he got up and saw the presents.

With a quick glance to make sure my door was closed, I snapped the phone up and swiped it to retrieve the message.

Hi.

One word. I tried not to be disappointed, and I typed one back myself.

Hey.

Can u meet for lunch?

Something wrong?

Yes.

I frowned and asked, *Work related?*

No.

One more word, but so much better than the first.

All right, I wrote. *Anywhere in particular?*

U know the crepe place?

I can find it.

Come a few minutes before the break starts.

Ok.

I stared at the phone for a few minutes longer, reading more into the texts than a hormone-riddled teenager would've.

What was wrong?

Why crepes?

What did she need to see me about that she couldn't discuss at the office?

I couldn't even come up with one logical explanation for a crepe-eating, early-break, non-work-related scenario. Well. One. But it involved whipped cream and a lot of dirty things that I somehow doubted she would decide to request spontaneously via text.

I finally gave up on sifting through my pile of emails and left for the restaurant a full thirty minutes before the official lunch hour started. On the way out, I spied Aysia in the copy room. From behind the in-office window, she issued me a friendly wave and the same heartbreaking smile she'd had on her face since Monday. It was a look that gave nothing away. Forcing aside the ache in my chest, I made myself not stop and beg to know how long she thought she would be. Or if she'd changed her mind.

When I got to the crepe place, the friendly host called me by name before I made it all the way through the door.

"Mr. Diaz? Your lady friend is waiting."

My puzzlement at how she managed to beat me there only lasted a minute. It wasn't Aysia at the table at all. It was her blond, sexy-dress-picking, coffee-delivering friend. Liv. She sat at a corner booth with a familiar, red-covered phone in her hand.

Shit.

If the host hadn't nudged me forward with a throat-clear and a murmur, I might've turned and run. Instead, I was stuck. Liv's gaze came up, her eyes narrowed, and she pointed imperiously at bench seat across from her. Stifling a sigh, I sat down obediently.

"Hello, Marcelo," she greeted.

"Liv. Couldn't find your own phone today?"

"Grabbed Aysia's by mistake while we were out for coffee this morning."

"Uh-huh. And you tricked me into coming here by accident, too?"

Her eyes narrowed even more. "I only tricked you into coming because I didn't think you'd show up if I just asked."

"I'm a surprisingly reasonable man," I said back. "Any particular reason for choosing the crepes?"

"I like them. And Aysia hates them. So I get what I want and I know she won't show up here and interrupt us."

"That doesn't fill me full of confidence. Should I check under the table for a weapon and a shovel?"

She sighed. "I know you think I hate you."

"Aysia assured me that you don't," I replied.

"And I guess you just believed her?"

"I've been assuming she's not a liar."

"Well. You've been assuming wrong."

The statement surprised me. "What?"

Liv twirled her stir stick in her coffee. "She *is* a liar. At least about some stuff."

"What stuff?"

"Just off the top of my head? Pretending like she doesn't have a heart."

I couldn't suppress a laugh. "I'm well aware that she has a heart."

"That's because she's a *bad* liar."

The server came by then, interrupting us temporarily. Liv ordered like an expert, and I just had them double it up. The brief interlude gave me enough time to get my thoughts together.

"Liv..." I said. "If you're here to give me one of those 'break-my-best-friend's-heart-and-I'll-kill-you speeches, you're barking up the wrong tree."

"I know you won't hurt her. She won't *let* you. And that's what I mean about her pretending not to have a heart," she replied. "We've been friends since kindergarten. Do you know how many boyfriends she's had since then?"

I stiffened a little as a trickle of automatic jealousy crept in. "No. How many?"

"Well. There was Walt. They went out when we were in seventh grade."

"Okay."

Was she seriously going to give me a list that started in elementary school? I waited. She said nothing else.

"Okay," I said again. "Walt. And?"

"And that's it."

"What do you mean?"

"Walt. She always liked him. And in seventh grade, he realized he liked her, too."

"What am I missing here, Liv?"

"That. Is. It."

"She hasn't had a boyfriend since seventh grade?"

The blond shrugged. "Dated enough to not be mistaken for a crazy cat lady. But no boyfriends. And before you ask about Carl…don't. He never earned the title."

"And I'm guessing she wouldn't be excited to know you're here with me, telling me all this?"

"I'm her best friend. So I *did* warn her I was taking matters into my own hands. And I'm only telling you this because she hasn't had this twinkly look in her eye since Walt. I think you should know that. And I think that she *deserves* that."

The server came by with our crepes, interrupting us once more. Liv dived into hers immediately, but I held off for a second.

"What happened to Walt?"

Liv paused with her fork halfway to her mouth. "He died."

"He *died*?"

"Yes." She chewed slowly and kept frustratingly silent.

I put my own fork down. "Uh. Little more info, please?"

"Cancer. A year-long battle."

"That's…"

"Terrible," she said.

Once again, I waited for her to add something else. She just chewed her crepes. Two more entire bites before she sighed loudly.

"I know I probably sound like I'm being insensitive," she said. "But I'm not. And I'm not saying she should've gotten over it by now or anything like that. I promise. It was over a decade ago, but it was awful and tragic, and I would never expect the loss to just go away. But between Walt's death and her dad taking off, Aysia built up a crazy wall of independence."

"Being independent is a good thing," I pointed out.

"I know. I wish I had half as much drive as she does."

"I don't know what it is you want me to do."

"You got behind it," she said, her voice low and hopeful.

"Behind what?"

"Her wall, dummy. I love her more than words, Marc, and I want you to stay there."

"Behind her wall."

"Yes."

I sighed, ran a hand over my chin and met her eyes. "I can't force her to be my girlfriend, Liv."

"But you'd like her to be."

"Yes," I admitted, realizing it was true—at the very least I wanted to give us a shot at having a relationship.

"So then can you do something for me?"

"Sure," I said, knowing she wouldn't let me go until I agreed.

"Next time you're alone with her...ask her about Walt?"

"I'm not sure if she's going to let the alone thing happen."

"I'll take care of that. You just promise to ask her."

"All right."

"Say it."

"I promise to ask Aysia about Walt."

Liv studied me for a minute, then nodded. "Good. And you should eat your crepes before they get cold. Seriously."

"Do you think maybe Aysia's independent streak comes from somewhere else?" I asked pointedly.

"What? From dealing with me?"

I shrugged. "Maybe."

She narrowed her eyes. "Shut up and eat your pancakes. I have to get this phone back to the office before Aysia notices I have it."

"Uh-huh."

"Crepes."

Dutifully, I lifted my fork.

* * * *

Aysia

A light knock on my office door—a space I'd taken over from the human resources manager who was currently on leave—made me lift my eyes from the overdue stack of performance reviews. It was a relief, really. I'd been working my way through the paperwork since Monday, and every time I thought I'd made some headway, another problem turned up. Apparently, for the six months *preceding* her leave, the manager hadn't filed a damned thing. So Eco-Go was behind on its raises, behind on its corrective action... behind on everything staff-related except for giving me a headache.

With a sigh, I slid my chair backwards, stood up, then made my way to the door. Putting on the best smile I could muster up, I opened it. And as soon as I saw who was on the other side, my smile turned genuine.

"Liv," I greeted. "Did you know that you're three months overdue for a raise?"

"Yep. I filed a complaint to the HR lady via e-mail. She didn't answer. Oh. Wait." She paused and lifted an eyebrow. "Well. This is awkward."

"Hilarious."

"The lower dregs of Eco-Go society are always behind by about a year."

"You're not the dregs. And seriously? A year?"

"Yeah. The retro pay is like a bonus."

I groaned and rubbed my temple. "That's *not* how it's supposed to work."

My friend stepped to my desk, snagged an apple from the top drawer, and held it out. "Eat this. You're cranky."

I stuck out my tongue. "You do realize you're not my mother."

"I know. She lets you get away with shit, and I don't."

With a sigh, I took the apple, then chomped down a noisy bite before speaking again. "What wonderful thing brings you to my office? Besides force feeding me, I mean. Please tell me it's something good."

She reached into her purse and dragged out a familiar phone. "I grabbed this by mistake when we had coffee this morning."

I reached for it, and she pulled it away.

"I'm only giving it to you if you say you'll call him," she informed me.

"I'm not calling him."

"Then at least text him back."

"Text him *back*?"

She shot me an innocent look. "I *may* have accidentally seen a message."

I narrowed my eyes. "You accidentally saw a message that requires you to enter my password?"

"I may also have accidentally entered your password."

"Liv!"

"He wants to talk."

"Too bad."

"Come on, Aysia. You like him. Why are you tormenting yourself like this?"

"Because it contravenes company policy. Because he's going to be my boss one day. Our boss, actually. And because it's up to me what I do with my sex life and not up to you."

"So you *do* like him."

I made a frustrated noise. "Did you hear anything I just said?"

"I only heard what you didn't say," Liv said.

"You're making my headache worse. Can I have my phone?"

"Are you going to answer him?"

"Fine."

She held out the slim device, but when my hands closed over it, she didn't let go right away. Instead, her face turned serious.

"You know that I love you like a sister, right?" she asked.

"Yes."

"So you know I'd never tell you to do something I thought would hurt you."

"I do know."

"Good." She released the phone and moved in for a hug. "I'm your favorite pain the ass, right?"

"A hundred percent," I agreed as she released me.

"Call me after work?"

"You got it."

I waited until the door was closed firmly behind her before I glanced down at my phone. My mouth was already dry, and I hadn't even tapped the screen yet. Marc wanted to talk.

So why didn't he just come and say so? I couldn't very well turn him away or cause a scene while we were at work. But he probably wouldn't use that to his advantage, either. He'd told me he could take no for an answer. And he'd been proving it all week. Not sneaking glances at mutual meetings. Smiling at me with his mouth but not with his eyes. And if I was being honest…I was more than a little disappointed at how easy he made it seem. Because for me, it wasn't easy at all.

I ached when I looked at him. I ached when I didn't look at him. I missed the stupid montage of romantic moments. I missed the feel of his hands on my body. I hadn't even been able to make myself use good old Francois-the-Vibrator in his place. I knew it was dumb to feel the emptiness so strongly. I'd made it two and a half decades without being aware that Marcelo Diaz existed. So why did a week and a half of knowing him make such a hole in my life?

C'mon, Aysia. Just look at the stupid phone.

With hands that actually shook, I lifted it up and swiped. Marc's name came up immediately. I was thankful that I'd forced myself to delete our previous conversation, glad that Liv hadn't gotten a glimpse of further evidence of me "liking" the man. But it made me feel strangely sad to see a blank slate of text. Just the solitary line.

I want to talk, it read.

I bit my lip and typed back. *Talk?*

There was a too-long pause before a reply came back. *About an HR issue.*

Which is?

The dress code.

I frowned and wrote, *What dress code?*

The one that requires u not to dress so provocatively.

In spite of the fact that I was alone, my face heated. I threw a glance down at my clothes. Sure, my skirt was a bit...I don't know...flouncy. If I spun, it might show some thigh. And my blouse was sleeveless and sheer at the shoulders. But my outfit wasn't *provocative* by any stretch.

I don't think that's an appropriate comment, I informed him, hoping the tone came across as cool and collected.

I don't think that's an appropriate pair of underwear, Marc countered.

I couldn't stifle a gasp. And I couldn't stop myself from trying to remember what I'd tossed on this morning, either.

A black thong, I thought. *Maybe with a little pink bow at the front?*

But how would Marc know that? The answer was easy. He couldn't.

Stop that, I typed.

Stop what?

Flirting with me.

I hate to break it to u, but after everything else I've done to u...flirting is the least of ur worries.

Now my face burned. My fingers flew furiously over the screen. But Marc was quicker.

Hot pink, he wrote. *Little strip of lace up the back.*

Automatically, my hand reached to the rear waistband of my skirt. A flick just underneath confirmed the familiar, stretchy tab at the back. Then I remembered. I'd been in a big rush this morning, and hadn't been able to find the black one with the bow. I'd grabbed the pink one at the last second. I'd asked Liv over coffee this morning if she could see it through my skirt.

"And apparently, she lied," I grumbled.

I turned to the side, trying to see my reflection in the stainless steel doorframe. I got nothing but a blur of black. I brought my attention back to my phone. Once again Marc was faster.

I like it, actually, he'd texted. *Wouldn't mind seeing it up close.*

What the hell is the matter with u? I wrote back.

Why are u pretending u don't like this?

WE'RE AT WORK. STOP.

U can't control my imagination. Work or no work.

STOP IT.

MAKE ME.

I couldn't keep my feet from moving, even though I knew I should've. They'd each grown a brain of their own, and they were currently in charge. They marched me across my office. They gave my hands an order, and my hands obeyed, flinging the door open with all the subtlety of a drunk elephant. The metal and wood flew backwards and smacked the wall hard enough to make me jump. But my feet were still the boss. They clack-clacked my high heels over the floor, past the row of offices beside my own, then kept going, all the way to the end of the corridor. They issued another command, and my hand again complied. Without even a single knock, I yanked on Marc's door. I stepped inside and slammed it shut. And there, my feet stopped at last. Just in time for my mouth to start.

"How dare you!" I yelled.

Marc eyed me nervously from behind his desk. "Aysia?"

"My underwear!"

"Your…what?"

"Underwear!"

He cleared his throat. "Um. Aysia."

"What?"

He nodded his head, and I adjusted my gaze to look where he'd indicated. *Shit.*

There was someone else in the room. A squat, bald man with a bowtie. Standing to the side near a shelf. Looking terribly confused and little scared, too.

And now my feet weren't in charge. They were paralyzed.

"Errrrr," I dragged out the strangled, nonsensical noise, my eyes flying from Marc to the stranger, then back again.

Marc stared back at me for a long second. Like he thought I might just dematerialize. When it became clear that I wouldn't move—or *couldn't* move, to be more accurate—he pushed up from his desk. He said something to the bald man. God only knew what. Then the man scurried out and Marc closed the door behind him.

"I'm guessing we won't be getting that ad account," he said dryly.

"That's *it*?" My words were just shy of a splutter. "That's all you have to say?"

"I'm not sure what *to* say."

He sounded so truly perplexed that I almost bought it. But as my arms dropped to my side, the phone I held in my hand reminded me why I was there.

"How about an apology?"

"For?"

"I hope you're kidding. You can't send me messages like that, Marc," I said.

"Like what?"

"Oh, please."

"What *kinds* of message do you think I've been sending?" he replied.

I ignored the heat in my cheeks. "Dirty ones."

"On your phone?"

"Yes."

"About your underwear?"

He looked amused for just enough time that my reply came out as a snap.

"Yes, Marc! My underwear. Is that *funny*?"

He ran his hand over his hair. "Look, Aysia. I haven't sent you anything. I've been in a meeting since I got back from—shit."

I waited for him to finish. Instead, he frowned. He stuck his hand into his suit jacket and pulled it out again. He frowned even harder. Then he moved back to his desk and slid one drawer after the other. When he'd looked into each one, he brought his gaze back up to mine.

"Liv," he said.

"What?"

"She stole my goddamned phone."

"You're kidding me."

"I'm not."

"*How?*"

"She tricked me into lunch using *your* phone."

"Of course she did," I said with a sigh.

Marc stepped closer, then stopped uncertainly a few feet away. "She's trying to get us to talk."

"By making me so mad that I humiliate myself?" I shook my head. "No. Never mind. I know her. She's devious."

"And devi*ant*, apparently. What did she say that got you so riled up?"

"Might as well look. It's not like I have any dignity left."

I held out the phone, and he reached over without moving any nearer. He even managed to keep our fingers from brushing, and I couldn't decide if that disappointed more or relieved me more. Once he had the phone, he pulled back and flipped through the messages, a small smile playing across his lips.

"She really is good," he said.

"She's horrible," I replied.

"She's your best friend."

I blinked at him. "What did she feed you for lunch? Eye of newt with a side of brainwashing?"

He chuckled. "None of that. Just crepes."

"Crepes?" I repeated, thinking maybe I'd heard him wrong.

"Sorry. I know you hate them."

"I don't hate crepes. I..." I trailed off as the world swam a little.

"Hey."

Marc's hand was on my elbow, steadying me, and I was too shaky to pull away like I ought to have done. Instead, I leaned into him, grateful for his strength. I breathed in through my nose and out through my mouth, working hard to get a hold of the panic before it got a hold of me.

"What did she want me to talk to you about?" I asked.

"She made me promise to ask about Walt."

"She said that? She said Walt? And she did it while eating crepes?"

"Yeah, honey."

I let the endearment slide. "What else?"

"Do you need to sit down?"

"No. I'm okay." I didn't let go of him, though. "Just tell me what else Liv said. Please."

"That he was your first and only boyfriend. That he died of cancer."

"That's it?"

He leaned away and gave me a look that asked if that wasn't enough all on its own, but all he said was, "That's it."

Unable to fight a sudden need to be close, I slid a hand to his waist and tucked my body against his. I clung. And he let me. It sent an unusual wave of sadness through me. I exhaled and let the feeling ebb and flow, tugging at the parts of my heart and mind that I usually kept under tight lock and key.

"I was five when they moved in next door," I said in Marc's reassuringly solid chest.

"When who moved in, honey?"

"Liv and Walt."

"They were brother and sister?" His surprise was evident in his voice.

I nodded. "Walt was eleven months older, and he never let Liv forget it. Even when they were little like that. He knew exactly how to push her buttons. Just how far to go before she'd run and tell their mom."

"And you liked that."

"I loved it. Liv was always a bossy, funny little person. So opinionated. She had to control everything. But Walt never let her. He used to make me laugh so hard. I mean, what kind of six-year-old knows how to drop an effective *wink*?"

Marc ran a hand over my hairline. "Haven't met one myself."

"Because it shouldn't be a thing." I smiled affectionately at the memory, the image of it filling my mind as I added, "I knew from the beginning that I loved him, even if I didn't really know what that meant. By the time I was twelve, I had this whole life planned. It's kind of embarrassing."

Marc's finger came down the side of my face to hit my chin. He didn't try to pull my face away from his chest, though. He just stroked back and forth soothingly.

"Not embarrassing at all," he said. "Better than a boy band fantasy, right?"

I surprised myself by laughing. "I guess. But just as cliché. Best friend's big brother and all."

"Still better than coordinated dance moves and a cheesy pop riff." He kissed the top of my head. "So when did he realize he loved you back?"

"It was his thirteenth birthday. Big party. Lots of people—family and friends, too—at this beach even though it was October. It was starting to get dark, and I was sitting by myself on a log while things were winding down. All of a sudden he was beside me. I can't remember the conversation, but it wasn't serious. Then boom. He kissed me."

"Boom, huh?"

"Pretty much."

"And that was it?"

I shook my head against him, enjoying the way the soft fabric of Marc's dress shirt rubbed into my cheek. "He said we were too young. Actually. That *I* was too young. But he didn't want anyone to kiss me before he did. Or after. He asked me to wait until I turned thirteen, too, the next January, before we made anything official."

"Patient for a thirteen-year-old boy."

"Frustrating, for a twelve-year-old girl who's already been waiting for seven years."

"And then he got sick."

"Yes." A thick lump formed in my throat. "Around spring break. It happened exactly the way it does in those sad, made-for-TV movies. The bruises. The tiredness. Not feeling well for months. Then he got a cut that wouldn't stop bleeding and they finally sent him in for testing."

"Leukemia," Marc said.

"Yes. Chronic lymphocytic leukemia. They caught it too late. The cells were too spread out, and his lymph nodes were overrun. Walt barely responded to treatment. But he still lived for a year."

"Hell of a fighter."

I closed my eyes. "He said right up to the end that he'd make it. He was so determined. I think that when he died, it was more shocking to him than anyone else."

"I'm sorry you went through all that, honey."

I'd heard those words a hundred times in the days after Walt died, from a hundred people. But for some reason, coming from Marc...they mattered for the first time. And it was like the metaphorical floodgate. It burst open, and a dozen emotion rushed in. Long pent-up grief. Relief. Something warm and deep and soothing.

"Thank you."

"You're welcome."

I leaned back and tipped my face up. With my three-inch heels on, our lips were already so close that I could feel the warmth of his mouth without any effort at all. And when he exhaled my name, I could practically taste him, too.

"Kiss me," I whispered back.

"You're sure that's what you want?"

"Right this second...it's what I need," I admitted.

Marc didn't hesitate. He tilted his head and dropped his mouth to mine. The kiss was thorough and tender. And strangely, everything else didn't slip away. It was all still there. Walt and the memories he filled. The office and the people I knew were just on the other side of the closed door. And I didn't mind. My whole life became a background for that exact moment.

Chapter 12

Marcelo

Aysia's lips were soft. Yielding. Vulnerable. Yet somehow, I was still under her control. Still kissing her on *her* terms. Which at the moment had nothing to do with sex.

And fuck did I like it.

Her arms came up my shoulders, and her hands caressed the back of my head, then teased at my hair gently. She pressed herself to me, her curves aligned with my planes, the grooves of our bodies locked together.

Even then, it still wasn't about sex. Need and release and comfort and nothing more. Or everything more. Hard to say which. I was damned sure, though, that it was a fucking *good* thing.

Not that I wasn't thoroughly turned on. I couldn't say I didn't enjoy it as much as I enjoyed taking her and letting her take me. Hell. Maybe, in some ways, I even enjoyed it more. So when she pulled away, kissing me lightly three more times in quick succession, I was disappointed. Until I looked down and saw the emotion in her eyes. Then I grinned like a fool. "Hi."

She smiled back. "Hi."

"Doing okay down there?"

"Been worse."

"Me, too." I kissed the tip of her nose. "And thank you for trusting me enough to tell me all of that."

She looked away and rubbed at the little tear-mark she'd left on my shirt. "Sorry about that."

"It'll wash out."

"It's silk."

"So it'll dry clean out."

"Still."

I studied her downcast face for second. "Are you really apologizing for making the world's smallest mess on my shirt, or are you apologizing for crying?"

She exhaled heavily. "I don't know."

"Well. For the record...you don't need to be sorry for either."

"You're only saying that because I'm wearing waterproof mascara."

"I'd like you even if you completely destroyed my shirt. And even if your mascara ran and gave you raccoon eyes."

The tension in her face eased. "Ah. You're familiar with the look. Made a lot of girls cry?"

"A few," I admitted. "But most of my experience comes from having a really blubbery sister."

"A sister?"

"Three years younger. Creative. Lots of emotion."

"You're close?"

"I like to think so."

"You haven't mentioned her before."

"I like to save a few details for the second illicit weekend away together."

Her face drooped, and she let out small sigh. "This is a mess, isn't it?"

"Which part? The making out in the office, the illicit weekend, or me being close to my sister?"

"Funny. I mean *us*, in general."

"I want to argue. But I'm too busy feeling smug that you said 'us'. Have dinner with me tonight."

"We still shouldn't see each other, Marc."

I dipped my head down and kissed her lightly. "Okay."

"Okay?" She leaned back, surprise evident in her eyes.

"Sorry." I covered a smile. "Did you want to fight about it?"

"No."

"Don't worry, honey. I'm just taking what I can get for the moment."

"And what do you think that is?"

"You. Blubbery. Kissing me in my office. Stubbornly refusing to admit that we can find a way around this." I shrugged. "I really do like you, Aysia. And I can be a patient man."

The look she gave me then was hopeful. Almost fucking heartbreaking.

"So," she said slowly. "If I tell you that's all you get from now on, you'll just sit around waiting?"

"Waiting...and possibly masturbating."

Her eyes widened and a laugh escaped her lips. "Pervert."

"No need for name calling. New studies show it doesn't actually cause blindness."

"Did you read that on the Internet?"

"How'd you know?"

"Lucky guess."

"Have dinner with me," I said again. "We can eat shrimp scampi and talk."

"Shrimp scampi?"

"First thing that came to mind."

She laughed and tucked herself into me again, her head resting on my shoulder, her arms under my suit jacket and encircling my waist. I pulled her even tighter, rubbing my hand in a circle against the small of her back. Under the attention, her breathing quickened. I knew I had to move away. If I didn't, the patience I claimed to have would evaporate. I was already eyeing my desk.

Toss aside the paperwork...lift her onto the edge...

I stilled my hand and cleared my throat. "Still doing okay down there?"

"I've been better," she replied.

Worried, I leaned back. She was smiling impishly. I narrowed my eyes. "Okay," I said. "I'll play. *When* have you been better?"

"Every time you've been inside me."

Under my zipper, my cock stirred. "Is that right?"

"Definitely." She leaned forward, eyes still fixed on me, and bit my lower lip.

"Are you trying to distract me with sex...again?"

"Distract you from what?" she asked innocently.

"From further baring your soul by baring your ass instead," I said, half-teasing, half-serious.

She snorted. "Nice."

My hands slid down to the ass in question, and I squeezed hard enough to make her gasp.

"Well," I said. "As tempted as I am, I'm not letting that happen."

"You sure?" She wiggled her hips, and the added height from the heels put her in *just* the right spot to make me growl.

"Aysia..."

"Marcelo."

"Tell me about the crepes."

She sucked in a breath. "Now?"

"Yes."

"They were Walt's favorite. A tradition. He insisted on having them every Sunday. Even on the Sundays when he was too sick from the radiation to eat. He forced Liv and me to have them, then. When he died...I swore I'd never eat them again. It's one of the few things Liv and I disagree about, actually."

"Because she thinks you're holding on too tightly."

She nodded, and I could see the unshed tears in her eyes. "But it was never on purpose. I *couldn't* eat them, just like I couldn't let go. I kept thinking I'd reach some place in my life where I could make it happen, but I never did. So I stopped trying to get past it and just focused on the things I could control."

"I don't think that's true, honey. Not the part about having stopped trying, anyway. I think you just buried the feelings so hard and deep that you thought you were numb."

"I'm not numb when I'm with you."

"Good."

I slid my hands down her arms, then under them. I ran my palms up her skirt-covered thighs. On her hips, I paused. Christ, how I wanted her. I thought again about my desk. About lifting her up and carrying her to it. The need to do it got worse as one of her knees slid up and hooked around my waist, and worse again as she pushed up for a fierce kiss.

Her lips weren't soft and yielding anymore. They were insistent and demanding. Still filled with need, but this time the pitch was different. It made me wish that I was the kind of man who kept condoms in his office. Or—for the first time in memory—that I was the kind who didn't give a shit about protection at all.

"Come to my house tonight," I urged against her mouth when she paused to draw in some air.

"For dinner?" she breathed back.

"And maybe a bit more than dinner," I agreed.

"Dessert?"

Her hopefully suggestive tone made me chuckle. "Or some conversation."

"Chatty bastard today, aren't you?"

"I like to talk to you."

She tipped her face up and gave me another kiss—lightly, this time— then wriggled free. She raised an eyebrow in that quirky way of hers. Then slipped her hands under her skirt.

"What are you up to, honey?"

"This." She slid a pair of hot-pink panties down her thighs, then down her knees, then bent to slip them over her heeled feet.

My mouth went so dry that I had to clear my throat twice before speaking. "And what are you going to do with *those*?"

She smiled sweetly. "They're a gift. An appetizer, if you will."

"Now who's the pervert?"

"Not me. I'm just a master chef."

She tossed the panties. They flew up, and my hand came out automatically to snatch them from the air. They were small and filmy and *warm* and sexy as fuck.

Aysia stepped toward the door, tossing her hair over her shoulder as moved. "Do those make you want to have a conversation?"

"No." My voice came out thick.

"What do they make you want to do?"

"So *now* you want to talk?"

"Only if it's dirty talk."

I laughed. "Come here for a second then."

She shook her head. "Uh-uh."

"Please?"

"Save it for tonight."

"Don't trust yourself if you get close again?" I teased.

"Exactly." She blew me a kiss, then closed her fingers on the door hand, where she paused. "Marc?"

"Yeah, honey?"

"I'm scared," she admitted softly.

My throat constricted, but I answered lightly. "Of dinner with me?"

"No. I love shrimp scampi," she joked, then sighed and shifted from foot to foot.

"But?"

"Well. I'm scared of the fact that I'm even willing to tell you I'm scared."

"You know that you don't *have* to tell me anything, right? I'll still feed you dinner. Even if you're just using me for *dessert*."

Her mouth tipped up. "Believe it or not, I *do* like talking to you, too."

"A compliment that involves my brain?"

"Definitely. And that scares me, too."

"You could work your way up. Start by telling me I have nice eyes. Then make your way to the part where you like the talking."

"I don't mean the compliments scare me, you big nerd."

"I know. Tonight at seven?"

"I'll be there."

I watched her go, admiring the smooth, panty-free curve of her ass as she exited.

* * * *

Aysia

The rest of my day flew by in a flurry of activity. I set up the reviews I needed to set up, powered through the overdue raises, then set aside the reprimands for a different day. Finally, I slipped out of the office, and made my way home.

Now I stood in front of the full-length mirror in my bathroom giving myself a final onceover.

My emotions flipped back and forth like a Ping-Pong ball. And not just a regular Ping-Pong ball. More like of the ones used in the Olympic Games, whipping around so quickly that it can barely be seen.

On one side, I felt guilty. Like I was betraying the unofficial pact I'd made to put my job first. And like I was betraying the job itself. Which was actually true, even if I wasn't being nit-picky.

But I was elated, too. Giddy with anticipation. And my libido was in overdrive. All of my body was on alert, the slightest rub of fabric making me want to gasp. As if it had been three months since I last gave in to temptation that was Marcelo Diaz rather than a mere three days.

Temptation. Is that all he is?

My hands and my heart both quivered at the self-directed question, and the Ping-Pong ball froze for a minute, hovering right over the little net in the middle of my metaphorical table. When I'd told him I was scared, it was the truth. Though maybe *scared shitless* would've been slightly more apt. The man officially knew as many of my secrets as anyone on the planet. As many as Liv, which was kind of crazy. What that meant, I wasn't sure. But heading to his house now was a definite way to find out. Dinner and conversation and 'dessert.' In the opposite order, if I had anything to say about it.

I leaned closer to the mirror and wiped my thumb over an invisible smudge. My makeup was actually perfect. Deliberately overdone. Lipstick the color of wine, eyes thick with charcoal liner. A burst of silver beneath my brow and even a sweep of blush over my cheekbones. Far more than I needed for a night in. But just enough to match the outfit I'd picked to wear. Black. Lace. A whole lot of exposed skin. And not much else.

"Perfect," I said to my reflection.

I exited the bathroom, snapped up my jacket from the bed, tugged it around my body firmly, then snagged my purse. I hurried out of the apartment, making it to the front step just as the cab I'd pre-ordered pulled about. Breathlessly—and with mine and Marc's first cab ride on my mind—I gave the driver the address. The ten-minute ride went by quickly, and I handed over my fare blindly, then rushed out of the tax and all but ran up the steps of Marc's apartment building. My eagerness made me so oblivious to the world around me that I didn't even notice the arguing trio at the top of the steps until I just about crashed into one of them.

"Whoops!"

A fiftyish woman with pale red hair put out a hand to stop my stumble. "Careful, honey."

"Thanks," I breathed, smoothing down my jacket.

"Do you live here?" asked the man standing behind her.

Shaking my head, I turned my attention his way. He was smiling at me from behind a pair of dark-rimmed glasses, and there was something vaguely familiar about him. I studied his salt-and-pepper hair for a moment. Did I know him? If I did, I couldn't think from where.

"You all right?" he asked.

I fumbled with my answer. "Yes. No. I mean, I'm fine. But I don't live here. I'm just meeting someone who does."

"Oh." The man's face fell.

"But if she's meeting someone," said the woman, "then she knows how to work the buzzer."

"No one in their right mind knows how to work that thing," interrupted a third voice, this one young and feminine.

And when the owner of *that* voice stepped into view...

Shit.

She was my age. Short, and pleasantly pump. A crown of enviably thick, gloriously auburn hair topped her head. But it was her eyes that pinned me to the spot. They were the exact same shade of brown as Marc's.

His sister.

It had to be. Which meant that the couple standing beside her had to be his parents.

The copper-headed woman was the one who supposedly called Marc special.

The good-looking man was his dad.

Not just shit. Crap-shit-damn-hell in a soggy cardboard box.

I swallowed. I needed to leave. Quickly.

"I can help you work the buzzer," I said, adjusting my coat self-consciously. *And then I can run.*

"That's a relief," replied Marc's dad. "We've been standing here for a good ten minutes. We wanted to surprise our son. Marcelo Diaz."

Dammit.

It would've been a lot easier to sneak away if they hadn't said his name.

I forced a smile. "Oh. That's a happy coincidence. I'm here to see him, too. We work together."

Not wanting to see their reaction, I turned toward the keypad and punched in his number. It only rang once before Marc's voice came through the speaker.

"Aysia? Why didn't you—"

I cut him off. "I'm here to pick up that thing for work. But your family is down here at the door, too. I can reschedule."

"My family?"

"Yes. Your mom and dad. And your sister."

"Lu?"

"Lu?" I repeated, utterly confused.

"Sorry. She probably called herself Mia."

"What?"

"Her name. It's Lumia. Mom and Dad and I call her Lu. To everyone else, she's Mia."

"Uh."

The curvy redhead finally interceded, putting her hand on my elbow as she called, "Hey there, Marshmallow!"

Marcelo's reply was dry, even through the speaker. "And that's what *they* call *me*. Thanks for that, sis."

"You don't have to reschedule," added his mom. "We'll bring her up with us!"

I stepped back and cast a vague smile in the direction of his family, waiting for him to protest. To tell them he and I could reschedule, just like I'd suggested. Instead, the buzzer went off, and his dad walked around me to push open the door.

"After you, ladies," he said.

I hesitated. Mrs. Diaz went first. Then Mia. But me...I had a chance to flee. To kick the door out of Mr. Diaz's hands and run away as fast as my feet could take me. Maybe wave my arms over my head and laugh maniacally as I did it.

My eyes flicked to my spiked heels. To the street. To the group of expectant faces. And I groaned. I was trapped. Bitten in the ass by the fact that I couldn't control my hormones.

"Come on," Mrs. Diaz urged. "We're excited to see Marcelo's new place."

Pressing my lips together, I decided *not* to act like a lunatic. I'd just make an excuse and leave the second I could. I squeezed my jacket tightly once more and followed the wave of Marc's mom's arm. Then stopped. Because I'd just realized where we were headed.

The elevator.

I was going to be trapped in a five-by-five room with his family.

C'mon, Aysia, I said to myself. *You can't handle two minutes in an elevator with a group of strangers?*

From the way my heart was thundering, the answer was no.

Maybe it has something to do with that fact that these particular strangers belong to a man whose tongue was between your legs ten minutes after meeting him.

I suppressed another groan as the doors slid open. *Yeah, that's what you should be thinking about. Why not just bring up the shower sex? Maybe the way he fucked you against the tree during that weekend-long romantic montage of his? How about the fact that you slipped him a pair of panties just this afternoon?*

We stepped into the elevator, and I could swear a cold sweat broke out on my upper lip. And when the elevator doors hissed shut, I just about jumped. A warm hand landed on my arm, yanking me forcefully back to the moment. Mrs. Diaz's hazel eyes were fixed on me, and full of concern.

"Are you feeling okay, honey?" she wanted to know.

For a second, I considered seizing on the opportunity. Pleading sick would be a good enough reason to hurry out of the apartment.

Mia jumped in before I could say a word. "Marshmallow is probably riding her too hard."

"Let's hope not," replied Marc's dad, smiling at me. "He's not, is he? Riding you too hard?"

Oh, god. A giggle threatened to bubble up.

"No," I got out the reply with a minimum of smoothness. Then immediately ruined it by adding, "He's riding me just fine."

I wanted to smack myself in the forehead. Especially when I caught sight of the puzzled look on Mrs. Diaz's face.

"Are you sure you're feeling okay?" she asked. "You look a little flushed. Maybe you should take off your coat."

I took a step back and clutched at the lapels. "I'm fine. Really."

The elevator glided to a stop, and I don't think I'd ever been so relieved to see the inside of a hallway before in my life. I practically leaped out, sucking in a deep breath as I did. But the oxygen didn't come. Because Marc was already standing at the end of the hall, propping open his door, and dressed in nothing but a pair of low-slung jeans and an unbuckled belt. The sight of his bare chest made me want to squirm.

Squirm?

Okay. No. Maybe that wasn't the right word. It made me want to toss aside my jacket and dry hump him in the hallway.

Stupid, unexpected family.

Behind me, Marc's sister cleared her throat. "You always dress that way when you're expecting company from work?"

"Spilled sauce on my shirt," Marc replied easily. "You always cop that attitude when you show up unannounced?"

Mia snorted. "Right. I'm the one with attitude."

"All right, kids," Mrs. Diaz interjected, her voice full of amusement. "I think that's good enough. Marcelo, aren't you going to invite us in?"

He lifted his eyes to mine for just a brief moment before flicking his attention back to her. "Come in, Mom. Dad, you, too. Mia...you can wait outside."

"Ha ha."

I hung back as they all laughed, then made their way into the condo. Marc continued to hold the door open and quirked a half-smile my way.

"You coming to get that work thing?" His voice was serious, but his eyes were sparkling with amusement.

I narrowed my eyes and answered in as sweet a voice as I could manage. "I'll just take what I need, then get out of your hair."

His voice dropped low. "What you *need*, huh?"

"Shut up," I muttered back.

"Aysia?" called his mom from inside.

"Yes?"

"You have to join us for dinner! Marcelo made shrimp scampi and it looks delicious."

Marc's mouth twitched with a muffled laugh, and I shoved by him, careful to give him a solid jab in the ribs as I went past.

Chapter 13

Marcelo

I probably shouldn't have been so amused by the fact that Aysia's game plan—whatever that might be—had been hijacked by my parents and my sister. I probably shouldn't have enjoyed watching my mom hold out a linguine-wrapped fork and insist that Aysia try it before she retrieved the mysterious work item from its equally mysterious place in my condo.

Except it was impossible not to.

I liked the way her painted lips closed on the fork and sucked up the piece of pasta.

I liked the way her made-up eyes widened, and the way her tongue darted out appreciatively to lick away a drip of stray sauce.

I liked the way her gaze found mine and held it, and how she blurted out, "You can cook?"

I even liked the way Mom, Dad, and Mia burst out laughing, then clamored over one another to brag about my mad-crazy skills. They lauded my spaghetti and my barbecued steak and my Thai chili sauce. Aysia looked suitably impressed. So when my mom told her to take off her coat and stay a while, I was sorely disappointed that she shook her head and asked if "the file" was in my office, then excused herself to go get it. I stared after her for a second before remembering that I had an audience.

I turned back, expecting to find all of them staring at me. Not one of them was. My dad had slipped from the kitchen to the living room, muttering about a golf tournament on TV. My sister had plopped herself down on a bar stool and was glaring at her phone. My mom had started digging in the fridge in search of God knew what.

She spoke without looking at me. "You should probably go help her."

"I should?"

"I remember your office back in Los Angeles. Stuff everywhere. She's probably already buried in a pile of papers."

"Right."

"Go. It'll take an hour to find it without your help."

I bit back an urge to tell her it would take a lot longer than that to find a non-existent file in my barely-unpacked office, and acquiesced with an eye roll instead. "Yes, Mom."

Tossing another glance toward the rest of my blissfully ignorant family, I pivoted on a bare heel and headed up the hall. I paused outside the slightly ajar door that led to my office. I was suddenly cautious. I could feel the tension rolling out from the room.

"Aysia?" I called tentatively.

"Yeah, I'm in here."

"Can I come in?"

"It's *your* house, Marc."

"Uh-huh."

I heard her sigh, even from behind the door. "Fine. Come in, Marc. Please."

I pushed through and stood just inside the doorframe. Aysia was leaned up against my desk. She had her slim fingers pinched on the bridge of her nose, and her nylon-covered legs poked out from under her jacket. The sheer black material gave me a perfect view of her thighs. I knew those legs well. How they felt wrapped around my waist. How they looked soaking wet and how they shook when she came. Fuck. I wanted to see and feel all of that again. Right that second. I stepped a little closer, but her hand dropped from her face and came up firmly.

"Stop," she ordered. "And don't look at me like that, either."

"Like what?" I replied, grinning.

"Like you're ready to go straight for that dessert you promised me but won't be getting at all tonight because your *mom* is in the next room."

"That's not kind of hot?"

"Pretty sure I'm about ten years past the getting-caught fantasy."

Her gaze traveled over my chest, though, and her sharp inhale made me a little smug. I moved closer again.

"You sure about that?" I teased.

She ignored my question. "You have to get me out of here."

"It's not that bad, honey."

"Yes, actually, it is."

"It's just dinner."

"How long do you think they'll buy that for?"

"For as long as we eat?" I said.

She sighed and reached behind her back to pull out two wine glasses. "See these? I grabbed them from the table. I don't know if anyone noticed them and the uncorked bottle. But *I* did."

"So? Maybe I was getting ready to double-fist."

"It's not funny."

"It's kind of funny."

"How much shrimp scampi did you make? Enough to feed five of us? Or just the right amount for an intimate dinner?"

"Enough for an army. You're over thinking this."

She made an exasperated noise. "Okay, putting aside the wine, the over-sized portions, *and* the fact that I know your dad is besties with our mutual boss and could make every one of my worries come true…there can't be a dinner. Not tonight."

"Why not?"

"Undo my coat."

"What?"

She put her hands onto the desk on either side of her hips and pressed her heeled feet to the floor. "Just do it."

"Okay."

I closed the gap between us and put my hands on the top button. Her eyes dropped shut as I worked it free. When I moved to the second one, her breathing quickened. My pants were already feeling snug, and all I could see was a hint of collarbone.

"Hard not to think about dessert right now," I murmured.

"Just keep going."

I brought my fingers to the third button. The jacket bowed open, exposing a glimpse of cleavage.

Fuck.

"What're you wearing under here, honey?"

"Keep. Going."

"You being bossy isn't exactly a turnoff."

"I'm not going to say please."

Stifling a groan, I grabbed the fourth button. Now I was rock hard, straining against my zipper. The way the inside of her knee brushed the outside of mine didn't help at all. I tore the button free and spied a sliver of something lacy.

"Aysia." Her name came out as a growl.

She opened her eyes, the heat in them washing over me. "Did I tell you to stop?"

"Christ."

I undid the rest of the buttons in quick succession.

Five-six. Seven-eight-nine. Ten.

The jacket fell open on its own, and this time I couldn't hold back the groan. What she had on was strapless. It pushed her breasts to high alert, pooling them over the stiff edge of black lace. A ribbon criss-crossed the front of it, cinched tightly over torso and ending in a little bow just above her belly button, which was exposed. Below that, she wore a pair of low-cut panties. Black, too, and as sheer as the stockings on her legs. They were stay-ups, I realized then, rather than full-blown nylons. Capped in stretchy lace and pulled up devastatingly high.

My eyes traced the ensemble back up again, then came to rest on her face.

"See?" she said softly. "I'm not exactly dressed for dinner with your family."

"What the hell are you trying to do to me?"

"You mean what *was* I trying to do to you?"

"I'll tell them to leave."

A tiny smile lifted her lips. "Flattering. But unrealistic."

I put my hands on her thighs and ran my thumbs over the stretchy lace. "I'm sure they'll understand."

One of her heels came up to press into the back of one of my calves. She leaned back a little, too, widening her legs for a tantalizing view of the diaphanous strip of fabric between her thighs.

"What excuse would you give them?" she asked.

I bent down and dragged my mouth from her chin to her ear, then lifted her up to the desk. "That I need to be alone with you so we can *chat.*"

"And when they want to know why they can't be a part of the conversation, too?"

"I'd explain that it's a private, work-related matter."

"Work, hmm?"

Her heel dragged up to the back of my knee, then pulled me forward. My erection pressed into her, and her hips rocked up. I pulled her earlobe between my teeth and tugged hard enough to make her whimper, then soothed away the sting with a suck and a kiss. I eased back just enough to slip my hand in between us, my palm against her damp panties and my knuckles against my own thick cock.

"I really need to go, Marc," she breathed.

Her actions told a different story; that same heel was on my ass now, holding me tight against her.

"Actually, Aysia," I said, "I think you really need to *come.*"

"We've already been in here too long. Your family's going to get suspicious."

"Maybe we had some trouble finding the work file."

"Maybe."

It was my turn to rock, sliding my fingers back and forth as I did. "Do you really want me to stop?"

"No," she admitted.

"I won't, then."

I pressed a little harder, and she moaned. I cast a quick glance toward the door. Why hadn't I thought to close it all the way?

"It pains me to say this," I told her, "but I want you to be quick, and I want you to be quiet."

"Who's bossy now?" she retorted. "I don't think I—"

I silenced her with kiss. Hard and thorough, and I accompanied it with a finger slipped under her panties. She was wet and butter-soft, and I wished like hell it was more than hand giving her the attention. And apparently the feeling was mutual. Still locking her mouth to mine, she fumbled with her coat, and I heard the telltale crinkle of a metallic wrapper.

"Take this," she gasped, handing over the condom.

I released her—only so I could comply—and as I ripped open the package with my teeth, she made short work of my belt and jeans. She pushed them down just far enough to give me enough space to unroll the latex.

"Quick and quiet," she tossed back at me, a wicked glint in her eyes.

In reply, I slammed into her hard enough to make the desk rattle.

* * * *

Aysia

Marc filled me completely, the length of his erection driving so far inside me that I could feel it in my toes. In my fingertips and my scalp. Everywhere. And it was so good. I knew I wouldn't have any trouble with the *quick* part of his request. The quiet on the other hand…I was struggling with it. More than a bit.

"Oh, God," I groaned. "Marc."

"Shh, honey."

"I can't—oh!"

"Shh." But he didn't slow his rhythm, didn't ease back at all.

"Please," I whispered.

"Now?"

"Yes! Before I—seriously. *Please.*"

He slid his hands up the back of my neck and dug his hands into my hair. His mouth dropped to my throat. His lips were all I needed to send me soaring. Feeling porn-star-esque, I tossed my head back and dropped my mouth open in a silent cry. I felt him jolt and throb inside me, and just like that, we climaxed in unison. Pulsing in time. The everywhere-ache became an overall tingle. I might even have said it was damned near perfect in spite of the quickness and the quietness. Except for one little thing. As the last little shivers wracked my body, my hand came down and slammed into one of the wine glasses and sent it flying.

I watched in slow, post-orgasm horror as it lifted into the air, hit the wall beside the desk, then split into pieces. The noise echoed through the small room. But that was only my biggest concern for a few moments. As the glass cracked, the shards scattered. And one very large, very sharp piece ricocheted from the wall to the desk then back into the air. Finally, it took purchase in the part of my thigh that wasn't covered by my stockings. It hung there, kind of quivering. A thick, crimson pool formed around it, and my leg twitched involuntarily, dislodging the glass.

"Shit," I said, a little stunned by both the pain and the sight.

Marc leaped into action, pushing himself away from me and talking at the same time. "Sit really still, honey. I'm going to—shit. It's getting worse."

He moved across the room, buckling his pants as he went. He pulled a piece of white cloth from somewhere—I didn't know if it was a towel or a T-shirt or something else entirely, but whatever it was, he folded it up, lifted my leg and pushed it firmly against the bleeding. The white went pink immediately, then red.

Marc met my eyes. "Honey—Aysia—I think that's going to need stitches."

"But…"

"What?"

"My outfit. I can't go anywhere in this."

"Your… Christ." He ran his hand over his hair. "It's hardly an *outfit.* And I seriously think we need to go to the hospital. Like, now."

"But…" I trailed off, feeling a little woozy.

"Okay. Hang on. Ten seconds. Count them for me and push down on that wound."

"One…" I trailed off as he darted out the door, then tried again, mumbling to myself as both my eyes and hands stayed fixed on the reddened fabric. "One. Two…One. Oh, god. Three. Four." *Did I miss something?* "Four. Five."

Before I could hit six, he was back, a plaid shirt slung over his torso, a black shirt and a pair of boxers in one of his hands, a piece of gauze in the other.

"We're going to wrap that thing up to help keep the cloth in place," he stated. "Then I'll help you slip these on. And don't wriggle around too much in case it hit your femoral fucking artery."

"It didn't hit my—"

A voice in the hall cut me. "Marcelo? Is everything okay in there?"

He pushed the shirt over my head as he answered. "Just a little accident, Mom. Stay there."

"What kind of accident?"

"Hang on."

He slid my legs into the boxers, careful not to disturb the makeshift dressing, then tightened the waist using an elastic band.

"I'm going to lift you up now," he announced.

And before I could protest, he had me cradled in his arms and was carrying me out into the hall. His mom stepped back, her gaze going from mildly concerned to deeply worried as she caught sight of my leg.

"Oh, God," she said. "Should we call 9-1-1?"

Marc shook his head. "I don't think it's as bad as that. I'll take her myself."

"What about my femoral artery?" I interjected.

Mrs. Diaz's expression grew alarmed. "What?"

"She's fine, Mom."

"Fine?" I repeated.

Marc ignored me and slid past his mom, too. Snagging his keys from the counter, he instructed his dad on how to set the alarm, told his sister to save him some dinner, then carried me straight out to the elevator.

"Which is it?" I asked as the doors slid open. "Am I dying, or am I fine?"

He breathed out. "Riding the line closer to fine, I hope."

"So what was this…your ploy to get me away from your family?"

"You stabbed yourself, remember?"

"I hardly—"

For the second time in the last twenty minutes, he shut me up with a kiss. This one, though, was fiercely tender rather than just fierce. When he pulled away, he pushed his lips to my forehead then tucked me even closer to his body. He said nothing else as we reached the parking garage, and nothing as he settled me—carefully—into the passenger seat, or when he plugged in the hospital address to his GPS. His hands were tense on the steering wheel, and his jaw was locked. I swallowed nervously, a little jarred by his sudden intensity, and focused my attention out the front windshield. The familiar bits of city flicked by quickly, and we reached the emergency room in far less time than the speed limit should've allowed. As he parked, I bit back a question about what would've happened if we'd been pulled over by a cop, and just let him lift me out again, his warm hands gentle on my skin.

Thankfully, the hospital was slow, and we moved from triage to a treatment room quickly. And it wasn't until Marc saw the sign on the door—*Minor Trauma,* it read—that at last his face relaxed. Even then, it was only a marginal change.

"You okay?" I asked cautiously.

"I'm not the one waiting for stitches."

I flinched at his tone, and opened my mouth to say something back. But an aging doctor stepped into the room then, temporarily silencing me.

"Good evening, Ms. Banks," the white-coat-clad man greeted, nodding at me, then at Marc. "And, uh…Mr…?"

"Diaz. Ms. Banks's boyfriend."

My pulse jumped. "Boyfriend?"

Marc met my eyes. "What did you want me to say?"

"I don't know."

"Illicit lover?"

The doctor cleared his throat, and I felt my face warm.

"Boyfriend is fine," I said.

"Good." Marc faced the doctor. "So?"

The gray-haired man smiled and snapped a pair of gloves onto his hands. "Helps if I take a look."

Marc stepped away, his expression slightly chagrined. "Right."

I leaned back on the examination table and closed my eyes as the doctor unwrapped the temporary bandages that the triage nurse had put down. If he noticed my now-shorn stockings, he didn't say. But the air did sting a bit, and in spite of the way I fought them, tears threatened. I drew in a breath. It did nothing to steady me. But when Marc's hand landed on my shoulder and squeezed, I felt better immediately.

"It's all right, honey," he said. "The doc's just gonna clean it up a bit, then put in a few stitches."

"Twelve or so," the doctor confirmed.

My eyes flew open. "Twelve?"

"Did a pretty good number on yourself," he replied, dropping a few sharp and dangerous-looking objects into a metal pan. "I'm going to inject a little painkiller to make you more comfortable, then I'll get to work."

I swallowed nervously, fighting an urge to ask if the needle really had to be that big. "You know what I hated when I was a kid? That game… Operation."

"This isn't an operation," Marc said. "More of a procedure."

"Mr. Diaz is right," the doctor agreed. "Won't take more than a couple of minutes. Why don't you focus on your boyfriend so that I can focus on you, hmm?"

Boyfriend.

Yes. It was a distracting enough thought. It made me warm and cold at the same time, and filled my stomach with butterflies that could've been excitement just as much as they might've been from nerves. I didn't need a boyfriend. I *really* didn't need a future-boss slash career-ending slash turn-my-brain-to-mush-with-a-look boyfriend.

Really, Aysia? said a little voice in my head. *Aren't you past being that wishy-washy? You might not* need *a boyfriend, but you can't pretend the idea isn't straight-up appealing.*

As the doctor stepped near my leg again, I made myself study Marc's face. His eyes were on me, too. And his handsome features were pinched with worry, and even though he had a smile on his lips, I could tell it was forced. I started to ask him what was wrong, then stopped and shook my head instead.

"Oh. My. God." I broke the words off like an eighties sitcom heroine.

"What?"

"You're just as chicken shit as I am. This totally grosses you out."

"That's ridiculous."

"You don't like blood and guts and gore."

"Of course I do."

I snorted. "Do you even like action movies for real?"

"Yes, Aysia. I like action movies for real."

I thought about it. "What about *doctor* movies?"

"Doctor porn? Fine with that, too."

My face burned and I cast a quick glance toward the real-life doctor at my side. But he seemed thoroughly immersed in patching me up. He was even whistling a little under his breath.

Relieved but no less embarrassed—it was his attempt at payback, I was sure—I shot Marc a dirty look. "How about *real* doctor shows? Like the one where they removed the rebar from the guy's stomach?"

He winced, just barely. "Not my favorite."

I laughed. "You're squeamish."

"Your attempt to unman me isn't going to work."

"Oh, I think it is."

"And *I* think that if you keep teasing me, I'll feel an ape-like need to prove just how manly I am. Right here. Right now."

"I'm sure the doctor would appreciate that."

"The doctor definitely would *not*," added the man in question, leaning away and dropping a wickedly curved needle into his bin of horrors. "But the doctor is also done."

"That quick?" I asked.

"Said it would only take a few minutes, didn't I?" He patted my knee. "Lucky thirteen, by the way."

"That's a lot stitches," I said.

"Seen worse. But I'm still going to give you a prescription antibiotic to ward off possible infection, as well as a mild oral painkiller. You can grab the medication at the twenty-four-hour pharmacy near the exit, and I want you to take it easy for the next few days. Very easy." The doctor smiled at me, then directed a stern eye Marc's way. "Nothing *strenuous*. Got it?"

Marc's lip curled with amusement. "Got it."

"Good."

He issued a few more instructions about changing the gauze, airing out the wound, and wrapping it with plastic to bathe. Finally, he told Marc he'd get me a wheelchair rather than suggest he carry me out, and at last turned to go. But at the door, he paused.

"By the way..." he said. "It never happens the way they show it in the movies."

"What doesn't?" I asked.

"The doctor porn. It's never two sexy nurses and a hot young doctor. Every time I've caught someone going at it, it's been a really hairy intern of some kind and a woman with a penchant for clown-covered scrubs."

My mouth worked silently, and I heard Marc let out a choked laugh. Then the doctor slipped out, and a nurse—dressed in clown-themed scrubs, no less—slipped in.

Chapter 14

Marcelo

I pushed Aysia along in the wheelchair provided by the woman I'd silently dubbed the Circus Nurse. We'd filled the prescriptions quickly, and we were already back on our way back to my car. I'd even managed to convince her to take one of the painkillers, and I was still chuckling over the Circus Nurse as I swung open the Quattroporte's door. My amusement died quickly, though, when I started to help Aysia from the chair to the car and spotted a tiny, crimson mark on the gauze. I tried to push her back down into the seat.

Her hand came up and batted away my attempt. "What are you doing?"

"Taking you back in so that Dr. Not-So-Useful can redo his shoddy stitch job."

"I don't need to go back in," she said.

"We haven't even left the hospital yet and you're already bleeding again."

"I'm not bleeding."

"The blood on your bandage begs to differ."

"What blood?"

I pointed. "Right there."

She frowned. "That's not blood. That's not even a smudge."

"It's a drop."

"I think your fear of all things medical is getting to you."

"Aysia…"

"Unwrap it and have a look."

"I'm not going to unwrap it!" I said.

Before I could protest, she was unwinding the gauze. Three layers. I was sure there should be more like thirty.

"See?" she said, kind of lifting her thigh in a way that made me cringe. "You can look at it, Marc. It's not going to morph into a spontaneous appendectomy."

"Don't make me re-wrap that gauze around your mouth instead of your leg."

When I made myself look down, though, there wasn't much to see. A tidy row of blue stitches, and nothing else. No sign of where the reddish mark had come from.

"Are you going to faint?" she teased. "Should I get some smelling salts?"

"I'm not that bad off."

"Uh-huh."

I rolled my eyes and bent down to take hold of the gauze. "If you weren't injured and drugged up, I'd be doling out some serious punishment right now, you realize that right?"

"Like what?"

As I finished redressing the wound, I caught the entertained sparkle in her eye. "You're not supposed to sound *happy* about the idea."

"Maybe I'm just curious about how you think I should be put in my place."

"I'm not sure you *could* be put in your place."

"But you do think I have one?"

I noted the abrupt change in her tone. "Are we still talking about how funny you think my dislike of giant needles is?"

"Yes."

"You sure?"

"Yes," she said again.

I waited for her to retract the affirmation, but her eyes were trained out the front windshield now. So I just closed her door instead, then made my way around to the driver's side. We moved silently out of the parking lot, then out to the street. We got as far as our own neighborhood before she spoke again, still without looking my way.

"You just *had* to label yourself?"

"Label myself?"

"Boyfriend." It was almost a whisper—like she was saying the world's dirtiest word.

I wasn't going to back down, though. "Yes. As a matter of fact, I did."

The intensity of my statement made her blink, and she swiveled her face toward me and blurted, "Why?"

"You really have to ask that?"

"Boyfriend sounds so...ominous."

I might've laughed if she hadn't seemed so serious. "Hell of a lot better than fuck buddy."

From the corner of my eye, I spotted the flush that crept up her cheeks. Her attention moved to the window once more, and I didn't know if she was embarrassed or mad or something else completely. I didn't care. I had to lay it out. I lifted a hand from the steering wheel and ran it over my hair before saying what I knew I had to say.

"I needed to label myself because it's the only way I can justify how I felt when I saw all that blood rushing out of your leg."

"What do you mean?"

"It fucking *scared* me, Aysia. And not because I'm not crazy about blood. I was worried that you were really hurt. I made the femoral artery comment because for a second it crossed my mind. I know I said I could be patient, but fuck. What the hell would I do if something happened to you? Who would even know I *should* be doing something? And before you remind me again that we can't, shouldn't, or won't be together...just remember that you're not *numb* when you're with me, honey. Tell yourself whatever you want, but I know I mean something to you." I exhaled. "That's why I want the goddamned label."

We reached her apartment then, and suddenly, I was drained, and not just from the speech. From the stress of worrying about her. From feeling at least partially responsible for the giant gash on her leg. But mostly from pretending that the rush of emotion meant less than it did.

I might've said even more if my phone hadn't echoed noisily through the car right that second. Welcoming the distraction, I lifted it from the console and swiped the on-button. "Hi, Dad."

"Marcelo. Were you just going to let us wonder all night what happened to that pretty girl of yours?"

I tossed a glance Aysia's way. "The pretty girl is fine. But she's not mine."

"Better get on that, then, son."

"We work together, Dad."

"How do you think I met your mom?"

"I know. But this is different."

"Because she says so?"

"Exactly."

He went silent for second, then sighed loudly. "All right. Glad she's okay. We locked your place up and we're camping out at the Sheraton if you want to swing by."

I tossed another quick look Aysia's way. Her eyes were on her hands, her bottom lip sucked under the top one. The flush was still in her cheeks, and this time it sent a renewed trickle of worry through me.

"Thanks, Dad," I said into the phone. "I think I'm going to stick around her place and make sure she doesn't need anything."

"All right. I'll see you tomorrow?"

"Sounds good." I hung up the phone and reached over to touch Aysia's knee. "You feeling okay?"

"A little tired," she admitted.

"Okay. We can talk more about the B-word later. For now, let's get you upstairs and into bed."

I waited for an innuendo-laden reply. I didn't get one. With a stifled sigh, I unbuckled my seatbelt, exited the car, then came to her side and scooped her out. She didn't argue as I lifted her out, or as I turned her so she could key in her code, but once we were actually in the elevator inside her building, she let out a sigh.

"You don't have to come in," she said.

"I do, actually," I replied as the elevator slid open.

"I'm fine to take care of myself."

"That's clearly the meds talking."

"I'm not some needy invalid who—"

"Okay, stop right there. What's this really about?"

"What do you mean?"

"You are *literally* an invalid at the moment, honey," I pointed out, stopping in front of her door. "Your leg is frozen, the doctor made you use a wheelchair, and I'm pretty sure if I put you down right here, you'd be stuck in that spot for the rest of the night."

"I'm not going to apologize for that."

"Am I asking you to?"

"No, but—"

"But what?"

Her mouth set into a stubborn line. "If you put me down, I could just crawl inside."

I fought a laugh. "You'd have to reach the door handle first."

"I have long arms."

"Aysia…"

"Really long arms."

"You know, I happen to think it requires more balls to admit that you need help than to pretend that you don't."

Her mouth twitched. "More balls? Is that what you're after?"

"Lady balls," I amended. "Which I happen to admire greatly. So you don't have to be stubborn about it. You can just ask."

"Why am I asking? You've already decided you're coming in."

"Because it'll make me feel like less of a pushy asshole." I slid my hand over to her chin and leaned in for a quick, light kiss. "And talking to my dad reminds me that I'm supposed to have good manners."

"You *are* a pushy asshole."

"That doesn't mean I can't also be polite."

"I'm pretty sure impolite is the very definition of pushy asshole."

I might've argued further, but a door up the hall swung open, and a familiar voice carried through the corridor. "Some of us prefer to carry on our conversation *inside* our homes."

I swung sideways and spied a tiny, wizened old lady with her hands on her hips and her feet planted on her doormat. I knew who she was even before Aysia groaned and issued a greeting.

Mrs. Fisk.

"Ms. Banks," said the old woman. "Just how late—and how long—are you planning on being out here causing a ruckus?"

"Just for a minute more," Aysia assured her, nudging me with her elbow. "C'mon."

I waited until Mrs. Fisk had huffed once more and closed her door before I spoke.

"You still haven't asked me to come in," I said.

"Seriously?" she replied.

"Yes."

"Fine. Marc?"

"Yes?"

"Will you please come in?"

"Glad to. But if you proposition me, I'm going to have to say no. Doctor's orders."

With an eye roll, she reached out to key in the second set of numbers, and when the automatic lock clicked, I pushed the door open with my shoulder and carried her inside.

"Where would you like me to put you?" I teased. "That fancy couch of yours, or would you prefer that I take you straight to bed? In a strictly non-sexual way, of course."

"Shut up. I'm probably going to go straight to sleep," she said. "But I should also probably try to get there myself."

"I can carry you."

"I know. But I need to be able to get up and down on my own when you go."

"I'm not going," I said.

"Yes you are."

"No."

"Marc."

"I'm like a vampire. Once you've invited me in officially, I can come and go as I please. And right now, I want to stay."

She didn't laugh, or even smile. Instead, she just looked up at me with worry-tinged eyes. "I don't want to be a burden."

The admission came out in a small voice that made me want to crush her to my chest and kiss the stupid out of her. My thoughts went to her father, and how he'd left. Right around the time Walt was dying. When she needed him the most.

A puzzle piece snapped into place.

Those pivotal events were exactly what made Aysia who she was. Losing her father and her first love. They created the tough and driven woman who was stealing my heart, piece by piece. But they were the source of her vulnerability, too—the part that she tried to hide and the part that made her tense at the idea of commitment.

I fought to keep my fist from tightening in anger at her father, and frustration at the universe for taking Walt away, and made myself channel the negative emotion into a need to protect her and reassure her instead.

I swept a wild curl from her face and met her eyes. "Honey, I'm just plain not easy to get rid of. There's nowhere I'd rather be than here with you."

"But you didn't even get to eat your shrimp scampi."

"So I'll make a sandwich. You hungry?"

"No."

"Me neither," I admitted.

"So…bed for both of us?" she asked.

"But no sex."

"You sure about that?"

"I refuse to answer on the grounds that I may be forced to lie."

She laughed, and I headed for the loft, taking the stairs as quickly as I could. I set her on the edge of the bed—black satin sheets now, instead of red, and no less sexy—and offered to help her get changed. As soon as the words were out of my mouth, I remembered what she had on under the borrowed T-shirt and boxers.

She lifted an eyebrow.

Shit.

Apparently she remembered, too.

In spite of the fact that it was my fucking *feelings* that'd been running the show for the last little bit, my body was totally happy to be reminded of its own wants. When she put her hands at the bottom of the T-shirt and started to tug it up, my cock immediately came to attention. I took a step back.

Think about something else, I commanded. *Sad puppies with big eyes. Hairy testicles. Anything.*

It didn't do much good. Especially not when the T-shirt came off and landed on the floor. Scantily-clad Aysia and my self-control were a bad combination. Almost as bad as her leg and the giant shard of glass.

That, I said silently. *Use that. You'd never forgive yourself if you tore her stitches.*

"Is that a 'no' to the help, then?" I made myself say.

In response, she pushed her foot to the floor, raised her injured leg, then shimmied out of the boxers.

Fuck.

I closed my eyes and counted to ten. When I opened them again, she'd already stripped off the stockings, and was unlacing the crisscrossed ribbon at the front of her sexy little top. Her eyes were fixed on me, their blue hue full of undisguised want.

"You know what?" I said. "I'm just gonna get in bed and wait."

"And if I decide to sleep naked?" she asked.

"I can handle it."

"Liar."

I shrugged, then slid out of my own clothes. Shirt tossed to the dresser. Jeans pooled at my feet. I shot her my best, cocky grin, then dropped my own boxers. I stood there for another ten-count, unreasonably satisfied by the way her eyes ran over my body. Pleased at how her gaze lingered on my full erection.

"Can *you* handle it?" I teased.

She drew in a breath. "No."

"Too bad."

I moved to the other side of the bed, lifted the sheets, and climbed in. I blew her an obnoxious kiss, then put my head on the pillow and closed my eyes. Aysia muttered something incomprehensible, and I felt the bed shift. I lifted one lid, just to make sure she was being careful. I watched as she hopped on one foot to the dresser, dragged open a drawer, and yanked out something shimmery. Her back was bare, the lace panties hugging her ass perfectly. I slammed my eyes shut.

Stitches, I snapped at myself.

Seconds later, the bed dipped down, and her scent filled my nose. Worse than that, her satin-covered ass filled my lap. She wriggled a little—just enough to drive my rigid cock into her back.

"Good night, Marc," she said sweetly.

"Good night, Aysia," I growled back.

She went still and quiet so quickly that I thought she'd was asleep, but after another minute, she exhaled, and her voice carried to me in the dark once more. "You said I wasn't your girl."

"To my dad?"

"Yes."

"Well. You seem determined not to be."

"That's not it at all."

"No?" I slung an arm over her and pulled her a little closer.

"No," she answered.

"So you *do* want to be my girl?"

"Don't you know that I do?"

"Maybe I do know," I said. "But you *wanting* to and you *willing to be* are two different things, aren't they?"

"Yes," she admitted. "But…"

"But?"

"I want to, Marc."

"Should I ask you, then?"

"Yes, please."

I inhaled. "Aysia…will you be my girl?"

"Yes, Marc."

"Good."

She went silent again, her breaths evening out. I pressed my chin to her head, and she didn't stir. She was asleep for real this time. It was probably a good thing. Because my heart ached in a stupid fucking way.

* * * *

Aysia

Thursday.
Friday.
Saturday.
Sunday.

Each morning I woke to an empty bed. And I felt it. The spot where Marc and his perfectly warm, perfectly hard, perfectly off-limits body had been. Somehow, he'd magically woken up before me each day.

Admittedly Thursday was already a write-off. My leg was too sore to do much but make me complain. And to appreciate the fact that Marc had taken the day off, rescheduled whatever he'd been planning on doing with his parents, and was totally willing to play nursemaid. I couldn't even muster up irritation at myself for needing him to help me in and out of bed. At the end of the day, I was totally worn out. And while sex might not have been the *last* thing on my mind, it wasn't at the top, either. I was just as happy to fall asleep in his arms.

On Friday, though, I'd rolled over expecting to help myself to a thorough groping. All I got was handful of air. When I dragged my ass out of the sheets and down the stairs with my leg aching—okay, maybe burning—I found Marc's sister sitting at my breakfast bar. She had a crossword book in one hand and a muffin in the other. And she wasn't the least bit perturbed by my cursing. She just shoved a cup of coffee and a painkiller my way, and told me sweetly that Marc had threatened to shave her head if anything happened to me while he was at work. So I was on house arrest. And when the king of temporary celibacy came home from work, he dragged out my collection of board games and wouldn't let me sit in his lap no matter what I said to him. Apparently, strip Monopoly wasn't a thing.

Saturday and Sunday were no better.

On the former morning, Marc made me an omelette. Served me orange juice. Reminded me to take my antibiotic and even did a load of laundry. But I couldn't bait him into letting me have my way with him.

On the latter morning, I thought I could outsmart him. I set my alarm on my phone for five in the morning, thinking there was no way Marc would be awake before that. But sometime in the middle of the night, a power surge hit the building. It did something funky to my phone settings, and the alarm never sounded. And for the first time in my life, I truly knew what men meant when they used the phrase "cock block." Because the universe was giving me a royal one. Working in cahoots—yes, cahoots, dammit— with Marc to screw me over by keeping me from actually *getting* screwed.

Stupid Thursday.

Ridiculous Friday.

Damn-it-all-to-hell Saturday.

And Sunday could just plain bite me.

He just as effectively deflected me each night, too. Showering so long that I fell asleep. Telling me he needed to cuddle his girl, and being all sweet and making me look bad for wanting to tear off his clothes instead.

So when Monday rolled around, I really expected to find my bed empty again. Instead, as I sighed and stretched a little, I slammed into Marc's solid form. It startled me so badly that I skidded forward and just about fell off. His hand came out at the last second to snag my pajama top and drag me back.

"Don't need you injuring yourself again right before we go to the doctor," he said, his voice thick with sleep.

"The doctor?"

"Did you forget? You have your follow up this morning."

I groaned. I *had* forgotten. Because I'd been too busy thinking about getting into Marc-the-Monk's pants.

Speaking of which...

I pressed a hand to his thigh and slid it up. For a blissful second, he let me touch him. Then he pushed up, delivered a swift, far too chaste kiss to my lips, and climbed out of bed. With a frustrated mutter, I flopped backwards.

"Marc?"

"Yeah, honey?" I heard his pants zip up.

Damn him.

"I'd like it a lot better if you'd come back to bed."

He chuckled. Probably amused by my needy ache. It annoyed me. But it didn't make me want him any less. I'd take angry sex with Marc over no sex with Marc any day. In fact, the idea kind of appealed to me at the moment.

"Jerk," I grumbled as the sound of teeth-brushing started up in the en suite. "Big, giant, uncooperative jerk."

The water in the bathroom turned off, and Marc appeared beside the dresser again. "Are you calling me names, now?"

I propped myself up on my elbow. "Yes. Come over here and make me pay."

"How about *you* come over *here* and put some pants on."

"You're no fun."

"I have it on good authority that I am, in fact, fun. But I'm also a punctual adult. Your appointment is in thirty minutes."

"You. Are. No. Fun."

He grabbed the sundress I'd taken from the closet the day before and held it out. "You're wearing this?"

I considered tossing a childish denial back in his face, then thought better of it. I could be an adult, too. Sort of. I swung my feet to the floor and stood. I marched—with no limp, I might add—to the laundry basket in the corner. Then I stripped off my PJs and my underwear, slipped on the dress and smiled sweetly.

"I'm ready."

He swallowed, his Adam's apple bobbing up and down. "That's it?"

"Yes."

"You're not forgetting a little something?"

"Nope."

"Fine." With an irritated twitch of his mouth, he spun. "See you downstairs."

"Wait."

"Yeah?"

"You're not going to help me?" I asked.

"Call me if you get stuck."

I narrowed my eyes at his back as it disappeared out the French doors. But as I stood up, I found that my leg didn't twinge at all, and even going down the stairs didn't make it ache. Without any assistance, I made it all the way to the parking garage and to Marc's car. As I climbed in, I had to resist an urge to pretend it *did* hurt, just to spite him and his lack of willingness to be my personal sex slave. But he'd supplied a coffee in a to-go cup, and a fruit Danish, too, so it was kind of hard to stay mad.

Thankfully, the traffic between my place and the doctor's office was minimal, and since I was the first patient of the day, I got ushered in quickly. I expected Marc to insist on coming in, but as I stood, he got a call from Mike Roper, and he waved me off. I was almost disappointed to find myself facing my doctor on my own.

I made myself not overthink it, and greeted the familiar woman with a smile. "Morning, Dr. Link."

She positioned herself beside the examining table and smiled back. "Morning yourself, Aysia. Looks like you've been busy."

For a second, I thought she was talking about Marc. Then clued in that she meant my injury.

"I got in a fight with a wine glass," I joked weakly. "And I lost."

She leaned down to examine the stitches, then bent my knee up and down. "Looks to be healing well, though. Much pain?"

I shook my head, then answered a few more questions. She made a quick note in my electronic file before she pronounced me fit to get back to my regular day-to-day activities, smiled again, and told me to enjoy the rest of my day.

But I paused at the door as a request sprung to mind.

"Something else, Aysia?" she asked.

I hesitated, then told her what I needed in a rush. I was sure my face was redder than a teenager's as she handed over a sample. And it was still burning as I pushed through the door into the waiting room. Marc shot a little frown my way. I ignored it—and him, more or less—until we were out in the hall. And he was the one who spoke first.

"Well?" he said.

"Well what?"

"What did the doctor say?" he asked.

"Oh. I'm good."

"How good?"

"Cleared for normal activities."

His caramel eyes slid up and down my body. "How normal?"

A heated flush crept from my toes to my hairline. "I asked her to put me on the pill."

He didn't miss a beat. "Thank fucking God."

I might've laughed. But his face was more intense than I'd seen it since the second we met. His gaze was hungry. And then—without warning—he was on me. He grabbed me by the waist and dragged me close, slamming his lips into mine with heart stopping ferocity. His tongue danced through my mouth, warm and persistent, thorough enough to make me moan. Then he slammed my hands over my head and pinned my wrists to the wall. I fought a yelp.

"Hey!"

"Do you have *any* idea how crazy I've been going?" he growled.

"No." It was a squeak.

"Walking around in the short fucking shorts all day. No bra. Wiggling your perfect little ass against me in the night. Then coming here with nothing under that dress."

His free hand slid up my hip, then my stomach, then cupped my breast firmly. Possessively. His thumb flicked over the thin fabric, torturing my already taut nipple.

"We're in a public place," I gasped.

"Don't care."

"Someone could walk by any second. Someone probably *will* walk by."

"Still don't care. You told me you wanted to be mine five whole days ago," he said. "But I haven't been able to claim you even once since then."

"You could've," I managed to say.

"And risked tearing that wound of yours so that I had to start waiting all over again? Not a fucking chance."

"So what are you waiting for now?" I challenged, forgetting all about being in public.

His hands slid to the hem of my dress, then we both froze as the elevator dinged a warning. Any moment, it was going to open, and we'd have company.

Marc dropped my dress, grabbed my hand, and tugged. I stumbled along beside him, clueless as to where he was pulling me until we he shoved open a heavy door. A stairwell. Cool air blew up from below. But I didn't even have time to shiver.

He took a hold of me again, pressing me to the wall, the heat of his body more than enough to stave of the chill from the concrete.

"Tell me again," he commanded.

"What?"

"That you're *mine*."

The way he said it—all caveman and ridiculously sexy—took my breath away, and my reply came out in a quaver. "I'm yours."

"Fuck, yes, you are. I've been counting the seconds. Fantasizing about burying myself inside of you. Licking you up and down. Sucking on every bit of you."

My knees shook a little at raw-sounding admission. "Tell me more."

"I've been wanting to fuck you so hard that Mrs. Fisk calls that cops. That my parents hear you scream from their hotel."

"More."

"When I'm done with the hard and fast, I'm going to take you again, nice and slow." His tongue darted out to taste a spot just below my ear. "I'll make you come over and over, and just when you think you can't possibly handle any more…I'll make you come again. I'll use my fingers and my mouth and my cock. You'll be so full of *me* that there won't be room for anything else."

I was panting. My thighs shook. If I'd been wearing any underwear, they'd have been soaked through, and I wondered if Marc knew I was halfway to where he wanted me, just based on his words alone. And, damn, did I want to get the rest of the way.

I tipped my face up and spoke against his mouth. "Are you all talk?"

"Have I *ever* been all talk?" He pulled my lower lip between his teeth.

"People change," I teased.

He laughed, low and sexy as usual, then reached down, put both hands on my ass, and lifted me from the ground. He ground against me, his denim-covered erection driving forward in the most frustrating way.

"Your pants, Marc. Please."

"Hang on tight."

I clung to his shoulders and tightened my knees on his hips as he dropped his hands to unfasten his belt. The sound of his zipper coming down made my breath quicken once more. And then his tip was positioned in just the right spot. He circled lightly against my clit before he drew back and—

"Wait."

He paused. "Fuck, honey. *Why?*"

Had he seriously forgotten his own rule?

"Well," she replied. "I don't think the pill starts working the moment I ask for it."

One of his hands released, and when I slipped down a little, he immediately brought it back to keep me in place.

"Wallet," he said.

"Wallet?"

"Fucking condom in my fucking wallet. It's in my back fucking pocket, Aysia." His cursing was vehement, but not really directed at me. "Can you reach?"

I dropped my hand. My fingers just brushed the leather edge. I wriggled, trying to grab it, and I very nearly drove him straight into me. He growled and adjusted again, propping me up with his knee. His hand came around his back, meeting mine. Together, we yanked out the wallet, then Marc tugged it away from me and smacked it to the wall. He freed a metallic package and let the wallet fall to the ground.

So fast that I barely saw it happen, he unwrapped the condom, got it properly in place and met my eyes.

"Need me to wait for anything else?" he asked.

"Just one thing."

"What?"

"This." I pushed my lips to his. For ten seconds, the kiss was tender. Meaningful and definitely sexy. But not more. Then it intensified. Dragged into something else—something full of need.

Marc eased back, repositioning himself.

I closed my eyes.

And as promised, he filled me so well—so hard and so thoroughly—that there wasn't room for anything else.

Chapter 15

Marcelo

I snuck a glance Aysia's way, then smiled to myself. We were on our way back to her condo, and she had her hand out the Maserati's window, her fingers spread wide to catch the wind. Her hair was catching the breeze, too, whipping wildly around her face.

Fuck, how I loved the way she looked right then. Satisfied and free and happy. So goddamned beautiful.

I looked away again, focusing my eyes on the road, even if my mind preferred to stay on her.

I loved how *I felt* right then, too. My chest was tight and full. Swollen up with pride that I was the one who made her mouth turn up, that I was the one whose name she called out. I dragged in a deep breath, and instead of easing the pressure, I drew in a lungful of her sweet scent. It was on my skin, permeating my existence. Making her mine.

Mine.

I'd never used the word to describe a woman before. Not even Janie, when she'd told me she was pregnant. *My* girlfriend, yes. But not *mine,* not like this. I loved that, too.

In fact, I loved everything about being with Aysia.

Shit.

My foot just about flew off the gas pedal as I realized what I'd just admitted to myself. I tightened my grip on the wheel and steadied my driving path. I tried out the word again.

Love.

Hell, yes. That was it. *This* was it. A few insane weeks in, and I was falling in love with her. I drew in another breath and fought a need to turn and ask if she felt the same. I was pretty damned sure she did. I was also pretty damned sure bringing it up would make her open the door and jump out of the moving car. How long would it take before she knew it, too? And how long after that until she'd acknowledge it and accept it?

Patience, I said to myself.

She was worth the fucking wait. All good things were, right?

"Are we taking the long way home?" Aysia's question brought me back to the moment, and I realized that I'd managed to skirt around the turnoff to her street.

I tossed her a smile. "Guess we are."

A little frown creased her forehead, and she sighed. "I'm in a *really* good mood."

"Me, too."

"And I don't want to wreck it."

My ribcage compressed. "So don't."

"I just—"

"Seriously, Aysia. Now's not the time to break my fucking heart."

It must've come out with more emphasis than I intended, because her hand suddenly landed on my forearm, her fingers warm.

"Would you let me finish?" she asked.

I refused to let her see the look I knew had to be in my eyes, and kept my gaze fixed out the front windshield. "Fine."

"I was just thinking about what to do about work."

"Work?"

"Yes. I mean, this is still officially against the rules. I'm not quitting, and you're not quitting, but—"

Without even thinking about it, I slammed on the brakes and swerved onto the shoulder of the road. Behind us, someone honked, but I didn't care. Aysia's eyes went wide. Then wider still as I leaned over, took both her cheeks in my hands, and kissed her soundly.

"What was that for?" she breathed as I finally pulled back.

"For thinking about what we're going to do about work."

"All that for a thought?"

"A few days ago, you wouldn't even have considered the idea that there *was* something to be done about it. So I'm thrilled as all hell that you're opening this particular window."

She laughed. "Yeah, well. Don't jump through it yet. I want to be cautious. And practical. So I'm still trying to think of a way to make it work."

"Because I'm your boyfriend."

"Uh-huh."

"And you're my girlfriend."

"You're really pushing this, aren't you?"

"Yep." I kissed her again. "However we handle it…It'll be worth it, honey."

Her expression turned serious, her blues eyes searching my face for a long moment before she responded. "I know it will, Marc. That's why I want to do it."

My throat tightened. "Aysia?"

"Yes?"

"I—"

Her phone came to life in her purse, cutting me off.

Probably a good thing, I said to myself. *God knows what you were about to say.*

I gestured to her bag. "You gonna get that?"

"Uh. Sure." She pulled it out, glanced at the screen, then answered in a cheerful voice. "Hi, Mom! How are—what? Slow down. No, I'm fine. Yes. No. I'm with Marc. No. Yes." She paused and looked at me, bit her lip like she was going to add something else, then shook her head instead.

"You forgot to tell her I was your boyfriend," I whispered with a grin.

Aysia swatted at me, her face pink, but continued to speak into the phone. "No. Never mind. Mom. You were saying something about my condo? I said—seriously? Okay, we'll be there in a few minutes."

"What's wrong?"

"The alarm at my place went off. Apparently, the company tried my phone and couldn't get through. Must've been when we were—um—preoccupied? Anyway, my mom is the secondary contact. The police are at the condo now, and so is she."

"They actually sent the cops? It wasn't a false alarm?"

"Doesn't sound like it."

"Damn. Okay."

I guided the car back onto the road, my gut churning with worry. Her building was secure. Or should've been. Between the key coded entry system, the nice neighborhood, and the fact that she wasn't on the first floor, a break-in couldn't be a crime of opportunity. My mind darkened. I didn't know every nook and cranny of Aysia's personal life, but the last five days of all talk, no sex had given me some pretty good glimpses. And I could only think of one person who carried open hostility toward her.

Carl fucking Reeves.

I actually hadn't thought of him in days. Not since he'd brushed by me in the hall at the beginning of the week, and even then, it hadn't been in relation to Aysia. In fact, I'd been more amused than anything at the way he'd first apologized for bumping me, then jumped back when he realized it was me.

If the fucker is responsible for this, he's going to do a hell of a lot more than that.

I kept my mouth shut, though, as we drove the last few minutes. When— if—we found out this had anything to do with him, I'd deal with it then. For right then, I just wanted to make sure everything was safe and secure.

As we pulled up to her building, I spied a solitary cop car, and took that as a good sign. Two officers stood on the curb, too, flanking a woman who could only be Aysia's mother. She had the same wild hair, though hers was flecked with blondish highlights, and when her gaze landed on the Quattroporte, I saw that her eyes were the same too-blue shade as well. She lifted a brow in a familiar gesture, then put her hands on her hips and said something to the police officers.

Aysia leaped out the moment I put the car in park, but I followed a little more slowly, scanning the exterior of the building. I had no clue what the hell I was looking for. Building security was something best left to the experts. I just felt a serious compulsion to look for something—anything—that would guide me to her asshole non-ex. No matter what excuse he had, no matter what he threatened to blackmail me with, he couldn't walk away from a breaking and entering charge.

Fuck if I could see a thing.

I slid closer to Aysia, but addressed the nearest cop. "Find anything?"

The uniformed man blinked at me. "You are?"

"He's with me," Aysia said quickly.

Her hand snaked out as if she was going to pull me against her. Then it dropped to her side quickly. If the officer noticed the awkward motion—or my disappointment at the fact that claimed me verbally but not physically—he didn't say.

Instead, his face relaxed. "Evidence of a break-in. Door handle unscrewed and left on the front mat. Big electronics—TV, stereo, all that—still there, no one inside. Whoever the guy was, he was in and out in under ten."

"Could be personal," the second cop added.

I saw Aysia stiffen, but her voice was neutral as she replied. "Personal?"

"Jealous ex, old roommate."

Aysia's mother actually laughed. "Nothing like that kicking around for my daughter."

The first cop studied the two of them for a second, like he could sense that something about the statement wasn't quite true. He didn't comment on it, though.

"We're going to need you to come in and take a look around. Let us know if anything is missing or disturbed, all right?" He waited for Aysia to nod, then added, "While you take inventory, my partner will take notes. I'm going to ask a few questions of the neighbors, find out if the building security cams caught anything, stuff like that. Some guys'll be by to see if they can't lift some prints. Realistically, it'll probably be a few hours. When everyone's finished up—and assuming everything checks out—you're welcome to stay in the apartment, but a lot of people like a day or two to collect themselves. No shame in wanting that."

"She can stay with me," I said.

Her mom offered me the eyebrow lift. "My house might be the better option."

Aysia let out a noisy sigh. "Let's just get this over with."

"I'll lead the way," the second cop offered, and we all followed him upstairs.

Aysia was quiet as we moved through the condo. She pulled a coffee can full of spare change from the kitchen cupboard, and noted that a brand new credit card still sat in its envelope beside her coffee pot. A set of movie gift certificates hung on the fridge, untouched. In the living room, she lifted the removable lid on her table and pointed to her high-end tablet. As the police had mentioned, the television and stereo were in place and intact. A quick glance into the office confirmed that the computer remained just as she'd left it.

Upstairs, things were the same. A painting she said was worth five grand sat on the wall. The bed was made.

"That's it," she finally said. "Everything's here."

The cop cleared his throat. "The underwear drawer, please, Miss?"

Aysia went pink. "Excuse me?"

"Surprisingly common thing," the man replied, shifting uncomfortably. "Panty theft."

"Oh."

Woodenly, without a glance at me or her mother, she moved across the room and slid open the top drawer of her dresser. She moved things around a bit, then frowned.

"Something missing?" the officer asked.

"No, I just—no." She shook her head firmly, then stepped back. "Can we go?"

"Sure can. If you like, we can give building maintenance a call and have them seal up the door with some tape when we go," the policeman offered. "We'll contact you directly if we find anything. And vice versa, all right?"

"Sure."

A few short minutes later, Aysia had an overnight bag packed, the correct contact information exchanged with police, and we were back on the front step. There, her mother turned my way and stuck out her fingers.

"Crystal," she said.

I took her proffered hand and shook it. "Marc."

"Well, Marc. You can follow us home." Her eyes were shrewd. "And I hope you like playing cards, drinking wine, and sleeping in a guestroom."

Then she grabbed Aysia's bag, stuffed it into my chest, spun on a designer heel, and led her daughter away.

* * * *

Aysia

Normally, I would've fought my mom on her insistence that I ride with her rather than Marc. It would make more sense. I could give him directions. Warn him that she probably wasn't kidding about the guest room. And of course, avoid her questions about Marc himself.

But I had a feeling *his* questions were going to be worse. More pointed. More insistent. And the last thing I wanted to do was confess what had crossed my mind when the police said "personal." What I thought might be confirmed when I rooted through my underwear drawer.

I shook it off now, too, telling myself it was nothing more than supposition. A hunch. And I knew from years of watching crime dramas that facts and evidence were the only thing that could get people arrested. Everything else just got people in trouble.

You sure about that? The police also need leads, *don't they?*

I shoved aside the little voice in my head and focused on my mom instead.

"Sorry," I said. "What was that?"

"Well. I asked how you met Marc and what's going on with him. But now that your face has gone the color of the kale smoothie I had for lunch, I want to know if you're okay."

I lifted an eyebrow. "Kale smoothie?"

"Trying something new. Healthy."

"Gross."

"Have you tried it?"

"No."

"Then don't knock it." Her manicured hands tapped on the steering wheel. "You haven't answered my question."

"About Marc?"

"About whether or not you're okay."

"I'm fine, Mom. Just a little shaken up. Even when I lived in that miserable apartment my first year of college, I didn't get broken into."

"It's definitely a bad feeling. Do you remember that old Chevy I drove when you were a toddler?"

"Kind of."

"*It* got broken into once. They jimmied the door open, took the two quarters I kept in the ashtray, rifled through the glove box, and left a dirty old mitten on the front seat. It took me weeks to feel comfortable driving it again."

I made myself smile. "Don't get your hopes up. I'm not moving in for *weeks*. Just long enough to get my door fixed."

"Or just long enough to sneak out to Marc's house?"

"Mom."

"Aysia."

I sighed. "Okay. Don't get the wrong idea, but I met him at a bar a few weeks ago."

Now *she* lifted *her* eyebrow. "Is there a right idea about that?"

"You're so old-fashioned."

"I'm not old-fashioned. I had a kale smoothie for lunch."

I couldn't help but laugh. "Okay. Fine. I'll give you that. But that doesn't mean you don't sound *motherly*."

"I *am* your mother," she pointed out. "Do you meet men in bars often?"

"Mom! No. And even if I did, I'm a grown woman. Meeting men in bars is normal."

"A smart, grown woman. Who's never introduced me to any of the men in her life—bar-met or otherwise—before this one, no matter how normal it might be. And even now, the introduction wasn't on purpose."

"It's still really..." I trailed off helplessly.

"Really what?"

"Really I don't know."

"Really you don't know, or really you don't want to say?" She glanced in my direction, her face softening. "I take it this is the same guy who was making you giggle over text?"

"That's him."

I hesitated. Would it be so bad to tell her that he wasn't just some guy? That we'd already labeled ourselves. That I might as well have been pinned, or wearing his letterman jacket, or possibly had his name tattooed on my left butt cheek? But I couldn't make the words come. It seemed almost harder to tell my mom than it was to think about disclosure at work.

Maybe just invite her by when you have the neon, Marc + Aysia sign installed below the Eco-Go headline at the office.

And in the end, I went for distraction.

"Hey, Mom," I said. "Wanna see something gross?"

"Not particularly."

"Have a look anyway." I lifted my dress hem to expose my stitches.

She glanced down and her face filled with concern. "Oh, my God! What happened?"

"Accident with a wine glass."

I launched into explanation—minus a few, torrid details—and the story took me all the way to my childhood home's driveway. But as we pulled in with Marc's Maserati close behind, my mom adjusted the rear view mirror to watch as he climbed out and moved toward the trunk.

"Maybe this is the wrong moment to bring this up," she said, "but I'd rather mention it now than wish I had later. And I'm allowed to be overprotective."

My pulse fluttered nervously, but I made myself answer lightly. "Spit it out, Mom."

"This is the first time you've brought a guy here in more than ten years." She paused and met my eyes. "Since Walt."

My chest squeezed, but only a little. "It's not the wrong moment."

"No?"

"No." I took a breath and added, "And *he* knows, too."

Her expression became surprised. "He does?"

"Everything."

"So you would've introduced us eventually? On purpose?"

"Yes." Even though I hadn't thought of it until right that second, it was true. "I would've introduced you *soon*. And you're going to like him, Mom. I promise."

"Not as much as you do," she teased.

My eyes followed him as he approached. He had my bag on his shoulder, and a smile that was just for me on his face. My body warmed.

I exhaled, not caring how sappy I sounded as I swung open the door and answered her over my shoulder. "No. Not nearly as much as I do."

It should've been awkward. Spending hours with my mom and the man who made my skin tingle. Instead, it was just comfortable. Grilled cheese sandwich, tomato soup comfortable. Wood-burning fireplace, footy pajamas cozy.

My mom beat the metaphorical pants off Marc at rummy, and he lost gracefully. We ordered Chinese food and we fought over the last wonton in the wonton soup. Then Marc made us watch my mom's grainy, old

VHS copy of *Life of Brian,* and we all laughed as we sipped our wine. We somehow managed to avoid the topic of where Marc worked, though he did tell her he was in marketing, and they compared notes from her days in advertising. And it was all kind of like living in an alternate universe. A good one, full of unicorns with rainbow manes.

Finally exhaustion won out—at least for me—and I drifted to sleep on the familiar, floral-print couch. I didn't even worry about what they would talk about without me. If my mom decided to pull out embarrassing family photos…that would be just fine.

The whole thing was a bit surprising to me.

I was surprised, also, to wake up in my own childhood bed, and to find Marc stretched out beside me. His big body hugged the edge of the twin-sized mattress, and his manly features looked comical on top of the pink pillowcase that had been mine since I was ten years old.

Automatically, my eyes flew to the door in search of my mom. The white-painted wood hung ajar slightly, the butterfly-themed wind chimes hanging on the knob like a makeshift alarm.

Nervous, I brought my gaze back to Marc and whispered, "What are you doing here?"

He looked far too amused for his own good. "Well. We met a few weeks back. I'm Marc. Your boyfriend. And usually you *like* to have me in your bed."

I slapped his shoulder. "I don't mean like that. Didn't my mom insist that you sleep in the guest room?"

"I'm not sleeping."

"I'm being serious."

"About kicking me out of bed?"

His hand tickled my thigh, and I swatted it away.

"Stop it," I said. "Or my mom will hear us and make you leave."

"Nah. She likes me."

"Not if she finds out you're in here trying to seduce me."

"Actually…she gave me permission."

"To seduce me?"

"To tuck you in."

I narrowed my eyes. "And how long have you been lying there, tucking me in?"

He grinned. "An hour."

"Probably not what she meant."

"Probably not. She's already come by once to check on us."

"Really?"

"Afraid so."

"So she doesn't like you *that* much," I teased.

He traced my jawline with his thumb, then tugged on my bottom lip. "Sure she does. She just doesn't trust me."

"*Can* you be trusted?"

"A hundred percent." He bent his mouth to mine and gave me a slow, shiver-inducing kiss. "What about you?"

I pressed my hand to his outer thigh and slid it up. "Nope."

"What?"

"I can't be trusted in the least." My finger came up farther, slipping under his shirt to play over his rock hard stomach.

He groaned. "You should probably stop that."

"Is that what you want?"

"Hell, no. But your mom frisked me for condoms before I came in here."

"Shut up."

He chuckled. "Okay. Maybe she didn't go that far. But I wouldn't put it past her."

I leaned back to study his face, and I groaned. "Oh, God. She doesn't just like you. You like *her.*"

"Well. She's pretty cool."

"Great. Just what I need. The two of you working against me."

"We'll only work in favor of your well-being. I promise." His smile dropped for a moment. "Are you going to tell her?"

"Tell her what?"

"That we're a couple."

I fought the warmth that crept up my cheeks. "Don't you think she knows?"

He touched my face. "Yes. I think she knows. But that's not the same thing as telling her."

"You remember what I told you about my dad?"

"He left your mom for another woman."

"After he made her quit her job," I reminded him.

He studied me for a second. "You're worried that your mom will react badly if she thinks you're taking the same path."

I exhaled, relieved that he understood. "Exactly."

"Did I tell you that *my* parents met at work, too?"

"No."

"They did. My mom was my dad's boss. At Dairy Queen."

I laughed. "Not quite as serious."

Marc shook his head. "You'd think. But there was an anti-fraternizing policy there, too. And since my mom was the junior assistant manager…"

"Okay. I'll bite. What happened?"

"Well. They were sixteen. So they quit and went to work at Burger King instead."

I gave him a playful shove. "You're awful."

He laughed. "But it worked. They got married at twenty. Had me at twenty-two and my sister at twenty-five. Thirty-four years later, and they're still going strong."

"So...you're saying we should go work at Burger King?"

"I'm saying that every situation is unique. Every relationship, too."

"I know."

"So don't you think your mom knows, too?"

The question was gentle but not condescending, and it made me pause. Of course she knew it. And of course *I* knew that *she* knew it. I'd just never really had a reason to think about it before.

"It's new for me," I said softly.

"I know." He offered me a smile. "But if it would make you feel better, I could have my mom call yours."

"Um."

"What?"

"You want to introduce our mothers to each other? See if they get along?"

"Yes."

"Are you also naming our unborn children?"

It was a joke. But Marc's face was utterly serious as he answered me.

"Not Liv, if we have a daughter," he said. "Because she's already got enough of an ego. But Walt would be nice for a boy."

My throat didn't just tighten. It constricted completely, and I could feel the tears forming in my eyes. I drew in a shaky breath.

"Are you for real?" I asked.

He brought my hand up to his chest and flattened my palm over his heart. "Don't I feel real?"

I swallowed. "Very."

"I like you, Aysia."

"I like you, too, Marc."

"I think I *more* than like you, Aysia."

My heart danced a nervous jig. "I think I more than like you, too, Marc."

"Think?" he repeated.

"Your word, not mine."

"That's because I don't want to scare you off, honey. I can't even stand the thought that I have to stay in a bed that's two doors down."

"You can't scare me off."

He laughed in that low, sexy way of his. "That's complete bullshit and you know it."

I sighed. "Okay then. I don't *want* to be scared off. How's that?"

"Better."

"You don't have to leave just yet."

"No?"

"You can definitely stay for a few more minutes."

"Twist my arm."

I tucked my head against his chest and yawned. "This was the most interesting day I've had in forever."

"In forever?" I heard the teasing innuendo in his reply.

"I mean interesting in a way that's not related to having intertwined body parts."

"Hmm. Intertwined body parts. I like the sound of that."

"Me, too." I wiggled against him.

"I thought you *didn't* want me to get kicked out of here."

"I don't."

"Hmm. So you just forgot that rubbing your body on mine has led to some less than gentlemanly behavior in the past?"

"You promised me slow and thorough after the hard and quick," I reminded him.

"Trust me. I remember." He went silent for a second, then ran his hands over my hair. "Tell me something."

"Okay."

"When you looked in your panty drawer today...did you see something?"

I swallowed. "Besides my panties?"

He didn't buy my light tone. "Yeah, honey. Besides your panties."

I buried my face a little farther into his shirt and mumbled, "Francois."

"What?"

"Francois."

"Who the hell is that?" he asked.

"Not who. What."

"Fine. *What* the hell is Francois?"

"My vibrator."

His long pause just about killed me. So did his response.

"You saw your vibrator—which you *named*—and you didn't like it? Do you *usually* like it?"

"Yes."

"Ohhhh-kay. What didn't you like about it this time?"

"This is going to sound dumb, but I don't think it was where I left it."

He moved away from me and propped himself up on his elbow, a frown marring his brow. "Explain."

"It's got a box. I always put it back inside, and I keep it at the back of the drawer. But when I looked today, Francois was near the front. Out of the box, and kind of wrapped up in a bit of lingerie."

His frown deepened. "And you're sure you didn't just forget to put it away?"

"I'm sure," I said. "I haven't even looked at it since I met you. And it'd been a while before that since I'd used it."

"How long before?"

"Marc!"

"Sorry. Couldn't help it." He flopped backwards, pulling me so that I was practically on top of him. "You think someone moved it?"

"I don't know. It would be weird as hell, wouldn't it?"

"Forgive me for asking this...but does anyone else know where you keep it?"

"No."

"No one?"

"It's a *personal* pleasure device."

"Doesn't mean you can't enjoy it with someone else."

"I can't tell if you're serious, if you're just fishing."

"Both," he admitted, winding a piece of my hair around his finger.

"Okay," I replied. "I've never used it with anyone else. Just myself. And I've never told anyone that I keep it there. Not even Liv. But I doubt I'm the only woman who puts her vibrator in her underwear drawer."

"I guess not."

"Do you think someone moved it?" I asked.

"I don't know, honey. Weird doesn't begin to describe the thought. But just to be sure...I'll buy you a new one."

"You don't have to—"

"I want to. I *really* want to."

"Okay."

He went quiet again for a long moment, then said, "I should go to bed." I threaded my fingers through his. "Can you stay until I fall asleep again?"

He cleared his throat. And for a second, I thought he might deny my request. I tensed. After another moment, though, I felt him nod, and his fingers started to circle slowly over the small of my back.

"You need a lullaby?" he teased.

"No," I replied. "Just you."

"Well. That's something you've definitely got."

I closed my eyes and smiled, and my worries slipped away as I drifted into oblivion.

Chapter 16

Marcelo

It was stupid.

It was reckless.

It was necessary as all hell to stop myself from going insane.

Lying in bed—the one in the too far away guestroom, instead of beside Aysia where I belonged—for an hour after she'd fallen asleep had been driving me closer to the edge. Thoughts of Carl with his hand in her underwear drawer almost pushed me over. It wasn't even jealousy. Though to say there was *none* would've been a lie. I knew there was more to it than something so simple.

I'd tossed and I'd turned, and his smug face filled my mind. She hadn't mentioned him. Neither had I. It felt dishonest. Especially in light of everything else. Of our semi-confessed feelings. Of how I knew exactly what was in my heart.

Climbing back into her bed had been a true temptation. Somehow, though, I was damned sure it would end in a fight I wasn't ready to have.

So I'd picked Option B. Sneaking out of the house like a derelict teenager. Rolling my car in neutral until I was far enough away to start it without attracting attention. And now I stood outside Aysia's apartment, staring up at it the same way I had when we'd been there with the police.

There were a few marked differences. I was alone, for one. For another, it was dark except for the streetlights and a few glowing windows, and there was even less to see than there had been earlier.

Might have something to do with the fact that it's two in the morning, I reminded myself, running a worried hand over my chin and glancing up and down the street.

I didn't really think I'd find anything. Whoever—whether that was Carl Reeves or if it was someone else—had broken in had done it in broad daylight. No lurking for the real fucking intruder. I'd saved that for myself. So selfish.

I tossed my car a final look, then stepped from the street to the sidewalk, then from the sidewalk to the front step. Guiltily, I plugged in the code that would let me into the building. Not that I thought Aysia wouldn't have given me the code on her own—okay, maybe not if she knew what I wanted it for that second, but in general, I was sure she would've told me—but because I'd deliberately watched her punch it in earlier. I'd deliberately committed it to memory. Even though I didn't know what I was going to use it for until she started talking about Francois.

Fuck.

Under normal circumstances, that would've been a very sexy little revelation. She kept a vibrator in her panty drawer. In pristine, boxed condition. She'd named it. I liked everything about that. Except for the part where she wondered if someone else had touched it.

I moved through the lobby, bypassing the elevator in favor of the stairs, gritting my teeth.

I believed her when she said she hadn't disclosed the sex toy's location to anyone. I was relieved that she hadn't used it with another man, and not just because the idea made me jealous. It meant Carl hadn't been near it. Which in turn meant that if he'd touched it...

Really, Diaz? That's what your plan is? I thought as I clued in to what my newly found, CSI-mind was concocting.

"Fucking fingerprints," I muttered.

If Carl had touched it without permission, he'd have left his goddamned whorls or loops or whatever all over them. All I had to do was carefully extract the thing from the drawer, mosey on down to the police station, and ask the nice guys with the magic dust to find them.

Aysia's going to kill you.

Yeah, she probably would. I was sure that she had deliberately left Francois out of her report to the police. In this case, though, I thought it was a hell of a lot better to be begging for forgiveness than to be asking for permission.

I reached the top step and pushed into the hall. Aysia's door loomed in front of me. It hadn't been roped off with yellow tape, or boarded up, or anything that screamed of crime. Instead, the broken handle had been taped on with good, old-fashioned duct tape. The door had been pulled shut, a single piece of the sticky silver stuff holding it on place. It sure as hell didn't seem secure. Or serious enough, considering how violated I knew Aysia felt.

At least it'll be easy enough to walk in.

Not a reassuring thought at all. I'd have preferred the place to be a challenge. For me. And for anyone else who felt inclined to take a peek.

Moving cautiously now—mostly because I was sure Mrs. Fisk and her radar hearing would be lying in wait just up the hall—I peeled back the tape. It came off without resistance, and the door swung open immediately, not even accompanied by a squeak. With a quick glance behind me, I stepped inside. I pulled out a flashlight from my pocket, glad I'd thought to grab it from my trunk, and flicked its narrow beam over the interior of the condo. It looked the same as it had this morning, and I wondered why I'd been expecting to find things different.

What did you think? He'd come back to finish the job?

I grimaced. What the hell had the job *been*, anyway? To touch Aysia's intimate things? Christ. The thought made me want to burn them all. Fuck just buying a replacement for Francois. I'd gladly dedicate an entire day to finding new bras and panties, too. Hell. I'd take her away for a whole week and help her pick out an exotic, for-my-eyes-only collection of lingerie. She'd need to start a second drawer.

With that in mind, I finished my sweep of the main floor and headed for the stairs that led to her master suite. At the bottom, I paused. I could swear I'd heard something. A rattle, maybe. Someone opening and closing a drawer?

I flicked off the flashlight and tucked it into my pocket. Above me, everything was quiet again. I moved up the first step. Then paused again. Silence still reigned. I lifted my foot, and the low noise sounded again.

Definitely a rattle.

My first instinct was to charge at the intruder. To rush up, knock the living hell out of him—especially if it was Carl—then drag him out to my car and toss him in the trunk. What I'd do with him after that was still up the air. A deep, dark hole somewhere wasn't out of the question. Neither was the Pacific Ocean.

I forced myself to curb my possessive, murderous instincts, and reached for a more reasonable weapon. My phone. Except when my hand got to my pocket, it came back empty.

Shit.

I'd left the damned thing at Aysia's mom's place. It was too late, anyway. A sweatshirt-clad figure appeared at the top of the stairs. Before I could react he was moving. Straight at me. Hood pulled low, shoulder down, a growl emanating from his chest.

At the last second, I ducked to the side. He missed knocking into me completely and just grazed my elbow. I cursed my own lack of reflexes.

As the other man stumbled, then recovered, then made for the door, I managed to collect myself enough to go after him. Using the stairs as a launch pad, I flew forward. My outstretched hand closed on the sweatshirt, yanking the man back with my grip. He let out another muttered curse and spun. His fist headed straight for my face. I dropped low and out of the line of fire. I tried hard to hold on, but I was forced to let him go in the name of not getting clocked.

With his hood still up, he spun again and made another attempt to hit me. This time I was a little more stable, a little more prepared. My hand came up quicker. It slammed into his forearm and knocked him back. He stumbled a second time, this time slamming directly into the coffee table. His reaction was a guttural yell and a pain-filled roll to his side.

I pounced. One palm landed on his shoulder, forcing him back. I was as determined to find out who he was as I was to subdue him. Hell. Maybe *more* determined. As if he could sense my urgent need to unveil him, both of his hands came up to block his face.

"Fuck you," I snapped.

He tried to drive a knee into my balls. I recognized the shitty trick before he completed it. I eased sideways and took the impact in my quad instead. It still burned like a sonofabitch. Pissed me off even more, too. With a snarl, I pulled my hand back and drove a flat-palmed blow to his chin. For a second, I thought I had him. His head flew back and his hands dropped. I caught a flash of him. Clean-shaven chin, split lip.

Then he twisted free. His body hit the floor and in two seconds flat he was up and running. I tore after him, but before I could catch up, my foot caught on a loose object in the doorframe. Stifling a holler, I fell forward. My knee slammed into the commercial-grade—definitely *not* soft—carpet in the hallway, then slid forward. When I looked up, the intruder was gone.

"Fuck. Fuck. *Fuck*," I bit off under my breath.

I pushed to my feet, and as I did, I spied the object that had sent me flying. *Fran-fucking-cois.*

The asshole *had* come back to finish the job. I snatched up the goddamned vibrator just in time to hear a familiar, huffy throat-clear from behind me. I knew who I'd find before I spun. And there she was. Velour robe tied tight, gray hair askew, and a dour look on her face.

Shoving the rubbery object into my pocket, I plastered a strained smile onto my face. "Sorry, Mrs. Fisk."

She didn't smile back. "Have you got something in your pocket?"

"No," I deadpanned. "I'm just happy to see you."

She eyed me up and down suspiciously. "Keep your funny business to yourself."

"Trying to."

With another huff, she kicked up a slipper-covered foot and disappeared back into her apartment. Sighing, I sagged against the wall and pulled the vibrator from my pocket.

I gave it a disgusted look. "You weren't much help, were you?"

I still didn't know if the hooded man was Carl, or just some run-of-the-mill perv. I glared up the hall. The guy was long gone. My own prints were all over the stupid fucking sex toy now, too. I'd have to wipe the damned thing down in case Aysia changed her mind about telling the police it had been disturbed.

Even more annoyed, I made my way back into the apartment. I headed straight upstairs, where I grabbed a towel and prepared to do the deed. As I walked past the open underwear drawer, though, I spotted something hanging over the side, and it that made me pause.

A red negligee.

Just like the one Aysia'd been wearing in Carl's home video.

My hands came out on their own to snap it up. My stomach roiled, a sick, oily feeling making it unable to settle. The fabric was soft and silky. It should've been a nice thing to touch. Instead, it made me want to vomit. And punch something.

Was this piece of lingerie that the vibrator had been wrapped in? If it was, that was proof—in my mind anyway—that Carl was responsible. Of course, acknowledging that meant the possibility of discussing the video with Aysia. Guilt nagged at me. Yeah, it was her who'd been insistent about not talking about him or the things he'd done. But maybe I should've pushed it, even if just to let her know that I was aware.

I squeezed the negligee harder, its deep red pooling between my fingers. In the dark, the color reminded me of blood.

Blood.

A slow smile tipped up my mouth as I remembered something. The vibrator-stealing fucker had a split lip. Sure as hell wouldn't be quite so easy to rub off as fingerprints.

I was suddenly looking forward to calling Carl in for a Tuesday morning meeting.

* * * *

Aysia

My phone woke me up unpleasantly, pinging to life and dragging me from a dream that involved Marc and a brand new vibrator.

"Really?" I groaned.

Dream-Marc had been about to test out a setting called *Ecstasy*. And dream-me had been awfully excited to be rendered ecstatic. With an annoyed grumble, I rolled over and snapped up my cell from the white-painted nightstand.

Marc's name flashed across the screen.

Hi, baby.

My irritation wiped away as I typed back, *Baby? Is that what we're doing now?*

Dunno. Just felt right.

Well. Baby. R u texting me to invite me from next door for a thorough good morning?

Sadly...no. Left for work early. Had something to take care of.

I'm pouting. I typed.

I bet that's sexy, he answered.

Hmm.

Hmm...what?

Hmm THIS.

I flopped back and held the phone up to snap a quick picture. I glanced at the shot—my hair was wild on the pillow, my cleavage suitably emphasized, and my lips turned down. I hit send. But I didn't get the response I was expecting.

Be careful what u send out there, Marc said.

Why? U going to use that pic to announce to the company that we're a thing?

Is that an option? He wanted to know.

Definitely not!!!

Relax.

I sighed. *I'm relaxed.*

Liar.

Shut up. Do I need to send u a pic of me relaxing?

Thx. I'll keep this one.

Something about the text made me narrow my eyes. And a second later, I knew why. He sent my own photo back to me. Only he'd zoomed in on the mirror behind me. The small, round one just above my night stand. And somehow, the angle managed to capture me from the knees up, exposing the fact that I wasn't wearing anything but a T-shirt.

God! I typed, glad he couldn't see my red face.

I told u to be careful.

Delete it.

No way.

Marc!

Fine. He answered.

Thank u.

Another few seconds went by and another picture came through, this one of him. He was in his office, leaned back in his leather chair, one hand on head. He wore a crisp shirt, and I swear it was *ochre.* A color I'd only seen inside of my crayon box, and which would've looked terrible on anyone but him. But it was almost the same shade as his eyes and contrasted perfectly with his tanned skin. A thin black tie was tight around his neck, and he had a small, lopsided smile on his face. Lust shot through me immediately.

I don't think that's what u were wearing last night, I wrote.

Stopped by my place.

How early did u leave?

Early, he admitted.

Well. I like it. But I'd like it better if I could take it off.

Is that right?

A half a dozen thunderous heartbeats passed, and a second picture came to life. Marc again. His tie loosened. His top button undone.

Something like this? He wanted to know.

I swallowed. *It's a start.*

Lunch today?

I'm definitely hungry.

Oh, yeah?

I could practically hear his chuckle. It made me shiver, thinking about how it would fill my ear if he was next to me, and I shifted a little on the bed.

What were u thinking about eating? I typed.

What I'm thinking about eating...nice guys don't write down.

R u back to that? Pretending ur a nice guy?

U saying I'm not?

I'm not falling for that.

So we're at an impasse then, he texted.

Does this mean I don't get lunch? I replied.

U pouting again?

Possibly.

3321 Alice Street.

What?

There's a nice little bed and breakfast there.

U rented us a by-the-hour place? Trashy.

B&B.

I smiled. *Technicality.*

It's ours from now until Sunday, he sent back. *Unless u want to keep staying at ur mom's?*

No. But if it's a B&B...are u sure they serve lunch?

Yes. And it's the only place I know for sure I can eat what I want.

Another delicious lick of heat zapped through me. *Which is...*

It's pink. Sweet. And right between those sexy fucking thighs of yours.

Now I didn't just shiver. My whole body quaked, and a little gasp escaped my lips. I thought of Marc's mouth. Of where he'd put it. Of how damned good it would feel.

My phone buzzed in my hand again, sending another wave of want over my body. I peeled open my eyes—which I hadn't even realized I'd closed—to read the text.

Really gotta work now, honey. Baby. Honey-baby.

U really want to leave me like this?

No. But I've got a meeting in an hour. See u at lunch?

Fiiiiine.

More than like u, he told me. *TTYL.*

I smiled. *More than like u, 2. Bye. Baby.*

As I pressed the phone to my chest, my stomach filled with butterflies. Giddy ones. They were almost as good as the desire-laden tingles.

Almost? asked a voice in my head.

I didn't argue. There was no point in lying to myself about it. The rush of my heart wasn't just a literal one. I could feel that warm, ready to explode with happiness sensation all over. It was the kind of feeling that made it seem not-so-strange—or so bad—to be curled up in my old bed. Even if I was there because I'd been broken into. And even if some pervert had rifled through my underwear drawer. Because being with Marc made everything else seem secondary. It was a weird feeling, to know that someone was there for me. And he was so patient. So understanding.

Feeling determined to reciprocate in some way, I threw back my sheets, stretched quickly, and grabbed the clothes I'd packed. I dressed as fast as I could and tossed my hair into a bun. I took a breath. Then I marched from the bedroom to the kitchen. There, I found my mom exactly where I knew I would—sitting at the table with her coffee and her paper and her muesli.

"He's my boyfriend," I announced without preamble.

She set down her mug. "I figured."

"And we work together."

"You didn't meet at the bar?"

"No. I mean, yes. We did. But he turned out be the new marketing manager. At Eco-Go."

"Not at the sex shop where you moonlight?" she asked.

"What? Mom!"

She lifted and eyebrow and took a sip of her coffee. "Just pointing out that I know where you work, Aysia. There's no need to remind me."

"So…"

"So…what, sweetheart? Are you not okay with it?"

"Me?"

"You look worried"

"I just want to make sure *you* were okay with it," I said. "I mean. I know it was a huge source of conflict for you and dad."

"That's what you think?" she replied.

"Isn't it true?"

She shook her head. "It's factually true, I guess. I was damned good at what both of us did and would've been a hell of a piece of competition for him. But when your father asked me to leave the advertising business, I said yes so that I could stay home with you."

"But you didn't have me yet when you quit."

"Seven months later I did." She smiled. "Your dad always liked the idea that he *won* because he got to stay at work. I let him think what he wanted. But he didn't win, sweetheart. I got to spend the next eighteen years dedicated to you. I've never regretted it."

"That's…" I trailed off, unsure what to say. I stared at her. Hadn't she been the one who'd told me she'd quit because of him?

Maybe not, I admitted silently.

Maybe I'd just filled in the blanks over the years, letting my own resentful feelings toward my dad cloud my view. It was like a curtain had just been drawn back, revealing a deep truth. One of the building blocks that made me who I was…wasn't. But instead of it being a bad thing, it was a good one. All I felt was relief.

"Are you all right, Aysia?" my mom asked.

"Fine," I managed to say. "Just…thank you."

"Words every mother longs to hear," she replied with a smile. "Are you staying home today?"

I shook my head. "The doctor cleared me."

"Cleared you for work? Or for Marc?"

"You're almost as funny a Liv."

"Speaking of Liv..."

"She knows. She even approves." I said.

"Well. Just this one time. We agree."

"You approve?"

She flicked open her newspaper. "He likes *Monty Python*. How could I not?"

I snagged a piece of toast from her plate and brought it to my mouth to cover my smile. I didn't need her approval, just like I didn't need a boyfriend. But it felt damn good to have both.

Chapter 17

Marcelo

I folded my hands on top of the little table in the corner of the coffee shop and waited. I had it on good authority that each morning *after* he checked in at work, he headed to this very spot. The woman at the front desk had been more than happy to exchange that tidbit for nothing but a smile.

I glanced down at my watch.

8:31am.

Any minute now, Carl would come through the door. Something made me sure he wasn't just a plain black coffee kinda douchebag. He'd get something deliberately overdone. Maybe something he didn't even like. Something he used just to make himself feel complicated and superior.

Asshole.

Under the table, my leg twitched with anticipatory irritation. I knew I was being a judgemental jerk myself. But it was the only thing keeping me from thinking of plowing my fist through Carl's face.

Another look at my watch told me it was now 8:34am.

What's the hold up, Carl?

My eyes lifted toward the entrance. From my spot, I could just see the top of the glass and the bells hanging off the frame. I was positioned so that he wouldn't be able to see me as he ordered, and probably not even while he waited for his drink to be prepared. Once he picked up his stupidly detailed beverage, though, he'd have to turn around. Then I'd be right in his line of sight. He'd spot me. Maybe spill his coffee a little. With any luck, scald his hand and yelp like a baby.

I forced aside the smug satisfaction at the imagined scenario. My goal was to keep calm. To catch him off guard and use his arrogance against him. I hadn't been all that surprised that he hadn't called in sick. He was so full of himself, so confident that he held all that cards that he'd never expect to be called out for his actions. I had some of my own ammunition, though. All I needed was to see that fucking split in his lip.

I looked down again.

8:37am.

Then the bells on the door jangled, and I heard him. His voice carried over the hiss of steaming milk and grinding beans.

"Decaf triple soy no foam latte," he said. "Medium, please, sweetie. And don't make it too hot."

I gritted my teeth. It almost annoyed me that I was right. His drink was as pretentious as the rest of him. I closed my eyes for a second, but I couldn't block out the sound of him as he tried to flirt with the barista.

"Hey Katie?" Carl's voice was full of inflated ego. "You think about what I said about you and me and the bathroom?"

"It's Kaylee," the girl corrected. "Like my nametag says."

"I'm more interested in what's *under* the nametag, sweet thing."

"Kaylee," she repeated, just this side of impatient.

"And the bathroom?" Carl asked, clearly not taking the hint.

"It's pretty filthy in there, Mr. Reeves."

"Just the way I like."

She sighed loud enough that I could hear it. "Here's your latte."

"Thanks, babe."

I opened my eyes just in time to see him reach out to take it. Only instead of grabbing the cup, he grabbed the girl's wrist. I was halfway out of my seat before she bumped the latte, sloshing some over the side and forcing Carl to jump back.

I forced my ass down and waited for their interaction to finish playing out.

The barista smiled and moved out of reach. "Oops. Sorry, Mr. Reeves."

Carl wasn't fazed. "If you ever want a hand getting out of this dead-end job, I can put in a good word."

The girl stared him down. "In exchange for what? A *favor?*"

"If that's a possibility."

"I'll tell you what. If I ever decide to leave my girlfriend, become straight, and get a hankering for an asshole in a cheap suit, you'll be the first person I call." Then she tossed her ponytail over her shoulder and flounced away.

Carl stared after her, muttering about his suit not being cheap. I noted that he didn't say a word about reporting the girl to her supervisor.

Because the guy knows *he's a giant fucktard.*

The thought added a tinge of self-righteousness to my smugness. Both fell away, though, as the other man snagged his drink and spun. Ice cold anger took their place as I spotted exactly what I was looking for—the raw red slice up his bottom lip. There was a surprisingly low amount of satisfaction in seeing the proof.

I lifted my eyes and met his gaze.

Immediately, he took a step back, smacking into a rack of mugs that rattled under the sudden assault and looking around in search of a hasty escape. A crowd of teenagers blocked the way back. His only choice was to push through them or walk straight past me. I didn't want him to do either.

Borrowing a gesture from Aysia, I lifted an eyebrow. Then I pulled out my secret weapon. I set the red-lingerie-wrapped item on the table and watched as Carl's eyes widened to caricature proportions.

I smiled. Slowly. Then I crooked my finger and gave him my best, mob-boss-esque come hither. Like he couldn't help it, the douchebag moved in my direction, his nervous stare flicking between me and the object on the table.

"What are you doing, Marcelo?" His question was a snarled whisper.

"It's Mr. Diaz, actually," I corrected, my own voice edged in steel. "Sorry that I don't have nametag like your barista friend."

"Fuck you."

"Likewise." I nodded at the chair across from me. "Sit down."

"Don't think so."

"You know what's under that sexy little piece of fabric."

"Like hell I do."

"Are we really going to play games?"

"Are you really carrying women's underwear around in your pocket?" he countered.

"Better than spending my mornings *going through them,*" I said back.

"I don't know what you're talking about."

"Cut the bullshit, Carl, and sit down so that you're not embarrassing yourself. People are starting to stare."

He cast a glance around the coffee shop, then yanked out the chair and seated himself on the edge. "Couldn't have had this conversation at the office?"

"I chose the public venue for *your* safety."

"What the hell—"

"Shut up and listen. I know you were in Aysia's apartment. Twice. That little booboo on your mouth was a gift *from me.* The only reason I haven't already called the police is that I'm genuinely unsure of your intentions. Are you just a pissant pervert? Obsessed, jilted ex-lover? Or are you actually dangerous? If it's the latter, you're fucked. But if it's one of the former two, I might be willing to make a deal. You can quit your job at Eco-Go, and I'll keep my mouth shut. So convince me that you're just a complete asshole, Carl. Because the other option is looking good."

Fury played over his features. "You're kind of forgetting something important, aren't you?"

I shook my head. "You mean your attempt to blackmail me? No longer matters. You committed a crime. Hell of a difference between that and dating a co-worker."

"Tell that to Miss High-and-mighty."

"I did. Or I should say that we decided together that we'll be coming clean about our relationship. You've got nothing to hold over us. So what's it going to be, Carl?"

"The video," he said.

I stiffened. The stupid thing kept biting me in the ass. And it was about to again. A soft, familiar voice came from over the other man's shoulder.

"What video?"

Aysia. Shit.

She stepped into view, a reusable coffee cup clutched so tightly in her hand that her knuckles had turned white. Her pretty blue eyes moved from me, to Carl, then back again.

"Honey..." I started.

She put up a hand and said again, "What video?"

"She doesn't know?" Carl suddenly looked entertained.

"I don't know *what*?"

"Honey," I repeated. "Give me a second."

"Stop calling me honey," she snapped, then looked taken aback at her own tone. "Sorry, I just...what video?"

"The one where you're wearing *that*." Carl nodded at the table.

Aysia drew in a sharp breath. "Is that my lingerie? And my *vibrator*?"

She asked the questions so loudly that three people turned our way. She didn't seem to care. With another inhale, she inched closer to the table. "Someone tell me what's going on. Please."

"You?" Carl asked, throwing a shit-eating grin my way. "Or me?"

"Shut the fuck up, Reeves." I snarled, then turned to meet Aysia's eyes, guilt eating away at my anger. "I found the video that night I met you at the bar."

"Carl's video? The one of me?" Her face had gone pale.

"Yes. It was in his e-mail."

Her gaze flashed to him, but when she spoke, it was to me. "And when you came into the bar…"

"I recognized you. And him."

"And you didn't think you should *mention* it?" she asked.

I shook my head. "I *did* think I should."

"Until you took me out to the alley."

"I didn't know at that point that you worked at Eco-Go."

"And that made it okay?"

"Can we talk about this alone?" I sounded desperate because I felt desperate.

Her responding gaze was cool. "Sure. Right after you tell me why you didn't fire Carl. And why the two of you are sharing coffee with my vibrator as your centerpiece."

"The video." For some reason, it was all I could get out.

Understanding dawned on her face. "He blackmailed you."

"You made it pretty clear that you didn't want anyone at work to know what was going on between us," I answered.

"So you let him *blackmail* you?"

"Aysia. Let's go somewhere else."

"Francois?" she whispered insistently.

"It was Carl," I replied. "I caught him in your place again last night, trying to steal it."

"You went back?"

"Yes."

"So why don't the police have him?" She stepped back, her face crumbling for a moment before she composed herself. "I'm going to go."

"Don't. Please don't."

But it was too late. She whipped past, her expression stony, and she was gone so quickly that I couldn't even follow the blur of her disappearing back. I rounded on Carl.

"You're fired, asshole. And the cops'll be by to drag your ass to jail before the end of the day."

I slid my chair back and tore out the door.

* * * *

Aysia

I pressed myself to the brick wall outside the coffee shop, my breaths coming in shallow gasps. My chest ached. Each inhale made it squeeze. Each exhale made it want to burst. Tears pushed to the surface, then overflowed. Despair rocked me, and there was nothing I could do to hold it back.

I'd only felt this way once before. Twelve years ago when Walt lost his battle. And that's how I knew what it was. The burn of a broken heart.

A broken heart.

It confirmed what I'd been refusing to admit to myself. I loved Marc. And God, how it hurt right then.

It wasn't supposed to be this way. This moment of realization should've been sweet rather than sorrowful. My mind knew it. So why couldn't my body keep up?

I gasped, trying futilely to snag enough oxygen to ease the pain. But no matter how hard I sucked in the crisp, morning air, nothing changed. If anything, it was growing worse. Filling the rest of me with pain.

I breathed again, and the lungful seared. Then froze. Marc had stepped out onto the sidewalk, and from my vantage point, I had a clear view of his face. It was ragged. A perfect match for the emotions swirling through me. I wished it felt good to see him hurting the way I was hurting. But there was no satisfaction in seeing his eyes pinch with worry and his shoulders slump in defeat. It just felt awful instead. Not because I wasn't angry. I was. Maybe more than I'd been, ever. He'd betrayed me. Not trusted me enough to tell me that he knew about the stupid, meaningless video. And instead of calling the police on Carl when he should have, he tried to take matters into his own hands.

Didn't you do the same thing? Take matters in your *own hands?*

I shoved down the silent, pointed question. That was different. I'd made a choice for myself. I was allowed to do it. Marc, on the other hand, had no right to make decisions on my behalf. Not when they affected my job, or my life, or my safety.

But I could hardly resent the fact that he wanted to keep me safe. Even if he had a shitty, caveman, Alpha-dog way of doing it.

I swallowed against a new lump in my throat and watched as he took a step forward, then back. He ran a hand over his hair and scanned the street. He looked lost. But I knew he was just searching for me. It made me ache even more.

I closed my eyes, willing myself to hold onto the anger, hoping that not being able to see him would dull the need to reach out.

Except it had the opposite effect. Not having my eyes on him made me want to see him even more. Nothing undermined how much I cared about him.

Love, apparently, trumped fury.

I needed to talk to him. I pushed off the wall and moved forward, his name on my lips. But before I could even take a full step, a rough hand reached around and clamped down on my mouth. As the person attached to the hand dragged me to the narrow space between the coffee shop and the neighboring boutique, the taste of sour sweat exploded on my tongue and made me gag.

Realizing too late that I should be fighting off my assailant, I lifted an elbow and tried to throw it back. A second hand came up and stopped me.

"Stop it." The low, growled order was issued unmistakably by Carl.

My heart paused in its burn to thump erratically against my ribcage. *Shit.*

I fought a little harder, driving my heeled boot into his foot. He dropped an angry curse, then tipped me sideways and lifted me from the ground. He spun me around and slammed me to the wall, his hand still covering my mouth.

"I just want to talk to you," he said.

No fucking way.

I pulled up my knee, planning to use the small space between us to my fullest advantage, and jammed it straight between his legs. But my effort was in vain. Before I could connect, Carl's sleaze ball self was ripped away.

I heard him hit the opposite wall, then saw a blurred form draw back a fist and deliver a solid punch to the asshole's chin. Carl slumped to the ground. And Marc appeared in front of me, those warm brown eyes of his filled will worry. I looked up at him. And I yelled one of the dumbest things I'd ever said.

"I do *not* need your help!"

He blinked. "What?"

"I don't need your fucking help, Marcelo! I was just fine until you came along."

"Carl..." His gaze flicked to the barely conscious man on the ground.

I waved my hand impatiently. "I don't just mean now. Although you did completely rob me of rendering him incapable of having children. I mean all the time, Marc."

"I didn't mean to—"

"Yes, you did. Before you came along, I had my whole life sorted out. My job, my friendships, where things stood with my mom. But now...I feel clueless. Like I'm second guessing every move I make."

He flinched, then stiffened. "Fine. I'll just wait here until the police come. I'll give my statement, then I'll go."

My chest compressed painfully again.

Why, Aysia? Were you expecting him to protest? Wanting him to?

I refused to think about it. This was clearly a sign that I'd been wrong to bend both my own rules and the rules at Eco-Go. It was just too complicated.

"Does that work for you, Ms. Banks?" Marc prodded.

"Yes," I lied. "That's perfect."

The next thirty minutes went by in a blur. Marc told the police—quietly—that we were co-workers. That he'd caught Carl pulling me into the alley and had just reacted. By the time they'd finished giving me a quick but thorough medical assessment and moved on to questioning me directly, he was already shaking hands and handing over his business card in case they needed him later. Then he was just…gone. And the alley felt terribly, overwhelming empty even though it was full of police. Full of Carl in handcuffs. And even full of a few curious bystanders. I was alone.

It was that feeling that sent me home instead of back to the office. If I was going to feel alone, I might as well be alone. I placed a quick call to Liv to have her pass along the message that I wouldn't be there for the day, and was glad that her phone went to voice mail. Then I let one of the police officers drive me back to my apartment. I refused her offer to see me upstairs, and slipped into the building with a forced smile. But as the cruiser disappeared up the street, I couldn't quite make myself move. My gaze swept over the lobby, and I wondered why it seemed like a whole different place.

"Stupid," I muttered.

My condo was the same as it had always been. Built by my favorite company. Designed with all the things that mattered to me in mind. Sustainability blending with beauty blending with usefulness. Perfect. Except it was somehow empty.

"Extra stupid," I added.

Any second, Mrs. Fisk would use her weird, sixth sense to tune in to the fact that I was just standing around. She'd tap her foot and remind me that normal people weren't afraid of going into their own apartments because it felt odd to do it alone. Then she'd cackle. And possibly fly off on her broomstick.

The mental image was enough to let a small smile through. "Yeah, I'll show *you* normal."

I forced one foot to move, then the other. Step by leaden step, I managed to make it to the stairs. At the top, I almost panicked again. The last time I'd been inside—*was it really just yesterday?*—was the post break-in walkthrough. I'd had Marc to lean on. And I hadn't felt anywhere near as much raw vulnerability as she did now. Tears threatened again. If they managed to overtake me, I could officially say that I'd cried more in the last hour than I had in the last ten years.

C'mon, Aysia. Get it together.

Taking a steadying breath that didn't quite cut it, I pushed out of the stairwell into my hall. My shaking legs might've taken me all the way to my door. But they didn't. Because Marc sat on my welcome mat, his head in his hands, his tie off and wrapped around his fist, his coat a rumpled heap beside him.

And if I'd thought my heart was an aching, broken mess before…it had nothing on the implosion it experienced at the sight of him.

Chapter 18

Marcelo

It's funny how quickly you can become attuned to someone else. The way they move. Their unique scent. How they fill a space. A month ago, I didn't know Aysia Banks existed. I didn't know about her soft lips or the way her body fit so perfectly with mine. I wasn't aware of how empty a space could seem when she wasn't there, or of the fact that I could feel it when she walked into a room. If someone had told me any of that would be true today, I would've laughed my ass off, then asked if I could have a shot of whatever they were drinking.

Right that second, though, my life was proof positive that the made-up, fairy-tale love stories were true. The moment Aysia stepped into the hall, I knew. I didn't have to look up to confirm that it was her. The air around me just changed.

"I know I shouldn't be here." My statement came out rough and raw. I pushed on anyway, keeping my head down because I knew I'd fall the fuck apart if I had to see the cool detachment in her eyes again. "But I just needed a minute to explain. To apologize. Then I'll be out of your way."

She said nothing, so I went on.

"I came into Eco-Go on that first Friday to get a feel for the company. I went through some emails because I wanted to know if there was anything that might bite me in the ass when marketing the company. When I saw that video, my immediate instinct was to fire the man who made it. I wasn't expecting him—or you—to come to life in the bar. I didn't know you worked for Mike. I wasn't even sure if you knew about the video."

Aysia interrupted with a soft throat-clear. "Marc."

I knew she was going to dismiss me any second, but I had to get it all out. "I should've brought up the video before I even went home with you. And again when I found out you worked at Eco-Go. Hell. I was *going* to tell you before Carl busted in and made the blackmail threat. He had another video, too. One of you and me dancing that first night at The Well. He made a big point of telling me how much your job meant to you, and you said as much yourself. All of this sounds like an excuse. Maybe it is. But I just need you to understand that I was sincerely trying to protect you and your feelings and your career. It was shitty. And machismo. And stupid."

"Babbly, aren't you?" said an annoyed voice. "Especially for a man."

My head came up in surprise, and instead of Aysia, I found Mrs. Fisk. *You've got to be fucking kidding me.*

My mouth worked silently for a minute. Had I just imagined the whisper of my name? Was I bat-shit crazy? Then the old woman shuffled sideways, and I exhaled. Aysia *was* there. Her face worn, her eyes sad, and her cheeks pink.

"Can't decide if he just likes the sound of his own voice, or if he thinks if he talks more, you'll take his sorry ass back," Mrs. Fisk added.

"Probably both," Aysia replied, a tiny smile tipping up her mouth for just long enough to give me hope.

"Hmph." Mrs. Fisk crossed her arm. "Well. Take it inside. No one wants to see you make a baby out here in the hall."

"Thanks, Mrs. Fisk. We'll take that to heart," Aysia replied, nodding toward her still-duct-taped door. "Do you want to come in, Marc?"

"Do you *want* me to come in?" I asked cautiously.

"Oh, please," Mr. Fisk interjected. "Just go in the damned house."

I pushed to my feet and stepped away from the door to let Aysia lead the way. I followed her inside, waiting for the other shoe to drop. For her to tell me take my lame apology and stick it up my ass. Instead, she excused herself for a moment, hurried into her office, then came back with her laptop.

"I'm going to show you something," she said. "And it sounds dumb, but I'm breaking Carl's confidence by doing it."

I forced my hands *not* to ball up into fists, but my reply still came out through gritted teeth. "All right."

She clicked through a few screens and finally settled on a tab labeled *VIDEOS*. "I'm guessing this is what you saw?"

The window became animated, and yep. There it was. Aysia in the red negligee, stroking her hair. Moonlight streaming through the big window behind her. As beautiful as she'd been the first time I'd watched it.

"That's the one," I confirmed.

She sighed and leaned back. "About ten seconds after that recording ended, I realized what he was doing. He tried to shove his phone into his pocket, but dropped it instead, and the video replayed. I was pretty pissed off. What kind of sleazy guy records a girl in her underwear without her consent? I realized right then how stupid I'd been to get involved with him. I broke it off that very moment. I asked him to delete the video. He did. Except he somehow e-mailed himself a copy before removing it from the phone. I came into work the next day and found one in my inbox, too, with a note saying that if I didn't keep seeing him, he'd send it to everyone."

"What the fuck," I muttered angrily.

"Pretty much what I said." She shrugged.

I stared at her, wondering how the hell she could be so nonchalant about it. It made my gut roil. Before I could ask how she managed to hold her shit together, she leaned over the computer again and pulled up another video.

"I happened to also get *this*," she told me.

The screen came to life again, this time showcasing Carl. On a bed. Naked. Back turned away, thank fucking God. He was leaned down, staring at what could only be his own dick. Then Aysia's voice came through, tinny, but still audible.

"What's wrong?" she asked.

"It's too big," was Carl's response.

"Oh, hell no," I said, pulling away in disgust and slamming the pause button with a little too much force.

"Just keep watching," Aysia said.

"No! Christ."

"Please, Marc."

"Fuck."

She un-paused it, and her voice came on again.

"Too big? What's too big?"

"Goddamn it." Carl turned a little, and his face was almost purple. "The condom."

"The..." Aysia trailed off, clearly bemused, then cleared her throat. "Maybe you grabbed the wrong size?"

"I grabbed the smallest size they had. Just—goddamn it!"

"It's okay, Carl. Really."

"Can you just leave?"

"Sure. I'll...uh...wait out in the living room."

Carl's gaze found the camera then, and he muttered a curse right before the video cut off. Aysia closed the laptop, and I didn't know whether to laugh my ass off or just be disgusted.

I forced myself to speak as neutrally as possible. "And you got that how?"

"It was attached to the same e-mail as the first video. Along with one of him and another girl who didn't seem to care that they don't make condoms in a mini-sized."

I fought a chuckle. "Carl's pretty fond of recording shit, isn't he?"

"Yes. And that one I just showed you...he recorded that four nights before the other one of me in the lingerie. It was supposed to be our first time."

"I take it things didn't work out as planned?" I couldn't hide how entertained I was by the revelation.

"No," she replied dryly. "Not at all."

"So you never..."

"No. We tried one other time and he couldn't even get it up. Not for lack of trying. It was almost as comical as the condom. But that wasn't why I showed you the video. I just wanted you to know that Carl never actually had something hanging over us."

"The bastard was playing me." I shook my head in disgust.

"Until today, he probably thought you told me about seeing the video. And he probably thought I'd shown you the other one in return. He was desperate to keep it quiet, I guess. And counting on the fact that I cared more about my job and my reputation at Eco-Go than anything else."

I studied her face. "You said *cared*."

Her eyes held mine for a minute, then dropped to her hands. "I'm sorry about today."

"*You* are?"

"I just...I got freaked out. When you pulled Carl off me, I kind of lost it. And I know I probably sounded like a crazy person. But everything I said was true. Before I met you, I really did have my shit together." She paused, swallowed nervously, then went on. "I love you, Marc. And I'm having a hard time processing that."

She kept talking. But I had no clue what she was saying. Something about appreciating the fact that I cared enough about her to try to protect her, and about being grateful that I'd pulled Carl away from her when I had. Then a bit more about how overwhelmed she was and how quick it all happened and how I derailed her plans but that she *liked* it. Except none of it mattered. All I heard were those three little words.

She loves me.

My heart filled like a balloon. A helium one. Filled with glitter. Or something equally soft and sparkly and decidedly unmanly. The glitter-rainbow-helium floated up somewhere near my throat and threatened to burst outwards in a pile of sickly sweet happiness.

Ignoring whatever else was tumbling from her mouth, I dropped my hands to her face and tipped my mouth to hers, cutting her off. I kissed her hard. Fast. And thorough. So fucking thorough. I tasted every little bit of her lips and her tongue, and Jesus was it good. That much better because she *loved* me. When I finally pulled away, she was gasping for air.

"You love me," I growled.

"I know," she breathed.

I kissed her again. Soft. And tender.

"I love you back," I said. "So fucking much."

"So fucking much?" she teased.

"Yeah. I'm romantic as all hell."

Then her face fell again. "But it doesn't change anything."

I cupped her cheek. "It changes everything."

"No, Marc. There's still the work policy."

"I thought we decided we didn't care about that."

"We said we were going to try and find a way around it."

"And we will." I stood up then, and grabbed her hand. "C'mon."

"Where are we going?"

"Upstairs so I can show you exactly what *so fucking much* means when we're in the bedroom."

She started to stand. I wasn't that patient. Like the overprotective, love-blind caveman I was, I grabbed her by the waist and threw her over my shoulder.

* * * *

Aysia

Marc's mouth and hands were everywhere. For each piece of clothing he discarded, he placed a trail of kisses on the newly naked spot. My shoulders. My collar bone. Each of my breasts, then down my stomach to my belly button. Each touch made me gasp. By the time he got my pants unzipped and pressed his mouth to the sensitive spot just above my panty line, my blood was molten lava, rushing through my veins.

As he dragged the pants down to my calves, I started to quiver. When he pulled them to my ankles while simultaneously sliding his tongue along my thighs, the quiver became a shake.

"Do you remember that first night?" he asked, his voice rumble against my legs.

"Yes," I managed to get out.

"Sweetest fucking thing I ever tasted," he said. "And that was even before you were mine. Now…"

His tongue came up to graze me through my underwear. I couldn't hold in a moan.

"Now?" I whispered.

"It'll be even better. Lie down, Aysia."

I collapsed backwards on my bed, unashamed at how needy I was, unembarrassed by his chuckle.

Marc dropped down on top of me, suspending his still-clothed body over mine for a moment before kissing my lips.

"Mine," he said with a wickedly sexy grin. "And this, too."

He nibbled an earlobe.

Then my throat.

His lips seared along my skin in a slow dance, his arms holding him up as he tattooed me with kisses. And with each little lip, each little tug, he declared aloud his claim. Finally, he reached my stomach a second time. There, he paused. But only long enough to slide to the floor and grab a hold of knees. He pulled me to the edge of the mattress, his mouth hovering just above me. When he exhaled, his hot breath made me ache. My hips wanted to lift already.

"Tell me again," he ordered softly.

"That I'm yours?"

"The other thing."

I didn't have to ask what he meant. "I love you, Marc."

"I love you, too, Aysia."

Then his tongue plunged into me, and I lost all reason.

Hours went by, some slow, some fast.

We spent the rest of the day in bed. Or on the couch—which Marc swore he'd replace—or on the plush rug in front of the TV that I so rarely used. At one point, the maintenance guy came by to replace the door handle, and Marc dragged me into the bathroom. Later my mom called, and Marc took the phone to tell her that he loved me. I had no clue what she said back, because he hung up. Then pulled me to the couch once more.

I didn't think about work. Or if I did, I didn't dare bring it up. But when the day dragged to evening, and evening became a too-late night that stretched into morning, I knew I'd have to deal with it. And with Marc sound asleep at seven a.m., I decided to do what I always did, and come at the problem head on.

I placed a call to Mike Roper and asked him to meet me. I wrote Marc a note and signed it with a cheesy, filled-in heart. And twenty minutes later, I walked into my boss's office at Eco-Go, and I blurted it out.

"I've been dating Marc."

Mike's mouth quirked up on one side. "Congratulations."

I shook my head. "No."

"No?"

"It goes against company policy."

"Okay."

I grabbed the chair on the other side of his desk and pulled it out. I sat on the edge. I took a breath. "There's more."

My boss's smile didn't falter. "All right. Spill it."

I told him about Carl. About how it started and ended, and about the things he'd done over the past few weeks. I apologized for putting the company at risk by breaking the rules, and I told him I'd understand if he wanted to let me go. When I was done, he frowned at me.

"So Carl's no longer working here?"

"No. He's a liability."

"And you're wanting to continue to see Marcelo?"

"I'm *going* to keep seeing him," I corrected.

"You're in love with him."

"Yes."

He shrugged. "I don't see the problem."

"We have an anti-fraternizing policy in our employee manual," I reminded him.

"So?"

"I'm acting manager of human resources."

"Manager."

"What?"

"I got official word last night. Your predecessor isn't coming back."

"But…" I trailed off, willing myself not to cry in front of my boss. *Soon to be* ex-*boss.*

It was my dream job. Being handed to me. And I knew Marc wouldn't dream of asking me to walk away from it. But there was no way for me to take it. If I had to choose, it would be him over work. There was no doubt in my mind. Other jobs would come along. But there was only one Marcelo Diaz.

"I have to turn down the offer," I said firmly.

"Aysia. You're the most qualified person for this job. You've been *doing* this job for months. It's a raise. A renovation for your office. Isn't it what you want?"

"Yes. But how can I take the job *and* be with Marc *and* be an example to the company?" I shook my head. "I can't. And I won't be a hypocrite."

My boss pulled off his glasses and pinched the bridge of his nose, and when he met my gaze, his eyes were a little glassy. "Ruby—my wife—is ill. I'm assuming Marcelo told you?"

My chest ached immediately, and I nodded. "Yes. I'm sorry."

"Me, too. And I wouldn't dream of taking away a minute of happiness between you and Marc. Who wrote the policy, Aysia?"

"I did. It was one of the first assignments I was given."

"So change it."

"For selfish reasons?"

"Love isn't selfish."

I blinked at him. "I..."

He put his glasses back on. "The policy is there to stop personal relationships from interfering with professional ones. Reword it so that's the only caveat. It's your first official job as manager."

"Seriously?"

"Hell, yes." He tapped something into his desktop computer, then spun the screen my way and lifted the keyboard. "Do it here. Now. Before you talk yourself out of doing it."

With shaking fingers, I reached out to do it. Then paused.

I lifted my eyes to meet my boss's. "Can I print a copy of the old one and the new one?"

"Sure can."

I selected the original page, and seconds later, the printer came to life. Quickly, I deleted the four-sentence policy and wrote a new one. It was almost too easy. I inhaled, then hit the save-button. Finally, I printed out the new version and grabbed both sheets of paper. I couldn't hold in a grin as I folded the pages and shoved them into my purse. "Thank you, Mike."

"You're welcome."

I pushed out of the office. I only made it two steps before smacking into a familiar, warm body.

"Marc!"

"Hi, honey." He smiled his usual, heart-stopping smile.

But I frowned at the single piece of paper in his hand. "What's that?" He inched away. "Nothing."

"No, really. What is it?" I moved to grab it, and he danced out of reach. "Are you kidding me?"

"Is Mike in there? I've got to talk to him. I'll only be a minute."

"Okay."

I made as if to get out of his way, but the moment he sidled past, I snapped the page from his fingers.

"Hey!" he protested.

I scanned the paper before he could grab it back. "You're trying to resign?"

"Mike will understand."

"I know he will. But you don't have to."

"I want to."

"No, you don't."

"Aysia…"

"Come with me."

I grabbed his hand and pulled him up the hall to his own office. I yanked him inside, then shut the door and pulled out the freshly printed pages from my purse.

"Here," I said eagerly.

"What is it?"

"The old dating policy. And the new one."

Marc read the first one. Then the second. And a smile just about split his face in two as he grabbed me by the waist and dragged me flush against his body for a deep kiss. But after a few breathless minutes, he pulled back again, a tiny frown etching into his forehead.

"What?" I asked.

"Just one thing," he replied.

"Okay."

"Well. According to this old policy, we could've solved the problem from the beginning."

"I don't understand. How?"

"Simple. We could've just acted on the marriage clause."

And the serious look on his face made my heart thunder.

THE END

Keep reading for a special preview of **Until Dawn,** *the next book in the* **Business or Pleasure** *series by* **Melinda Di Lorenzo!**

"Kiss the next man who falls into your lap." When Mia Diaz agrees to the dare, she doesn't expect it to happen so literally. But suddenly, there he is—stubble-dusted jaw, sexy half-smile, and lips that make her appreciate the benefits of acting on impulse. Her long-buried libido certainly thinks it's the right move...as long as what comes next is strictly a one-night affair. Mia has dedicated the last few years to building her jewelry store. She's not about to put her heart in a stranger's hands, no matter how skillful they might be...

Ethan has made his fortune by seizing opportunities. So when he finds himself tangled up in long legs, red hair, and satin bed sheets, he doesn't complain—until he finds out the redhead in question is Mia Diaz. The same Mia who's been dodging his emails and calls for weeks, ignoring all his offers to buy her out.

Ethan is a master of the takeover. Mia refuses to give in. And what started out as a simple dare has become the ultimate challenge, where the only way to win may be to surrender...

Available to order now!

Ethan

With a wordless growl, I stepped back on the sidewalk and scanned the row of boutique-style shops, trying to discern which one might be Trinkets and Treasures.

It was an impossible endeavor. They all looked the same. BoHo-trendy. Brick fronts with varying shades of trim, no names hanging above the shops. I was sure the last bit was a trick. A subtle marketing ploy. The lack of signage forced the casual passerby to stop and look inside in order to figure out what the hell each store specialized in.

Another damned good reason to do my job from behind my desk.

I *liked* my desk. It had a nice, comfortable leather chair. It was in my office, which had a view. A panoramic one of Toronto. Nice, reassuringly solid concrete buildings as far as the eye could see.

And very few bad omens.

Which seemed to be plaguing me in droves since leaving the comfort of my office this morning.

First came the accident on the freeway, which delayed me so badly that I had to run to make my flight. Literally run. Through a goddamned airport in a three-thousand dollar suit. Next there was a mechanical issue that forced us to change planes in Winnipeg. The flight in question had zero seats available in business class, which resulted in me being trapped between an asthmatic octogenarian and a woman with a none-too-pleased infant. After that, a lengthy stop on Calgary to de-ice, and finally a fifty-minute delay at YVR *after* touchdown due to staffing issues. I'd finally stepped onto solid ground in Vancouver a mere six hours behind schedule. My car rental had been given away when I didn't turn up to retrieve it on time. Some kind of job action had the limo drivers running a skeleton crew, which in turn meant the taxi drivers were run ragged, and the wait to get one had been an outrageous hour and a quarter.

Like living in the fucking dark ages, I thought bitterly.

So why wasn't I holed up in my five-star luxury suite at the Regent Inn? The answer was simple. Mia Diaz. The thorn in my side who'd forced me to leave Toronto in the first place. I fought a need to curse the woman aloud. After making initial contact three weeks ago – and receiving a flat-out rejection of my offer – I'd tried dozens of times to get in touch with her.

The phone was a total no-go. Her business line was screened by some kind of answering service, and after putting me through just once, they'd subsequently rejected every call after. So I'd switched to email. At first, I'd been triumphant. Ms. Diaz sent polite, personal answers. To start, anyway. Then came the automated out-of-office replies. On my last attempt to get through, my email had been bounced. It didn't take a genius to figure out that she'd blocked my address.

A less determined person – a less successful businessman – might've taken that as a sign to let it go. I saw it as a challenge. My own company, Stuff, Inc., hadn't become the third largest distributor of unique, handmade products in Canada through a willingness to give up.

The last few hours, though, were a real test.

That's what makes it worth it, I reminded myself.

It was true that most of the businesses I took over were parted with reluctantly. The owners knew their product had potential. They fully believed in it. The harder they fought, the more profitable it usually ended up being for me. In the end, the quick buck I offered – combined with the promise of improved distribution and potential popularity – always won out.

Except with Mia Diaz and Trinkets and Treasures.

The mental reminder made me grit my teeth and turn my attention back to the row of shops. I squinted against the dim sky and took a step closer to the buildings. Everything was dark. Which I supposed was to be expected at eight o'clock on a Thursday night. I'd assumed, though, that I'd be able to get a good look at the shop in question. Or at least enough of a glimpse to let me know what I was up against. Having an edge meant no surprises. So far, the edge seemed damned far out of reach.

Then, as if to drive home the pervasive futility of my efforts, a car – the only one I'd seen since on this street other than the taxi that had dropped me off just a few minutes earlier – flew by and sent a spray of water in my direction.

"You've got to be fucking kidding me," I muttered.

My gaze turned down in disgust. The mess wasn't just wet. It was dirty. My suit was officially a total write-off, and I hadn't even made it to the hotel yet.

The hotel. My stuff.

"Shit." The whip of a sudden gust of wind carried away my curse as I spun on my heel.

Sure enough, my small suitcase, which I'd yanked out of the taxi and unthinkingly set on the ground, was covered with the same garbage as my clothes. And the bag was wobbling. Hovering right over the edge of the sidewalk.

Sensing its imminent demise, I took step forward. My reward was a soggy splash as my foot slammed into an ankle-deep puddle. The split second of ice-cold pant leg sucking against my calf was all the suitcase needed to complete its suicide attempt. It toppled over. It bounced. Then it sprung open. A crisp, white shirt tumbled out alongside a pair of dress socks.

I narrowed my eyes at the ruination. "What? That's all you've got?"

The universe decided to respond with a metaphorical middle finger directed straight at me.

A second heavy gust of wind kicked up and sent the top of the suitcase flying all the way open. A stack of paperwork – everything I'd collected about Trinkets and Treasures and its elusive owner, and that I could swear I'd secured – was loose. It lifted into the air, and before I could react, it sailed past me, hit the stream of water that bounced against the sidewalk, and started on a path toward a catch basin a few feet away.

"Shit," I said again.

With my feet sloshing unpleasantly through the water, I dived forward and bent my knees in an attempt to grab the paperwork. I failed in an epic way. One foot caught on a rock. The other stretched out far enough that it made me close my eyes and groan in pain.

"C'mon, Burke, get your shit together," I commanded.

Yanking as hard as I could, I pulled my foot out of my shoe and drew my sock-clad foot forward, stumbling a little as I did. Both hands hit the ground.

"Fuck."

I drew in a shallow breath, and tried to get up again. My body protested heartily, and it took everything I had just to keep from letting my chin slam into the concrete. All I could do was lift my eyes and watch helplessly as the precious sheets of paper danced over the grate, then slipped inside.

This...I thought, dropping my lids closed again. *This is why I like my desk. It's why I leave the grunt work to the grunt men. It's why I write persuasive emails and drink hot cappuccinos and –*

The silent tirade cut itself short, choked off by the fact that I lifted my eyes to find a redheaded woman in a slash of hot pink that could barely be called a dress. She was standing under an awning just a few buildings up, and as my gaze traveled the length of her body, I half-expected her to disappear in mirage-like fashion. She didn't. Her mile-high heels and crimson hair stayed put.

What was she doing there?

It only took me a second to decide I didn't even care. She was captivating as all hell. Long, slim legs that disappeared under the miniscule strip of fabric, and full hips that pressed against it at the same time. A slim waist showcased nicely by the dress, and a chest that rose and fell temptingly.

Hell. She was one of the most beautiful women I'd ever laid eyes on, and I didn't even have a clear view of her face.

Forgetting my overstretched body, I righted myself and took an automatic step forward, trying to catch her features. Were they soft and delicate? Or classical and imperious? Did she have full, kissable lips? For no good reason – aside from lustful self-indulgence – I hoped to God the answer to last question was yes.

Unfortunately, I didn't get a chance to find out. She straightened her shoulders, shook her head a little, then spun on one of those tall heels of hers, apparently unaware that I was standing there gaping at her. I had a strange—and admittedly irrational—feeling that she was deliberately avoiding turning her head in my direction. Irritation niggled at me for second. Going unnoticed felt like a slight, especially considering how aware *I* was of *her* presence.

I took another step forward, watching as she disappeared around the corner.

What waited for her on the other side of that building? I felt compelled to know.

Without even being conscious that I was doing it, I moved to catch up so I could find out.

ABOUT THE AUTHOR

Amazon bestselling author **Melinda Di Lorenzo** lives on the beautiful west coast of British Columbia, Canada, with her handsome husband and her noisy kids. When she's not writing, she can be found curled up with (someone else's) good book. Visit the author at melindadilorenzowrites. blogspot.com, find her on www.facebook.com/MelindaDiLorenzo, and follow her at twitter.com/melindawrites.

Printed in the United States
by Baker & Taylor Publisher Services